ORACLE

BOOK ONE OF THE MULTIVERSE SERIES

JOHN R. KOWALSKY

jrk media

Published by JRK Media

For more information:
Website: johnrkowalsky.com
Facebook: facebook.com/johnrkowalskyauthor
Newsletter (get FREE first-in-series): johnrkowalsky.com/signup

1

Sixth Verse
Sophia, Gaia

The kidnapper flashed into the Sixth Verse. As the sphere of blue and red light dissipated around him, he inhaled sharply and waited for an alarm to trip. After several moments of holding his breath and listening, he allowed himself to relax a little.

Once he was certain his jump was undetected, he shuddered from head to toe. He didn't know why, but jumping between the Verses always gave him the willies. It shouldn't have; the technology had always been stable, but there was a first time for everything.

In the middle of the night, the air had enough chill to it that he could see his breath. He did a quick equipment check. The zip drive first. The charge read sixty-seven percent. Enough to carry out his mission. Next, his sidearm. The stun magazine was fully charged and his ballistic magazine was at full capacity. He chambered a ballistic round and made sure the safety was on with the trigger set to stun mode. He had orders not to use lethal force unless absolutely necessary.

He approached the house with as much stealth as he could muster. Not the easiest thing in this Verse, but the new tech was supposed to help with that.

His intelligence told him that the husband was out on assignment in the Third, so there should only be two Gaians in the house—mother and daughter. He flicked on the infrared in his visor and confirmed. Two bright orange, warm bodies in separate areas of the one-level house. "At least they got *that* right," he muttered.

The larger body was in the front of the house, so he chose to enter through the back. The less time spent creeping around a strange home looking for the child in the dark, the better. He could probably just smash his way in and grab her, but he liked to think of himself as a professional. Brute force was a good tool, but in his opinion, it should be used as a last resort.

He started the hack on the lock and, with minimal effort and time, the door opened. He entered the kitchen which was open to the living room. A hallway led back to the bedrooms. He started down the hallway when he saw the child, standing at the end of the hall in her bedroom doorway. He smiled, attempting to appear as friendly as possible. *Maybe this will be easy*, he thought. The girl turned and ran back into her room slamming the door behind her. He heard the locks engage. *Maybe not.* He would need to move fast now.

. . .

Cara woke to her daughter, Mina, knocking in her mind. Her head was fuzzy, still partly asleep in that space between dreams and reality. Mina had been waking up with nightmares for the last few nights, and Cara was starting to get used to the late night interruptions.

"*Mommy, Mommy... There's a strange man here,*" Mina sent.

Cara bolted upright in her bed and threw back the covers. She reached out into the flux field and felt the disturbances of the Terran standing in front of her daughter's room. A cold tremble ran down Cara's spine. This was definitely not a dream. "*Run and hide, Mina! Don't come out for anyone but me!*"

What was a Terran doing here on Gaia? Cara summoned her rage as she moved through the house toward where she felt the intruder. Whatever his reason, she would make him regret coming here tonight.

The Terran was walking down the hallway toward Mina's room as she reached the kitchen. "I don't think so!" she yelled, reaching her hand toward the stranger, using it to guide the flux energy she accessed. She flinched involuntarily as her attempt to grab the Terran by the throat failed. She tried again.

Nothing.

It was as if her abilities were on the fritz. She'd never experienced anything like it. The flux was always there, like the air she breathed.

Cara took stock of what she could feel in the flux, trying to identify the cause of the problem.

She could feel her daughter and all of the things inside her house. She could vaguely feel the Terran, but she couldn't make contact with him. It was as if her invisible fingers kept slipping off him, almost like he was a phantom—a flux phantom.

While she pondered her dilemma, the Terran raised his weapon. The barrel flashed with blue light and Cara ducked as the weapon discharged. She felt the sonic stun waves speed toward her and used her flux to deflect as much of the blast as she could. The remaining energy was still enough to send her flying backward across the floor and into the wall. She winced and reached out once more feeling for the Terran. He was closing the distance, trying to get a clear line of sight on her.

She reached for a chair in the dining room and felt her flux connect with it, grateful that something in her world was still working. She hurled the chair at the advancing Terran, and then reached for the table, hurling that as well.

The Terran brought his arms up to fend off the attack, but the force of the blow managed to knock him down.

Cara stood and made her way toward her daughter's room. As she ran, she kept flinging whatever she could find nearby. Her aim was not as good as it normally was. It was much harder to hit a target that she couldn't locate in the flux field. She felt like a young woman again, newly bonded with the flux field and trying to gain some mastery of her newfound abilities.

She glanced back as the Terran got to his feet. She hurled a picture off the wall, some kitchen utensils, and a few unidentifiable objects. Some, he dodged, while others hit his body armor and deflected, not carrying enough energy behind them to do any damage. He brought his weapon up and fired. Cara felt the blast wave knock the air from her lungs as it hit her.

She slammed into the wall and slid down, stunned. Her arms and legs were heavy and unresponsive as she tried to stand up and defend herself. Her heart flooded with fear as she saw the blue flash of the muzzle.

Cara felt nothing as the final blast wave concussed her body, shutting down her nervous system.

THE TERRAN STOOD over the Gaian mother and whistled in admiration. "Tough gal," he said, checking the remaining charge on his weapon. Three shots were two too many as far as he was concerned. Lucky for him the new body armor seemed to do the trick. He'd never gone up against a Gaian before, but he'd sat through all the briefings about what they could do to a person with that flux shit they used. The researchers back home swore that it operated on some kind of scientific properties, but it was straight voodoo to most of the boys back home, including him. Picking up objects and flying them around the room—messing with people's minds—it gave him the heebie-jeebies. Then again, the Gaians felt the same way about the nanites that were coursing through his veins, augmenting everything from his vision and breathing to his fine motor control and heart rate.

He tried the handle on the girl's bedroom door, even though he knew it was locked. Force of habit. He then put his shoulder into it several times to no avail. Not so much as a budge. The door might have been a concrete wall for all he could tell from the attempt. "Jesus, what do they build shit out of around here?"

No matter, he had the answer.

He fished around in his cargo pockets until he found

what he was looking for. He placed the breach charge along the seal of the doorway, attached the detonator, and set the timer for a long enough delay that he could retreat down the hallway a few paces.

The charge blew, and the door flew inward. The girl screamed from inside.

He entered the room, hoping he wouldn't encounter any surprises. The smoke from the blast charge swirled around as he searched the room. No sign of the girl. At least not from where he was standing. He slung his weapon around to his back and crouched down on his hands and knees. *Predictable,* he thought. There she was, under the bed.

"Come on out from there, and I won't have to hurt you," he said. As soon as the words were out, he wondered if he'd made a mistake. "I'm not going to hurt you, either way," he corrected. *God, this is off to a bad start.*

"What did you do to Mommy?" the girl asked. "I can't wake her up."

"That's right, you're a smart girl. Your mommy is sleeping. Now, come on out from there. You and I are going to take a little trip together."

The girl shook her head. "No, I don't want to go. I want to stay here with Mommy."

The Terran sighed. "Alright, enough of this."

He needed to get this done before the mother came back around. He pulled the bed out from the wall, exposing the frightened child in the corner. He activated the zip drive around his wrist and received the all clear ping from his landing site. He then set a delay for ten seconds and picked up the girl who immediately began wailing and writhing around. He squeezed her tight to his chest and hoped that he didn't hurt her, but he couldn't let her scramble out of his grasp either. He counted off the seconds in his head as he took the girl outside to a clear jump point. When he reached *one*, the zip drive engaged and he and the child flashed out of the Sixth Verse.

CARA ROUSED SEVERAL MINUTES LATER, disorientated. The air was heavy with dust and the smell of smoke. Why was she sitting on the floor in the hallway? The pain in her head and the memory of what happened came to her at the same time. She rushed to her daughter's room and took in the scene, praying that it had all been a bad dream and Mina would be sleeping soundly in her bed.

The bed was pulled out from the wall, and several shards from the door and frame were lying about, but other than that, Mina's room appeared like it had the night before when she'd put her baby to sleep. Cara stepped over the fallen door, sat down on her daughter's bed, and began to sob.

She didn't know how long she cried before she called Emergency Services.

"What's your emergency?" a woman's voice said.

Cara sniffled and wiped a tear running down her cheek. "It's my daughter… She's been taken."

The woman's voice was slightly muffled like she'd turned her head away from the receiver. Cara overheard her say, "*Sir, I have another one.*"

2

EXCERPT FROM *THE MYTH OF THE ORACLE*

WHILE MUCH DEBATE still ensues as to whether the Oracle was a real person or just a figure of myth, passed down from generation to generation, the existence of the Enclave at Sophi Rock is not in doubt. Mentions of the Oracle stretch back over 4,000 years ago, but the Enclave was formed nearly 1,200 years ago. It consisted of a sect of Gaian scholars and holy men who believed the Oracle's prophecies were truth. They structured their entire settlement according to the Oracle's teachings.

Much of what we know about the disappearance of the Enclave comes from their own writings that were left behind. They were particularly enraptured with a passage from the scriptures that came to be known as the Oracle's Warning:

AT THE TIME OF TRANSCENDENCE, THE POWER YOU SEEK WILL HAVE POWER OVER YOU.

IN ORDER TO KNOW THE TRUE POWER, YOU MUST BECOME THAT POWER. ONLY THEN WILL YOU KNOW THAT POWER TO BE TRUE.

THE TRUE POWER REQUIRES ALL THAT YOU GIVE AND ALL THAT YOU HAVE. WHEN YOU KNOW TRUE POWER, NOTHING WILL BE HIDDEN FROM YOU. EVERYTHING THAT YOU DESIRE WILL BE EVERYTHING YOU HAVE, FOR YOU WILL HAVE EVERYTHING.

HEED NOW, MY WARNING: BE TRUE OR BE DESTROYED. THE TRUE POWER CANNOT LIE. WHOEVER IS BORN IN TRUE POWER CAN NEVER DIE.

AFTER THE ENCLAVE'S DISAPPEARANCE, *the passage was removed from the scriptures for fear that it was responsible for the Enclave's demise.*

In truth, no one knows what happened to the Enclave. Some theorize that they got lost, attempting to teleport themselves to Transcendence. While others believe that they staged their disappearance to lend credence to their claims, and that they lived out their lives quietly while their legend grew.

One of the more interesting theories claims that the Oracle laid out a method of melding directly with the flux energy. The purpose was to become one with all things. But the feeling was extremely euphoric and therein lied the danger. This theory's proponents believe The Enclave, caught up in a narcotic state of bliss, gave too much of themselves to the flux meld and simply ceased to exist.

What really happened to the Enclave? And what did the cryptic passage known as the Oracle's Warning from the ancient scriptures have to do with it? These are the questions that we will attempt to answer...

3

Sixth Verse

60 miles outside of Cairos, Gaia

Desmond Bishop smelled the coffee brewing from out on the deck. The mid-morning sun peeked out from behind a cloud and lit up the view of the lake in front of him. The sun was warm on his skin. *Going to be a hot one today,* he thought. He marked his place in *The Myth of the Oracle*, a commentary on one of the more popular Gaian religious figures. Desmond wasn't particularly religious, but he loved a good mystery. This one happened to be written by his old trainer at the agency. Scholars and holy men had been debating the Oracle and her prophecies for years, and there were far more questions raised than answered. He'd been meaning to get around to reading it for years, but something had always seemed to come up.

He let out a lazy yawn and wondered what he was going to do with the rest of his day. After careful consideration he decided—nothing. He would do absolutely nothing today. After all, that was one of the main perks of being retired. Sure, he would occasionally go out of his mind with boredom, but for the most part, Desmond had enjoyed not being involved with any facet of the government or the GDA. He definitely missed the action at times, but he didn't miss the endless meetings and debriefings where the Council would drone on and on about the most mundane details.

Two years ago he'd finally had enough of the bureaucratic red tape and put in his notice. It took almost another year before he was able to disentangle himself from the active missions he was a part of, but at long last, he'd made it. He'd sublet his penthouse in Cairos, the capital, to his twenty-three-year-old daughter, Celia, and moved out to the lake house about an hour away.

Some days he'd fish, or paint, or catch up on some reading, but mostly he spent his time struggling to stay away from the latest news feeds. Once an info junkie, always an info junkie, he supposed.

His stomach growled. He went inside to pour himself some coffee and ponder whether or not he was hungry enough to cook something. On his way to the kitchen, he walked through the living room where a live newsfeed was already playing.

"...reports of multiple kidnappings across the globe. I'm told that several of those occurred right here in Cairos. We expect more information to be released from the Director of the GDA later today."

Desmond shut off the feed, lest his curiosity get the better of him and compromise his plans of doing nothing for the day. He sipped his coffee and was about to go back out to the deck when his datapad alerted him to an incoming message. It was from his daughter, Celia. He answered the call.

"Celia, to what do I owe the unexpected pleasure this fine morning? Don't tell me the sanitizer broke again in the penthouse—that guy swore to me it would last for at least ten years before it needed to be serviced."

His daughter laughed. "Hey, Dad. No. Nothing like that. Sorry to interrupt your peace and quiet. I know how much you've been enjoying the retirement."

"That's all right. I've always got time for my favorite daughter." Desmond smiled.

"Thanks. You do remember that I'm your only daughter, right? Or has retirement and old age started to take its toll?" Celia cracked a smile of her own.

"No, all of my marbles are still right where I left them, at least as far as I remember. So, what's going on? How are you doing with everything?" He tried to get a sense of what was troubling her, but even though their connection was stronger than most Gaians, he was unable to deduce anything through the flux field. The distance that separated them was too great. Even if it wasn't, Celia had grown pretty adept at hiding her emotions from just about everyone.

"Let's not make this about me. I'm fine."

"Take it easy, tiger. You've been through a lot over the last year, it's perfectly natural to—"

"What do you want to hear? Jacen's never coming back and my life will never be the same. I'll always have a hole in the space that he filled. Why does everyone in the world want me to talk about it? I just want to move on, but everyone keeps bringing it up!"

"I'm sorry," Desmond said. "I didn't mean to—I thought maybe that was why you were calling... It's just, well, it's not like you to call for a chat."

"It's okay, I'm sorry. A little on edge, I guess. It's not your fault."

"The GDA keeping you busy?"

"Funny you should say that..." Celia said.

"Why do I have the feeling I'm not going to like what you're about to say, all of a sudden?"

"Like I said, I hate to bother you, and I know that you're enjoying yourself out there on the lake, but I don't suppose you caught the news stories about the kidnappings last night?"

"As a matter of fact, I did hear something about that, but I just caught the tail end of it. Wait—have they assigned that to you?" Desmond frowned for a brief moment, puzzled. While he had all the confidence and trust in his daughter's abilities, she was only a few years removed from her bonding, and last time he'd checked, she was still being assigned the more minor cases—typical for an agent of her experience level. And after watching her partner, Jacen, die in front of her, she'd just been cleared for active duty recently.

"Err, well, kind of... I guess." Celia's cheeks grew red as her face flushed. "The Council hasn't so much assigned the case to *me*, as much as they have assigned *me* to *you*." Celia pulled her lips back wide exposing the biggest fake smile she could manage.

Desmond's gut feeling had been correct, he didn't like this at all.

"I'm not sure what I'm supposed to say," Desmond responded. "They do remember that I don't do that kind of thing anymore, right? I'm *retired?* As in, *someone else's problem?*"

Celia's face fell. She had hoped that this would be easy, even though in her heart she had known what her father's response would be. "Believe me, everyone is aware of your position. I, myself, told them what your response would be if they asked you, personally. Which is why they decided to task me with getting you in front of them at the next council meeting." Celia forced another smile. "Which, incidentally, is this evening in Cairos."

Desmond laughed. "Well, good luck with that. Now, if you'll excuse me, I'm going to get back to enjoying my retirement. Have a good day, Celia." Desmond ended the call and made his way out onto the deck to resume what he hoped was still the makings of a beautiful and relaxing day.

An instant later, Desmond felt her enter the local flux field and turned to see his daughter standing on the deck.

"Listen, Dad—"

"Getting better at that," Desmond said.

"Thanks," Celia grinned, basking for a moment in the praise of her father. "I've been training a lot. After all, you left some pretty big shoes to fill. Everyone at the agency is always, '*Your dad did this, and your dad did that, and your dad took down that guy, and your dad saved us from this,*' it's kind of gross the amount of man crushes you have in that place..."

Desmond sighed, throwing up his hands. "Okay, you're here, and I don't really feel like jumping across all of Gaia to try and lose you. So, I assume you have an argument in mind that is supposed to sway me?"

"I wasn't supposed to go into too much detail if I

could help it, but there are some things that were not mentioned in the news reports."

"Such as?"

"Such as, the kidnappings were done by Terran agents."

"Well, of course, they were. Doesn't take a special investigator to figure that much out. Who else would it be? A mentally healthy Gaian would never dream of harming a child, and the bi-monthly screenings usually find the unhealthy ones before they hurt anyone. Besides that, the Third is still trying to solve hunger, disease, and world peace. Who knows how long it will take before they discover the multiverse, let alone ours? The other Verses are wastelands... Only the Terrans have the ability to travel to our Verse."

"Of course, you're right. And while I know you've been retired for a little while now, did the question happen to pop up in the back of your mind of how lone Terran agents were able to break into multiple Gaian houses and overcome either one, or both, Gaian parents? All without being killed, knocked unconscious, picked up and flung into a wall, or simply held in place in the invisible grip of the parent's flux, waiting for the authorities to arrive?"

To be honest, Desmond *hadn't* given it any thought. His brain was entirely in retirement mode. The revelation left him with mixed feelings. On the one hand, it had taken him a long time to disentangle himself from his former life. But on the other hand, he liked to think that his reflexes would have remained sharp and in their peak state indefinitely, despite no longer being on the job.

"I had assumed there were teams," Desmond mused.

"You mean to tell me that the kidnappings were all carried out by single Terran agents?"

"That's not all. They were wearing some new kind of armor that disrupted our control of the flux."

"Disrupted? How?"

"The parents all described it differently. Ranging from ghostly to vague to slippery. They claimed they could still feel the Terran's presence, but when they reached out to manipulate them with the flux, they were unable to. One woman said it was like trying to grab a handful of water."

"What in the world could do such a thing?" Desmond wondered aloud. His mind began to race down a thousand theoretical rabbit trails.

Celia shook her head, unsure of the answer. "It would appear that they've finally started to unravel our genetic abilities with their science. And there are a lot of nervous people back in Cairo..." She paused. "Come on, do it for me... Come to the Council meeting."

Desmond groaned. He *really* didn't like the way this day was turning out.

"Does that mean you'll go?" Celia did her best to look hopeful and pitiful all at the same time. A look that every daughter usually masters and begins using on her father shortly after birth.

"You'd better get a promotion for pulling this off," Desmond said.

Celia jumped up and down with joy. "Oh, thank you! Thank you! Thank you! I can't tell you how much I was dreading this."

"Yeah, me too," Desmond said. "Everything was going so great today. Remind me to disconnect my comm service out here after this is over. Speaking of which—"

He was interrupted by the chirp of Celia's comm. She apologized before answering the call. "Yes, he's agreed to come... What? Now? Why? Has something else happened?" She listened intently and nodded a few more times. "Okay, I understand. Yes, sir." She ended the call.

"Let me guess... I'm not going to like this either, am I?" Desmond asked.

"They've moved the meeting up. The coverage on this is spreading like wildfire and the Council wants to try to get out in front of it before there's a mass panic."

"Moved the meeting up to when?"

"To as soon as we can be there," Celia said.

Desmond cursed and swallowed the remainder of his coffee which had gone cold. "Alright, let's get this over with. Where are we jumping to?"

4

Sixth Verse
Cairos, Gaia

The central courtyard of the Council Chambers in Cairos was bustling with activity as Desmond and Celia jumped in. Major and minor representatives hurried to and fro with their various assistants in tow. No doubt off to another endless meeting or education session, where every elected official would brief all the members of their district on every new proposal that was brought up for legislation. It was painstakingly slow work and another reason that Desmond was glad to be done working for the government. Every decision had to be weighed, ever so carefully, and run through a committee and then another, to ensure that the action was endorsed by the people. He had learned long ago that it was almost always easier to act without permission and ask for forgiveness, rather than wait for the bureaucracy to make a decision.

Celia led him into the Chamber Halls which led to the grand foyer. Marvelous staircases flanked the large circular room on both sides, leading to the second-floor offices of various officials and the Council's private conference room.

Inside, the Council was already seated around the long oval table. Chancellor Anselm Pearson sat at the head of the table, and the eleven other members from various districts filled the remaining seats. Everyone looked up as Desmond and Celia entered the room, creating an awkward silence.

"Hope we're not interrupting," Desmond said, trying to break the ice.

"Of course not," Councillor Evelyn Krystniak stood and motioned for them to take a seat. "Please come in, we were just discussing the recent events."

"Events which have led us to call you here, Desmond," Chancellor Pearson took over. "Please, be seated."

Desmond and Celia took their seats. Desmond nodded around the table at the Council members with whom he was familiar. There were only a few remaining who he still recognized. The rest were new additions to the Council. It wasn't uncommon for the entire Council to turn over every two to four years. The people were fickle masters, their desires ever-changing.

"Well, I'm here," Desmond said, expectantly. He leaned back in his chair and propped his feet up on the council table. "Anyone want to tell me why?"

The Councillor two seats to his left cleared his throat,

preparing to speak. Desmond didn't recognize him, but his name plaque read Thomas Skizak.

"By now, you know about the kidnappings, and perhaps you have an inkling of how they were carried out. There are those around this table who are more than familiar with your warnings over the past twenty years that we need protection from an outside threat like the one we encountered last night. To that end, we would like you to head up a new branch of the GDA."

"Getting right to the point, eh? You're new around here, aren't you?" Desmond only half-joked.

Several chuckles sounded from around the table.

Desmond didn't know what he had expected to hear, but it sure as hell wasn't this. He had tried and failed for years to establish a more flexible force that would be capable of defending the Sixth from any Terran threat. An organization that would answer only to the Council and was able to respond to situations much more quickly than the current protocols that were in place for the agency. An organization that would live in the shadows. "I'll be honest, I'm more than a little surprised."

"I know you and the previous Councils have had your issues over the years, but in light of the new circumstances we find ourselves in, I'm hoping that we can all put the past behind us, and look to the future of protecting our world."

"Your districts must be hitting you pretty hard if this is the best solution you could come up with," Desmond said.

"Mr. Bishop, I can assure you, that the pressure from the population is only one part of this equation. While it is true that there has been a large uproar over these attacks, there is a good reason for why."

"And what would that reason be?" Desmond asked.

"The people are scared. Terrified, in fact. And to be honest, we are scared as well. There has never been an attack of this magnitude before. When we first discovered the Terrans, or rather, I should say, when they discovered us, the Terran scout teams were easily overpowered and subdued by common Gaian adults. They were wise to sue for peace as quickly as possible. But over the last 50 years, and even more so over the last few, relations between our two Verses have become more and more strained. Despite all outward appearances, we have been afraid of something like this happening for quite some time."

Desmond scratched the stubble around his chin. "I get that you don't trust the Terrans, but that's nothing new. What haven't you told me yet? What am I missing?"

Skizak looked to Chancellor Pearson.

"Go ahead, Tom. Tell him," Chancellor Pearson said.

"The Terrans have figured out a way to somehow negate our natural abilities to affect their persons. As their science is light years ahead of our own, our best people can only guess as to how they have achieved this."

"Yes, I've heard about the new technology," Desmond replied. "So what?"

"So, the attacks of last night were bad enough in and of themselves. What if they have found a way to affect our abilities on a larger scale?"

"Do you have any proof of that?" Desmond asked. His heartbeat quickened at the prospect that the Terrans might possess something that would render almost all of Gaia's defenses useless. They were almost entirely dependent on their manipulation of flux. It was another reason he'd pushed so hard for some diversification of defense.

"No, no proof. Nothing like that. We are just guessing at the next worst thing. But, you can see why it is crucial that we have more information; why we must begin proactively protecting ourselves from this latest Terran aggression?"

The Chancellor took over, "Your past experience, truth be told, is only one of the reasons why we've asked you here today."

"And here I thought it was just for my good looks."

The Chancellor continued, ignoring Desmond's attempt at humor. "The other reason is that of your ex-wife. How often do you keep in contact with her?"

Desmond looked at his daughter. "What is this?"

Celia shrugged with a frown. "Beats me. They didn't mention anything about her to me."

"Please just answer the question, Desmond."

"Or what?"

"Look, Desmond, we didn't invite you here to threaten you, or to interrogate you, but at the same time, we do need to proceed with a certain level of precaution. So, again, when is the last time you spoke with your ex-wife?"

"Julia and I haven't spoken for almost a decade, by my count. We don't keep in touch. Which would be kind of hard anyway, her living in a different Verse and all."

The man addressed Celia. "And what about you?"

"My mother packed her bags and abandoned both of us two weeks after my thirteenth birthday. She can go fuck herself," Celia said with a snarl.

Chancellor Pearson raised his hands to pacify them.

"Sorry, I believe you both, but we had to ask out of due diligence. I hope you understand."

"Any other personal questions?" Desmond asked.

"I do apologize, but since her appointment as Prime Minister on Terra—well, we need to be sure that there won't be any problems of a personal nature for you moving forward. Either of you."

"None here," Desmond looked at Celia, "how about you?"

Celia shook her head. "Nope."

Desmond looked back at the Chancellor. "Satisfied?"

"Yes, I believe we are. So, you'll do it then?"

"Whoa," Desmond waved his hands. "I didn't say that... I have some demands of my own; certain provisions that I'll want in place before I agree to anything."

"Mr. Bishop, we don't have time for this. *You* don't have time for this."

Something about the way the Chancellor spoke left Desmond with an uneasy feeling. "What do you mean *I* don't have time for this?" His curiosity was piqued, like a fish swimming back around toward the hook for a second look.

"After your separation, we put Julia under surveillance."

"You what?" Desmond exploded.

"We were taking precautions against any secrets of state falling into the wrong hands."

"How did you even manage? She vacated her post here as Ambassador and went back to Terra. Any of our people would have stuck out like a sore thumb."

"It wasn't easy, believe me. But we managed to find a

few sympathetic natives and—anyway, that's really beside the point. The point is, you have a son."

Desmond went numb and silent. A chill spread across his body. He stared at the Chancellor for what felt like an hour.

The Chancellor continued. "Our contact learned that Julia was pregnant around the time she left. And not wanting another child, she removed the embryo and had it cryogenically stored. We liberated the embryo from the storage facility and managed to take it to the Third where it was given to a fertility clinic and implanted in a woman who was unable to conceive on her own."

Desmond opened his mouth to interrupt but realized that he didn't know what to say.

"We've watched over him, taking care to keep him hidden from any Terran operatives. We couldn't risk the child falling into Terran hands. God only knows how they may have tried to use him against you."

"Jesus Christ!" Celia cupped a hand over her mouth like she might be sick at any moment.

"Oh, you mean like the way *you're* trying to use him against *me*?" Desmond had found his voice and his anger along with it. "You had no right to keep this from me! To keep *him* from me!"

"No right?" the Chancellor replied. "Yes, I suppose you're correct, but we didn't feel like there was a choice in the matter. It was the only way to keep him safe; to keep him hidden from Julia. If you'd known about it, you would have moved heaven and earth to get to him."

"Damn right, I would have!" Desmond pounded his fist on the table.

"Which is why we want you to get to the bottom of

whatever this Terran plot is and take steps to ensure that something like this will never happen again."

Desmond sat, fuming in silence as he considered the Chancellor's words.

"So, Desmond... What do you say?"

Desmond knew what his answer was already, but he made them wait for his response.

"Here are my conditions," Desmond began. "I get to hand pick my people from whatever branch or agency I choose."

"Done," the Chancellor responded.

"I have full authority over operations."

"Done."

"And we'll have access to whatever equipment and funding we need for active missions."

"Of course. Any equipment we have will be at your disposal. As far as funding goes, for now, we'll need to funnel everything through the GDA. But eventually, we'll sort out the logistics. Is there anything else?"

"I'm sure there will be more, but at the moment, no."

The Chancellor stood to call the meeting at an end.

"Actually, wait. There is one more thing," Desmond said. "I want to pick what we'll be called..."

"Did you have something in mind?"

Desmond nodded. Something from earlier in his day that just wouldn't go away. "Oracle," he said. "Like the scripture..."

A puzzled look spread on the face of several councilors, including the Chancellor. "An odd name, but I suppose we'll need to call the agency something," Chancellor Pearson said. "Is there some reasoning behind it?"

A self-satisfied grin spread across Desmond's face as

he answered. "Because, if I have anything to say about it, we'll be so good at what we do that in the years to come, people will doubt our very existence."

A few chuckles sounded around the room.

"I admire your confidence and hope you're right. Now, if there's nothing else...?"

Everyone stood to leave.

"Wait! Sorry, one more thing," Desmond smiled. He could get used to this kind of control.

Chancellor Pearson sighed loudly. "Yes, Desmond, what is it?"

"I want to see everything you have on my son as soon as possible."

The Chancellor nodded. "It will be waiting for you at the GDA when you arrive. Now—" he banged the gavel on the table. "Meeting adjourned."

Desmond and Celia stayed seated while the room emptied out. Celia shot her father a look and spoke from the side of her mouth. "What the hell just happened?"

Desmond mirrored her incredulous look. "I'll let you know when I figure it out."

5

Seventh Verse
Civitas, Terra

Prime Minister of Terra, Julia White, stepped off the shuttle and onto the landing pad on the roof of Mescham Laboratories. She took a moment to take in the view. The lights of the city contrasted against the night sky. Flashes of light flew by as the hyper rails transported passengers to their destinations.

Julia ducked her head against the high altitude wind and hurried toward the door. She could see the lights from the transport lifting off in the reflection of the glass door as it opened. Inside, one of Dr. Mescham's lab assistants waited. A short woman with dark, shoulder-length hair pulled back into a ponytail. She wore a white coat that went down to her knees.

"Please, this way, Prime Minister." The assistant

showed her to the private elevator which would take them all the way down to the sub-levels.

Secrets were a necessary part of the Prime Minister's job. There were many things that the government took care of that the Terran people didn't need to know about. It was in their best interest not to have to worry about such matters of state, chief among them, their security. The subterranean labs were just one of many such covert facilities spread out among the capital city of Terra.

Civitas spread out for miles. The peaks and valleys of the spires of various districts throughout the city resembled a jagged mountain range when viewed in the distance. It was the oldest city on Terra by a few thousand years. Once construction could no longer spread outward, the city had grown upward. Its tallest buildings were nearly a mile high, while the average building height was around 2,000 feet tall.

Needless to say, the elevator ride took several minutes.

Dr. Mescham was waiting for them at the bottom of the lift when the doors opened.

"Prime Minister, I trust your journey was a good one?" Dr. Mescham asked. He had an average build and what hair he had left was dark and combed over as if to try to spread what little there was around.

While physically unassuming, Charles Mescham was Terra's leading expert in the field of nanotechnology and biotechnology. His team was responsible for the latest breakthrough in cracking the Gaian's abilities to manipulate the flux field.

"How is the treatment progressing?" Julia ignored the doctor's attempt at pleasantries.

"It's best if you see for yourself." Dr. Mescham led her

down a series of hallways before arriving at their destination.

Julia inspected the room. Part lab, part hospital from the looks of it. "How many of these rooms are there?"

"Three for now, but we have room for more if we're able to come by more subjects."

There were nine beds in the room, each with a child between the ages of six and twelve lying in them. "Are they awake? Can they hear us?" Julia asked.

"Their bodies have entered a coma-like state as they fight off, or at least *attempt* to fight off the strain of nanites that I've injected them with. We're currently on strain three point two."

"And what about the uplink? Are we able to start harvesting?"

Mescham's face fell. "Unfortunately, no. Not yet, anyway. We've been having problems with the nanites taking root. It seems that, even though the children's connection to the flux field hasn't formed yet, their genetics are still able to resist the nanites from taking control."

Julia gritted her teeth as she listened to the doctor make excuses. "What are you doing about it? Time is an issue here."

The doctor swallowed hard and wiped several drops of sweat from his brow. "We are doing everything we can think of, I assure you, Prime Minister. I have a team working on matching the bio-signature of the nanites to Gaian genetics, but this sort of work can take years. What we really need is a hybrid of sorts—" he hesitated, before continuing, "someone like your daughter."

Julia exhaled, annoyed. She had hoped that she

would be able to make due with the pure-blooded Gaian children, but now she would have to put her contingency plan in place. "No, I told you, the Gaian must not be bonded to the flux yet. Even a teenager would be too old, with too many genetic glimmerings of what they will soon become."

"Yes, you mentioned it, but you didn't say why... Perhaps, if I understood—"

Julia raised her hand, cutting him off. She felt the beginnings of a headache forming behind her temples. "Because the process would drain the life of a bonded Gaian long before we were able to siphon enough of their flux energy—" Julia massaged her throbbing head as the pain intensified. "Look, the details don't concern you. Just keep doing as I've asked and all will be well." She could feel him studying her like a subject.

"How long have you been having the headaches, Prime Minister?" Dr. Mescham frowned. "I'd like to run a diagnostic on your nanites. They should be handling any sort biological imbalance."

"No, I'm fine." Julia forced her hands down to her sides. She wasn't fine, but the pain had started to fade. Soon, it would be gone.

"As you wish." Mescham nodded toward the nearest child lying on a bed. "What do you want me to do with them?"

Julia considered his question. "What are you doing with previous strains of nanites that you've injected?"

"Nothing at the moment, we've extracted them, but nothing more."

"They are still active, yes? Or have they been rendered inert?"

"Yes, still active and functioning." The doctor nodded, his enthusiasm peaking. "But they had no effect, or should I say the effect they had was not the one we were after."

Julia smiled. "Good. I want you to see what they do to an adult—call it a hunch."

Mescham brought his hands together in front of his chest in an awkward, single clap. "Excellent, however, my supply of test subjects is rather limited at this moment." He gestured around to the children.

"Don't worry about that, I'll have Mallak round some up for you."

Dr. Mescham looked surprised. "Is that wise, so soon after the children? Surely, they must be on high alert?"

Julia laughed. "I bet they are... No, we'll take some of the Gaians who are stationed in the Third. They won't be expecting it."

The doctor nodded his approval. "The limbs are always weaker the farther from the body."

"Yes, quite." The Prime Minister turned toward the door. "If you'll excuse me, I have another meeting..."

"Of course, Madam Prime Minister, but..." Mescham cleared his throat. "About our original problem?"

"Leave that to me. I've been grooming someone to help with a similar problem. I had hoped to wait until after this was all over, but it seems that we can't always get everything we want." She stared off into the distance, losing herself for a moment before returning. "With any luck, you'll have your half-blooded child before long."

6

Fourth Verse
New Queensland

ASHER BANCROFT LET himself into the Princess's suite and locked the door behind him. He sighed as he saw the mess. There were clothes everywhere. Dresses, blouses, stockings, shoes, and undergarments of all sorts covered almost all of the floor and furniture. He allowed himself a moment's pity and then got to work straightening up.

As he cleaned, his mind drifted to what the next year would hold for him. He turned sixteen in a month and a half. After that, he would begin training for the trials along with the rest of his peers. Training would last for two years and then the trials would commence. He was not looking forward to it.

It wasn't just that he found the whole notion of the trials barbaric, he was also terrified. He had never known anything else but his life in the palace, serving the

Queen's household. To leave his life at the palace and begin training for a place in one of the Houses was unfathomable. If he won the Gauntlet, he would receive the ultimate boon that a male member of society could achieve: becoming a member of the breeding class. If he lost, he would be sterilized along with the thousands of other males and spend the rest of his shortened life in servitude in the buzz fields, planting sunflowers and hemp to remove the radioactive elements from the soil.

All in all, not how Asher wanted to spend the rest of his life, but he didn't relish the idea of running the Gauntlet, either. If only he could stay in the palace somehow, and continue doing what he was doing. "If only the sun didn't set in the west and rise in the east," he muttered. He might as well wish for wings to fly away on.

Asher lifted what appeared to be a nightgown off the bed and held it up against his torso, comparing the small fit to his larger frame. He would be a liar if he said that he had not thought of what the Princess would look like wearing such a nightgown and nothing else countless times over the last two years that he'd been assigned to her chambers. He felt the blood rush below his belt and quickly dropped the garment, trying to reverse the physiological process that was hijacking him.

All he needed in his life right now would be for the Princess to walk in on him and see him like that. If he were found in an aroused state with the Princess, he would be *lucky* to be banished to the buzz fields as a punishment. More than likely, he would be dismembered or put to death.

He managed to steer his thoughts back to the unwelcome idea of training for the trials, and to his relief, Asher's teenage body did him a favor.

In a more compliant state of being, Asher resumed his clean up efforts. He bent over to pick up the nightgown he had dropped and his foot bumped against something underneath the bed that was barely sticking out. Asher pulled it out and removed the crumpled dress that was partially draped over it.

It was one of the Princess's jewelry boxes. *What on earth was this doing here?* Asher had always known the Princess to be an untidy person, but if there was one thing she was meticulous about, it was her jewelry. Of all the things he had found lying about her chambers over the years, he had never once seen a single piece of jewelry out of place. Each necklace and set of earrings were either on her person or in their designated places in the Princess's vanity cases.

Asher took the wooden box and placed it on top of the bed. The box was beautifully crafted. Hand-carved and painted by one of the Queen's own artisans, no doubt.

A burning sensation coursed through Asher's head as he stared at the box. He knew he should put it back where he'd found it, but curiosity got the better of him, and he flipped open the lid, unable to resist the temptation.

The velvet-lined box held only one object inside, and Asher had no idea what it was.

"*What the—?*" Asher stammered as he picked up the object and turned it over in his hands. Whatever it was, it wasn't from around here. Asher thought it most closely resembled a wristwatch, but he had never seen one in person, only blurred and grainy pictures from a world that didn't exist anymore. The world before the war that had ended the world. Asher had heard rumors that the Queen had a private collection of objects from before the end of the world, but he had never been privy to that part of the palace.

He picked up the watch and examined it. The strap was one solid piece of dark, shiny fabric. He tugged on the closed loop, but there was very little give if any. He knew that it was supposed to be worn around the wrist, but he couldn't figure out how. There were no clasps, or buckles, or anything that indicated the strap was something other than a solid, closed loop. He tried to force his hand through, but it kept getting stuck at the knuckles.

His finger accidentally touched the face of the watch and it lit up brighter than a torch. Asher gasped in surprise. He squinted against the glare. *How the hell did the Princess have a working device?* The last time anything with electricity had worked was over 50 years ago. At least according to the tales that Asher had heard. He supposed it wouldn't be out of character for the Royals to keep that sort of information a secret from the public, but why bother?

Asher turned the watch over in his hands several more times. His index finger came to rest on the back of the watch face almost naturally, and the band opened, straightening out, as if by magic. In his shock, Asher fumbled the watch and nearly dropped it.

He heard a sound coming from out in the hall and his heart leaped into his throat. He stuffed the watch back in the box, slid it underneath the bed, and threw some clothes back over it.

In a state of panic, he looked for a place to hide. He didn't know why he felt the need, but at this point, his instincts were too powerful to ignore. As he heard the sound of the key enter the lock, he dove into the closet and closed the door, leaving a slight gap—he didn't want to risk the noise of the latch if he shut it all the way.

Asher heard the door open, and then the Princess bid a good day to her escort. He worked up as much courage as he could muster, and peeked out through the gap in the door.

Princess Avialle hummed to herself as she walked through her room. She glanced around, taking inventory of the mess she had left behind. She went around to the side of the bed and knelt down, peering underneath. She removed the jewelry box and placed it on her vanity. She sat down and opened the lid, frowning as she found the watch with the band open.

Asher's heart threatened to leap out of his chest. *Please don't call for the guards, please don't call for the guards...*

She removed it from the box and then glanced around the room checking to see if anything else was amiss. Satisfied, she slapped the watch down around her wrist and the two ends fastened themselves around her wrist, holding fast through some unseen force.

Asher didn't know whether to be astonished at what he'd seen or relieved that the Princess hadn't sounded the alarm.

A loud bell rang and Asher nearly peed himself in panic before realizing it was only the clock tower alerting everyone that it was now one hour until noon.

As the bell sounded, the watch face lit up again, and

Ava made a sweeping gesture with her finger on the face of the watch.

Asher's eyes widened as a face jumped out the top of the watch and spoke. "Ava, my darling, how have you been?" The face belonged to a woman, somewhere in her mid-to-late-thirties, with straight, platinum blonde hair, almost white in color.

"Lady Prime Minister," Ava began, "so good to see you again. I've been looking forward to speaking with you. I'm well, thank you. A little bored to tears around here, but what else is new?"

"Yes, well, I believe I can help you out with that. The time has finally come for you to join me here on Terra."

"You mean it?" The hope in her voice was unmistakable. "I'm so excited! What do I need to do? Should I pack? Or, do I need to bring—"

"Take a deep breath. Settle down…" The woman laughed. "I've arranged for everything. We have everything you could possibly want or need here. I just need to walk you through how to activate the zip drive."

Asher was confused. *What in the world were they talking about? It sounded as though Princess Ava was planning a journey. But to where? And what was a zip drive?*

Asher listened in fascination as the woman from the watch kept talking.

"Tap the menu on the face of the zip drive. You'll see several options. Here you can choose a destination, which can only be programmed with a master key. There is only one option for your destination, so you don't need to select it. It will automatically be selected for you. Among your other options, you can set a delay, or you can just activate the zip drive. A word of caution, though, you should only activate the zip drive without a delay in extreme circumstances."

"Why is that?"

"The delay allows the zip drive to scan the landing coordinates and assure that the jump zone is clear. If the zone is not clear—let's just say that the results can be a little messy. For the same reason, you should take care to be outside or at least in a room large enough that the effects of the zip drive will not be a problem."

The woman saw the confusion on the Princess's face and explained further. "When activated, the zip drive produces a concussive blast, that in the right or wrong environment, depending on how you want to look at it, can cause quite a bit of damage. Thus, outdoors typically works best, unless you have dedicated launch zones like we do here on Terra."

"I see... How long will it take?" the Princess asked.

"Travel is nearly instantaneous, but you'll be making a stop before coming here... Only a handful of people know about your Verse and where it's located, and I'd like to keep it that way. So, you'll jump to the Third, and I will send some of my best people to come and take you the rest of the way. That way no one will be able to track your starting point."

As Asher listened, an idea popped into his head that might solve his impending dilemma. It was bold and unlike him. He was certain that the Queen would not approve of whatever Princess Ava was involved in, and he prayed that he was correct, as he was about to stake his entire future and possibly his entire life on it. He stepped out from the closet. The door creaked slowly as he entered the room.

The Princess's head whipped around, searching for the source of the startling noise.

"What's that?" the woman asked.

"*You!* What are *you* doing here? You're not supposed to be in here!" The Princess was furious. She rose from her seat, dark lines forming on her face. "Get out of here right now, or I will call for the guard!"

"Ava, what's happening? What's the matter? Is there someone else in the room with you?" the prime minister asked.

Asher refused to let himself be intimidated. He shook his head. "I don't think so. Go ahead and call the guards. I'm willing to bet that your mother will be more than happy to learn about what I just saw. So happy, in fact, that she will grant me any posting that I choose."

The Princess froze for a moment, considering what Asher had said. "It's the chamber boy," Ava explained to the woman. "He was hiding in the closets. I'm sorry, I didn't know he was there. I should have checked. I know you said tha—"

"Listen to me very carefully, Ava. You must leave now before you are discovered with the zip drive. If your mother or her guards found out about it, you would never be allowed to join me here on Terra. And you'll never be able to discover the larger world that awaits you. Go now, and activate the zip drive. Don't set the delay—forget what I said earlier. Just jump, now! My people will find you at the jump point."

The Princess started tapping on the screen of the device and Asher's heart quickened. He couldn't let her get away. If he did, no one would ever believe his account of what had happened. And while he might be able to play dumb about the Princess's disappearance, it would do nothing to save him from taking part in the trials.

He reached the Princess just as she was about to tap the screen again and grabbed her arm, trying to keep her from finishing.

She shrieked in surprise, but he held fast around her arm. A smile began to form on his face. He was doing it... He was going to change his fate.

The world grew bright around him and the Princess, and his smile faded as fast as it had appeared. Lightning flashed and he shut his eyes tightly. When he opened them, he was standing in the middle of a field, surrounded by grass.

7

Third Verse
Outside Nashville, Tennessee

Asher felt a sharp pain on the side of his face as Ava's fist connected. "*Let go!*"

He released her wrist and attempted to shield himself from further blows.

"I'll have you beaten for this!" The Princess yelled, shaking out her hand. "You better pray to the gods that you haven't screwed this up for me." Ava tapped the screen of the zip drive around her wrist but it didn't respond. She slapped at it more forcefully. "What the hell is wrong with this thing?"

Asher rubbed his cheek and tried not to freak out about what had just happened. The grassy field that they were in was cut very low. Trees peppered the well-manicured lawn. They were in a park of some sort. It was surrounded by sidewalks and paved streets, and other people were walking and running about further off in the distance. Several vehicles were out on the streets. Asher stared at them, dumbfounded. *Where were they? Had they traveled back in time? To a period before the end of the world?* His mind was overwhelmed with the possibilities. *What did this mean about the trials?* Whatever had happened, Asher couldn't figure out whether his situation had improved or worsened.

"How do we get back?" he demanded. "Your mother is going to be furious."

"My mother doesn't know anything about this. And why would she? She barely knows that I exist at all. She's too busy running the country and visiting the breeding houses to take any notice of me."

"So that's what this is?" Asher asked. "You're running away? Poor little baby isn't getting enough attention from her mommy, so she's acting out?" The Princess took another swing at him, but Asher saw it coming this time and managed to duck it.

"Don't you dare speak to me that way! I am still your Princess, no matter what world we are on, and you will obey my commands!"

Asher tried not to laugh, but he couldn't help himself. "Oh, that's good! But who's gonna make sure I do what you say? The Queen and your guards are a million miles away or at least I assume that they're that far away..." His comeback lost steam as Asher looked around at their surroundings once more. "Wherever it is that we actually *are*."

A man and woman approached them from across the park. They were dressed in dark pants, shirts, and overcoats. They seemed a little out of place. It was warm and humid, and the rest of the park goers were in shorts and tank tops.

"Finally," Ava turned her back to Asher and waved at the couple. "Hello there! You must be the Prime Minister's people."

The woman raised her hand and waved back stiffly as if she'd never made the motion before.

The closer they got, the funnier Asher felt. There were butterflies in his stomach, and his brain felt like a cloud had formed inside of it. This was all happening too fast. The world started spinning and Asher felt his gorge rise. He vomited before he knew what happened.

"Oh, gross!" Ava jumped back, out of the way of the spray.

"Please come with us," the man said. "We need to move before the Gaians catch wind of us."

Asher wasn't finished. He threw up again.

The man sighed, agitated. "What you are experiencing is the effects of the zip drive. Some people have an adverse reaction their first few times. It will pass."

"Sir," the woman prompted.

"Right. We have to go. Follow me."

The man and woman led Ava and Asher through a path in the park. Asher did his best to keep his insides on his insides but he lost the contents of his stomach once more before they reached their destination.

They rounded a bend after several minutes of brisk walking and approached a box truck with the words UNIVERSAL CONTRACTING on the side of it.

The man opened the back of the truck and climbed in. "Get in. And try not to get sick."

Ava and Asher both hesitated.

"Just get in, and I'll explain everything to you." The man extended his hand, offering to help them up.

Ava took it and climbed up into the back of the truck. Asher followed her, not sure whether he trusted the man or not, but he didn't want to be separated from the Princess. Wherever they were going, she was his ticket back to home.

The woman closed the compartment door, sealing the three of them inside. Seconds later they heard the sound of the cab door opening and closing, and then the engine turned over. The truck accelerated quickly, jostling the inhabitants of the back around.

"Good, now we can relax a little bit. Sorry for the shortness and the haste, this area has been crawling with Gaian agents, and we were only expecting one traveler."

"And you are?" Asher asked.

"Of course, how rude of me. My name is Mallak. I work in the Ministry of Defense, directly for Prime Minister White." He nodded toward the front of the truck. "Kiri's driving, and you would be?"

"Asher Bancroft, Assistant to the Royal Family."

"He's my maid, basically," Ava said. "I'm Princess Avialle, but please call me Ava."

Asher's face turned red. "I have other duties as well, besides just cleaning up after you."

"Yes, well I'm afraid the addition of another person has caused our plans to change," Mallak said.

"What do you mean?" Ava's face creased.

"You won't be meeting the Prime Minister until after your mission is concluded here in the Third."

"Mission? What mission? I didn't sign up for any mission," Asher said.

"*You aren't even supposed to be here!*" Ava's anger flared up, but she quickly gained control of her emotions. "But he does raise an excellent point: *What mission?* The Prime Minister never mentioned anything about a mission to me."

"She was going to ask you in person, but with the recent developments, we can't risk the extra exposure of you jumping back and forth. And it's not safe for her to leave the Seventh." Mallak paused, expecting an interruption, but to the Princess's credit, she waited for him to continue. "She needs you to retrieve her long-lost son. He was stolen from her by the Gaians and hidden here in the Third. She's been searching for him for years, and now she's finally found him."

"That's great. So, why doesn't she just send some of her men to pick him up?" Asher asked. "I assume that she does have men, right?"

Ava shot him a furious look. "My housemaid forgets his place, Mallak. I'm sorry. I'm sure you were just about to explain why she needed me to carry out this task for her. After all, she does command forces more intimidating than myself, doesn't she? Why not send you, or your friend up front there?"

"It has to do with the Gaians. They have guards around him and are much more powerful than we are." It looked as though it pained Mallak to say it. "While we are making strides toward closing that gap, we're not there yet. Our only play would be with overwhelming numbers and firepower, but the fallout and the danger of her son being injured in the attempt is too great to risk. Not to mention, it would alert the people of the Third to our presence."

"What can I possibly do against them, that you can't?" Ava asked.

"The bulk of their advantage over us lies in their ability to affect physical matter through something they refer to as the flux field. Using it, they can detect our physical presence and—are you at all familiar with the concept of telekinesis?"

Ava thought about, and shook her head, no.

"It's when someone can control an object with their mind, right?" Asher spoke up.

"Very good. Yes. And I can see that you're about to ask, so I'll answer what that's got to do with you." Mallak took a deep breath, readying himself for the explanation. "We discovered your Verse decades ago along with the others, but we thought it was an uninhabited wasteland, like the First, Second, and Fifth. We picked up major radiation scans from other parts of the planet and assumed that the population had been wiped out. We only just came across your settlement a little over a year ago during a follow-up scan of the planet for raw materials. As far as we're aware, the Gaians don't know about your existence.

"We discovered that the inhabitants of New Queensland naturally disrupt a Gaian's ability to access the flux field in their direct vicinity. We don't know why, yet, but what we do know is that for all intents and purposes, you will be invisible to the Gaians' abilities."

"They won't be able to see me?" Ava asked, puzzled.

Mallak laughed. "No, they can still see you, but only with their eyes. They won't be able to spot you coming, and they won't be able to use their powers to control you."

"I see," Ava mused, thinking about the revelation. "I'll

want to hear it from the Prime Minister, herself, before agreeing to anything."

"Of course," Mallak agreed. "I'll arrange for a conversation as soon as we reach our destination."

"And where might that be?" Asher asked.

"Place called Texas," Mallak answered. "We have several bases set up in the Third that the Gaians don't know about and we work very hard to keep it that way. You'll be trained there—*if* you agree to the Prime Minister's terms."

"He's included?" Ava asked, surprised.

Mallak shrugged. "Have to run it by the prime minister, but I don't see why not. Two's usually better than one. And this way, you'll have someone to watch your back." He turned to Asher. "What do you think? Are you up to it?"

Asher didn't know what to say.

"You'll have some time to think about it. It'll take a few hours to get there."

"And if I decide I don't want to?" Asher asked.

"Then we'll make arrangements to get you back home. Although I must say, from what I've heard, there's not much opportunity for you to go back to... My advice? Stick around and see if you can't change your fate."

"Hmm..." Asher considered the man's advice. He was only in this mess in the first place because he'd tried to change his fate. But then again, his fate did need changing. There wasn't anything to go back to, as it stood. Not unless he could return with the Princess in tow.

Ava huffed, not happy with the development. "How is it that he's even here in the first place?" Ava held up her wrist. "I'm the one who was wearing the zip drive."

"I'm guessing that he was holding on to you at the time?"

Ava nodded. "He grabbed my arm."

"The zip drive transports whatever is connected to it —up to a certain mass limit, anyway. Is the zip drive also not turning back on now?"

"How did you know?"

"Each zip drive only has a limited amount of energy for transportation, and if you double the mass," he pointed to Asher, "then you use up the power reserve. Here, give it to me."

Ava deactivated the strap and handed it to Mallak.

"How—?" Asher watched as though he was seeing magic.

"Separate power source for the bands," Mallak explained. "There's a charging station at the base, but this one will return with me."

"Because of the coordinates," Ava guessed.

Mallak smiled. "Very good, Princess. Yes. Can't have the knowledge of your existence falling into the wrong hands."

The truck came to a stop and the engine cut off.

"Right, this is our stop then."

Kiri slid open the door and they hopped down.

They were at a small airfield. A private plane sat in front of them with the door open and a staircase leading up to it. "Kiri, please show our guests to their seats and tell the pilot to prepare for takeoff. I need to make a call and then we'll get underway."

"Aye, aye, boss." Kiri bowed slightly and motioned her hands toward the plane. "Right this way, guys. Your new life awaits."

Ava and Asher shared a nervous glance with each other.

"Beats doing dishes, I guess." Asher shrugged and walked toward the plane.

"But I've never washed dishes..." Ava sped to catch up.

8

Sixth Verse

Gaian Defense Agency, Cairos

Desmond's new office was his old office. The irony was not lost on him. Nice to see that some things never change. At least he had a window with a decent view. The early afternoon sun was just starting to dip towards the horizon, scattering light off of the surrounding buildings.

Oracle would be stationed at the GDA for the time being. The official story was that Desmond was being reactivated to head up a task force to look into the kidnappings. The easiest way to hide was in plain sight.

There was a knock at the door. "Come in."

A young, well-groomed man poked his head in, testing the mood of the room. Desmond didn't recognize him, but the man's timid reaction made him wonder who had occupied the office before him. "You asked for the file on your son, sir?"

"Yes, come in," Desmond repeated. He'd had to go through three separate channels before he was finally granted the security clearance to view the file. "What's your name?"

The young man coughed. "Lee, sir. Daniel Lee."

"Do you go by Daniel or Dan—"

"Danny, sir. Where do you want me to...?" He indicated the folder he was holding.

"Just hand it to me—unless there's some other protocol that we need to abide by. Do I need to sign something or...?" Desmond was only half-joking. He wouldn't have been surprised if the kid had pulled out a large stack of paperwork for him to fill out.

Danny laughed awkwardly. "No, nothing else. Just, uh, send word when you're finished looking through it, and I'll come take it back to Records for you."

Desmond couldn't tell if he was trying to make a joke or if he actually wanted him to call him when he was done. "Okay, will do, Danny. Thanks, and you have a good day."

"Oh, you too, sir. Thank you, sir." Danny backed out of the room instead of turning around, and Desmond briefly wondered if the guy had all of his marbles. He hadn't sensed anything funny, but sometimes subtle things slipped by. And some Gaians were better than others at hiding in the flux.

Desmond opened the folder and began sifting through its contents. It contained some local information on where his son was being held—or living—he supposed. He had to remind himself that his son was not a prisoner, that he had a life, no matter what the situation felt like to Desmond.

His son lived with his uncle, Jack Spader, about an hour outside of New York City near the Adirondack Mountains in New York in the Third Verse. He was eleven now, nearing twelve. The file held several photos at different ages. Desmond could see bits of himself and Julia there. His first name was John, after his mother's brother. His last name was Keller. *John Keller.* It was a good name, Desmond thought.

There was a note in the file. His son went by the nickname Kid, given to him by his uncle when he was a toddler. His parents had both passed away almost a year and a half ago in a car accident.

Desmond wondered what his son's life must've been like. Was he a good baby or a fussy one. How soon had he started to walk? What were his first words?

Desmond skipped ahead in the folder. There was information about the security detail that kept an eye on Kid. One of his neighbors directly across the street from his house and the neighbors on either side were GDA agents, all long-term assignments to his son.

He set the folder down and stood to stretch his legs. It was too much information to take in sitting down. He felt antsy and needed to move. To work out some of the nervous energy that he had balled up inside. In the end, he settled for some pacing as he thought through his options.

Fatherly instinct screamed for him to bring Kid to Gaia, but that would hardly be fair to him. After all, he had a life in the Third. Friends at school, people who loved him. To rip him away from that without any concrete reason would be wrong, despite how much Desmond wanted to meet him. Kid didn't deserve to have the knowledge of his biological parents and their problems dumped on him.

The other option was to do nothing. Kid was protected and hidden. The GDA had kept his existence a secret this long. And nothing Desmond did would make Kid's life any better... If anything, it would only complicate it. Besides, it wasn't like Desmond's plate was particularly empty right now. And with his Uncle Jack and the protective detail, at least Kid had someone watching out for him.

When Desmond finally stopped pacing and resumed pouring over the file, he found the section that detailed how Kid had come to be in the Third.

It felt so clinical, reading it in other people's words. These were events from his personal life. To see them reduced to concise words in a report, seemed wrong—disloyal to the pain of the experience. He recapped the notes anyway and tried to stay emotionally detached.

Julia had left him, pregnant, but at a stage too early for Desmond to have felt the development in the flux field. Julia was ramping up her political career, a move that, at the time, had seemingly come out of nowhere. When Desmond first met her, she was tired of the political games she had encountered thus far in her public service. She had stated time and time again that Ambassador was as high as she cared to rise on the political scene. But then again, she had said a lot of things back then that turned out differently.

Not wanting a child to interfere with her political ambitions, Julia had the embryo removed and cryogenically stored. A few Gaian sympathizers in the Seventh learned of the embryo's existence and managed to steal it and get it into the hands of Gaian agents in the Third Verse.

With Julia's newfound political ambition, the Gaian High Council decided it was best to hide the child out of reach of both parents. They didn't want the existence of a child to be used against Desmond or affect his official duties. Julia didn't discover that the embryo had been stolen for several years. By that time, she had already risen up the ranks, and the scandal of a stolen embryo was something that she didn't want to be publicized.

It was a more thorough account of what Chancellor Pearson had told him, but all in all, it wasn't very helpful to his current situation.

The rest of the file's notes skipped around a bit, backward and forward in time. There was a section on Kid's parents, but only a few comments about his uncle. Desmond made a mental note to learn more about his son's caretaker as soon as possible.

An alert from his datapad sounded. It was an encrypted message. He set aside Kid's folder and ran the message through the decryption program.

An older man with a white beard and wild, wispy hair filled the screen. It was Wizard, a former Terran Senator. Desmond had first met the man around the time he and Julia had gotten together. Before he got into public service, Wizard had run his own tech-consulting firm and spent some time teaching university students the trade. He'd had several government contracts, but mostly he consulted with the private business sector. His given name was Ander Wallace, but due to his excellent tradecraft and his eccentric appearance, everyone called him Wizard. After Julia left, formal communication between the two Verses screeched to a halt, but Wizard had cooked up a way to get messages back and forth without being flagged, so they were at least able to catch up once in a while. Desmond used the connection sparingly, for fear of the consequences if Wizard were to be found out.

"Desmond, my old friend. How are you?" Wizard's smile was warm and kind. *"I've missed you and Celia very much. I got your previous message about the developments on Gaia, and I have to say, I was very troubled to hear it. As you know, we've both been afraid of my government doing something like this for years now. And while I'm sad that it has happened under such circumstances, I'm glad that the Council has finally given you the freedom to protect your Verse from any such future threats.*

"Our goal has always been unity between our two worlds, a goal that Julia used to share in before..." he drifted off for a moment before coming back. *"Before whatever changed her mind so drastically. It still boggles me.*

"While today, they may think of me as treasonous, I hope that through our efforts to live together in peace, one day, my people will look back at what I've done and see it not as treason, but as heroic, if not patriotic. Not to say that I think of myself as a hero, far from it, but I do what I do because I believe it is the right thing to do. Both for me and both of our worlds." Wizard broke into a short coughing fit and then continued. *"Anyway, sorry for the long rambling greeting. I guess my brain needed to get some thoughts out into the open. From here on out, I'll be brief. I got your request to keep an eye out for anything amiss, and I've already received word that something is stirring in the Third. Julia's lapdog in the Ministry of Defense, Malcolm Mallak, walked out in the middle of a state meeting at the Prime Minister's request,*

apparently. One of my sources in Transit said he checked out two zip drives and had them programmed for the Third. They weren't able to catch the exact coordinates, just the prefix that denoted the Verse. That was a little over four hours ago. I don't know why he went, but if he's going personally, then it must be something big. Naturally, my first thought was your son. I know you said he was well protected, but... Well, anyway, I'll keep digging on my end and let you know what I find. Take care, and give my love to Celia."

The message ended and Desmond immediately picked up his comm. The agent answered almost immediately.

"Donovan, I've just received intel that something is going down in the Third. The Prime Minister's right hand has gone in person, so whatever it is, it's significant. I'm not sure if it has anything to do with the kidnappings or not, but I want two more teams posted on my son at all times, and make sure the existing teams are on high alert. If anyone so much as dreams about a Terran in the Third, I want to hear about it."

"You got it, boss. I'll make the calls."

As Donovan hung up to do his bidding, Desmond once more fought the urge to jump to the Third and see to his son's safety personally. But there was much work to be done in the Sixth. Oracle still needed to be fully staffed and organized if it was ever going to be an effective tool. He sighed, put Kid's file in a desk drawer, and pulled up the GDA's personnel roster on his monitor to begin sorting through more potential recruits.

9

Third Verse

Somewhere in Texas, Terran Base TX-14

Asher hit the ground and popped back up, grunting with effort. He was covered in dust and sweat from head to toe. His lungs were on fire.

"*Down!*" Kiri yelled again, for what felt like the hundredth time.

Asher was still out of breath from the first round of calisthenics, and now he'd lost track of how many rounds they'd done. Although he was young and healthy, his life of caretaking around the palace had not prepared him for the level of physical exertion that Kiri was demanding.

"While your mission may be a simple one in theory," Kiri yelled over the ambient noise of the camp. "I will be training you as thoroughly as possible for any contingencies."

"But with so little time, why are we doing so many exercises?" Ava gasped in between breaths.

"It's true that your bodies might not have time to adapt to the benefits that these exercises will give you, however, the exercise simulates the high stress and adrenaline environment that you will experience on the mission." Kiri paused, a smile spread across her lips. "Now, if you're done complaining. *Down!*"

She put them through two more rounds of bodyweight exercises and then gave them a water break and a much-needed rest. Next, weapons training began, Asher's favorite so far. There was something exhilarating about the feel of firing a rifle. The way his body shook with the recoil. The feeling of power in his hands.

They met Kiri on the range. The rocks crunched beneath Asher's boots and the dust swirled from a gust of wind. The range was empty except for one of Kiri's helpers who was setting up watermelons at distances of ten feet apart.

"For the last several days you've trained in general marksmanship with several different weapons—pistols, rifles, and various hand grenades. Today, we will begin your specialized training with the standard issue NK-43 assault rifle." She held up the weapon, modeling it as she went over various features. "The NK has a dual-firing capacity. It is capable of firing lethal, ballistic rounds, or —" she flicked the selector on the side of the weapon, "it can be set to the stun setting. When the stun setting is selected, the NK will fire subsonic blasts in a focused beam that will stun a target if they're hit in the torso, or completely knock them out if the target is struck in the head. Multiple stun blasts to the torso will render the target unconscious as well. While the stun setting is usually non-lethal, there can still be significant injuries from the concussive sound blasts at close range. So do not use it lightly."

Kiri pointed the rifle at the nearest watermelon which was just on the other side of the barrier separating the shooters from the active range. She pulled the trigger and a blast of blue light flew out. The melon exploded. Chunks of pink fruit flew in every direction, splattering the ground all around.

"The light acts as a tracer, so you can see what you're hitting."

She then fired at three more melons, each one a little farther down the range. The concussive blasts from each discharge of the weapon propelled the watermelons off their perch several feet through the air. The farthest melon, however, barely wavered, and for a moment Asher wondered if she had missed her mark or not.

"As you can see, from point-blank range, the stun blast can be quite damaging. The most effective stunning range of the weapon is between two and fifty feet. Anything closer than that may cause too much damage, and anything farther away has little to no effect on the target."

The other instructor laid out Ava and Asher's weapons and stacked several clips of ammunition beside them. There were stacks of what appeared to be smaller ammo clips as well.

"What are these?" Asher asked. He held up one of the cartridges on the table.

"Those are the sonic charges for your stun setting," Kiri said. "They look somewhat similar to the ballistic round clips, and they function much the same way. Eject the clip that is spent, and insert the new charge," she demonstrated, "until it clicks into place."

"How many shots does each clip hold?" Ava asked.

"Good question. The NK ballistic clip can hold 30 rounds. But each sonic clip only holds enough charge for five stun blasts. So use each shot wisely, and be sure you're in the optimal range before firing."

The other instructor set up more melons for each of them to practice on while Kiri continued.

"This is your final day of training before you undertake your mission tomorrow, so I wanted this to be as fresh in your minds as possible. You'll have as much ammo as you need here today in order to get the hang of the NK-43, and I won't leave here until you both feel confident handling the weapon. Because make no mistake—failure is not an option. Lives are at stake, least of all your own. So, let's get to work."

Asher loaded his rifle. He didn't feel great about Kiri's little pep-talk. Truth be told, he still wasn't certain whether or not he *wanted* to go on this mission. On the one hand, he didn't really have any other options. He was essentially alone in the multiverse. The closest thing he had to a friend was the Princess. Who, at times, treated him as a peer, but more often than not, she treated them like the servant he had been his entire life. On the other hand, the mission was no less dangerous than the trials that he would face back home. But if he was successful here, his life would open up to countless possibilities that were not available for him back home. From the way Ava had described Terra, there were endless opportunities and the standard of living was lightyears beyond anything New Queensland could offer. Still, he'd never really fancied himself a soldier, despite how much he liked firing a weapon.

When they'd first arrived at the camp, Mallak had arranged for Ava to speak with the Prime Minister. He then took Asher aside and gave him the choice to join in the mission or return home. At the time, Asher accepted his offer. Anything had seemed better than returning to the life that awaited him back home. Back in Ava's chambers, he'd thought he could maybe trade the information about Ava to the Queen in exchange for an exemption from the trials, but he knew he would still be treated like a second rate citizen, at best. Here, he still had people telling him what to do, but at least he had a shot at earning his freedom and improving his lot in life.

"*Hey! Earth to Asher!*" Ava smacked his arm. She'd already worked her way through an entire clip. "What are you doing?"

Asher snapped back to the present moment. "Sorry, I was just... thinking about home, I guess."

"What? Why? I would think you, of all people, would be happy to put that place as far behind you as possible."

"I guess... I don't know. I'm a little scared, I suppose." Asher was embarrassed to say it out loud, and he immediately regretted it.

Ava stared at him for a moment and then hugged him, much to his surprise. The hug made Asher feel warm and good and human. And Ava smelled wonderful, like flowers. He fought the urge to make it more than a hug. He didn't want it to end, but if it went on much longer he didn't know if he could resist trying to kiss her.

Finally, she pulled back, and Asher tried to make sure his face didn't betray his thoughts.

"I get it, Asher. Really, I do. Sometimes I miss home, too. But the places that we'll get to see, and the things in store for us—it's going to be better than ruling over a piece-of-shit world like ours. You'll see. *I promise.* After all, you don't think I'd pass up being queen for nothing, do you?" She smiled.

He smiled back. "Actually, I did kind of wonder what you were getting out this."

She ejected the spent magazine and inserted a fresh one. "Bet I can beat you best out of five."

"You're on," Asher grinned, relaxing. Maybe this would all work out after all.

10

Third Verse

Texas, Terran Base TX-14

Ava waited until she heard soft snoring coming from Asher's bunk. They were the only occupants of the barracks. There were six bunks, three on either side of the room. She slept on one side, while Asher slept on the other. She drew back the covers and tip-toed across the room, opening and closing the door as quietly as she could manage in an attempt to not wake him up.

Outside, the command center was a short walk away. The path was lit with overhead lights every forty feet or so. The night air was hot but dry. A few lingering fireflies lit up intermittently. She marveled at the luminous creatures. New Queensland didn't have any fireflies.

She nodded to the guard posted outside the command center. He should be expecting her, but she wasn't certain what would happen if he wasn't. Would he raise an alarm? Detain her? Would she have to raise her voice and demand Kiri's presence? Thankfully, he merely nodded back and waved her toward the door.

She *humphed*, disappointed that he wasn't opening the door for her. Patience, she reminded herself. She might not be a princess here, but soon enough she would climb back to her previous social ranking and doors would open themselves for her once more. Wait, what if they didn't have to open doors on Terra? She laughed at the thought, drawing a curious glance from the guard. No matter, she decided. Whatever the equivalent level of respect and fear was, she would have it. It was only a matter of time.

Inside were several tables with electronic equipment stacked on them. Some appeared to be organized intentionally, while others seemed to be junk piles and spare parts. She stood there, looking for someone that she recognized, but saw no one. Finally, one of the technicians who was seated in front of one of the organized stacks looked up and saw her standing there. "Ava, you made it. I was beginning to wonder if you'd manage or not."

"Sorry, he took forever to fall asleep. Can't really blame him though—big day tomorrow."

"Indeed. Come..." the man stood and gestured for her to take his seat. "Let me connect you with the Prime Minister." He left the front room and disappeared into the back somewhere, returning moments later. "Please clear the room."

The other technicians stopped their tinkering and filed out, one after the other.

Ava watched as the remaining technician produced a

zip drive from his pocket. He tapped on the device and several moments later a man's head projected out from the face. "*Outpost TX-14*... Is she there?"

"Yes. Is the Prime Minister nearby?"

"Standby... She's just finishing up another call. She'll be with you shortly."

"Thank you." The technician handed off the zip drive to Ava. "My counterpart will connect you as soon as she's available. When you're done, just let me know. I'll be waiting outside with the others."

Ava nodded and then spent the next few minutes wondering how long it would be. She wasn't used to waiting for other people and having tried it a few times now, she could say with certainty that she didn't care for it.

The Prime Minister's smiling face abruptly replaced the technician's. She always seems so pleasant, Ava thought.

"Prime Minister, hello."

Prime Minister Julia White wasted no time returning the greeting. "Did you do as I suggested?" she asked.

Ava nodded. "Yes, I did exactly what you told me to. I even gave him a hug."

"Splendid, dear. That's excellent. You'll have need of him, I'm sure. Always better to have something in your pocket and not need it, than to need it and not have it. And then, when you've returned tomorrow, if you still don't want him around, we'll make arrangements to send him home."

Ava winced at the mention of home.

"What is it, my dear?" the Prime Minister asked.

"Is there anywhere else you could send him? It's just

that—they really wouldn't be very kind to him back home. With my disappearance and all..."

"Where else would you have me send him? I can't have him blathering on about your Verse—even my own people aren't aware that we've discovered New Queensland. Not that anyone would believe his story here in the Seventh, but still."

"I don't know... I hadn't really given it much thought," Ava said. In truth, with all the training they'd been doing, there wasn't time for much of anything else. Ava had had her hands full just making it through the day. "I suppose he could stay, I just hadn't pictured myself having to babysit anyone."

If she needed to keep an eye out for Asher, it would detract from her own agenda. She'd still be able to make progress, she supposed, but it would slow her down considerably.

"I can see it matters a great deal to you. I'll tell you what—why don't we discuss it after the mission is completed? And I promise you we'll find a solution that works out for everybody. How does that sound?"

"More than fair, Prime Minister. Thank you, for everything!"

"Don't mention it, Ava. It's a small thing compared to what I've asked of you. And on that note, are you ready for tomorrow?"

Ava nodded. "Yes. Kiri has done a wonderful job of whipping us into shape!"

"She's one of our best. I want you to remember, someone will be with you the entire time on your comms and I will be listening in as well. You're not alone in this...

Now, walk me through the plan from start to finish. You can never be too prepared!" The Prime Minister smiled.

Ava really did feel prepared for the mission, and having the Prime Minister's approval was an added boost to her confidence. She began reciting the mission plan, "Okay, first, we jump in..."

11

Third Verse
New York State

Jack Spader pulled up to the pickup line at Crestfield Middle School and cursed. Back of the line again. He'd left early from the hospital, and somehow he still managed to catch every red light on the way. No matter what he did, he always seemed to end up in the back of the forty-five-minute line to pick Kid up from school.

After Bob and Mary's accident, Jack had started working at the hospital as an MRI technician in order to better take care of Kid. His previous life as an on-again-off-again security contractor was too unpredictable for a young boy. So Jack had given it up in an attempt to provide Kid with some stability in his life.

That was almost two years ago, and now Kid was rapidly approaching his teenage years. Most days, Jack felt like he still didn't have a damn clue what he was doing. Today was one of those days.

He fiddled with the radio as he inched closer to the school entrance at a snail's pace. Children milled about on the sidewalk as he flipped through the top-40 stations, the oldies, the classic rock station, and talk radio. Each one he flipped to agitated him more and more. He finally just turned the damned thing off and sat in silence.

He smiled, nodded, and waved at the various teachers who were helping with the pickup lines today, playing the part of the willing participant. They were spaced out every twenty feet or so, like a small invasion force. He wondered if they could tell how much of an act he was putting on.

At last, he made it to the front of the line where Kid was waiting with a handful of teachers and three or four other students, the only ones left. Jack reached across the center console and pushed open the passenger side door.

"Hey buddy, sorry it took so long again," he said as Kid climbed in the car. "I even left work fifteen minutes early, but it still didn't seem to have any effect on what time I got here."

"It's okay," Kid said. "I know you do the best that you can."

Jack couldn't tell if Kid was being genuine or sarcastic, and almost as if reading his mind, Kid went on, "Really, Uncle Jack. You're doing the best that you can. And it's a pretty good job at that."

Jack shook his head and chuckled. "Thanks, bud. Sometimes I wonder if your mom made a mistake putting me in charge." Jack immediately regretted saying it out loud. He could see the emotions flash across Kid's face as he dredged up the heartbreaking memory of the loss of his parents. "Shit, man. I didn't mean to say it like that... You know me and my big mouth, always saying things first and thinking about them second."

To the boy's credit, Kid shook off the feeling and got himself back to neutral within moments. "It's okay. I just miss them still sometimes, I guess."

"I know, I miss them too," Jack said. "And there's nothing wrong with missing them, either. Don't let anyone tell you otherwise."

Kid nodded as he stared out the window, too uncomfortable to make eye contact.

Jack checked that Kid's seat belt was buckled, and then pulled out, heading for the practice field. "So, you ready for your game tomorrow?"

The change in subject brought Kid back around. "As ready as we'll ever be. Coach said that if we win this game, we'll play in the championship next week."

"That's exciting," Jack said. "When I was your age, my team was never good enough to make the Little League playoffs at the end of the season. Best we ever did was fifth-place if I remember correctly."

"Yeah, but your high school team won the state championships," Kid pointed out.

"That's true, but we never took the Crestfield Little League by storm like you have. You guys keep winning and you might make it all the way to Williamsport!" Jack reached over and messed up Kid's hair. Kid giggled and squirmed away, attempting to flatten his hair back out.

Like many youth leagues, the practice field was the same as the game field. The teams alternated days for access. Today was Kid's team's day.

They pulled into the parking lot and Kid jumped out and ran around to the back of the car, opening the trunk and getting out his bat bag. Jack turned off the ignition and slowly got out of the car.

Kid was already running off toward the practice field. "Hey, don't forget your glove!" Jack yelled out.

Kid kept running but turned his head and yelled back, "It's in my bag!"

Jack laughed and went around the back of the car to close the trunk that Kid had left open. He then settled down on the bleachers with a few of the other parents who were attending the practice. Jack had other things he could be doing at home while Kid practiced, but watching a couple of kids play the game of baseball was the perfect way to unwind from any day, in his opinion. Everything else could wait a little while longer.

Kid changed into his cleats, grabbed his glove, and ran out to take infield practice with the rest of the squad. Kid currently rotated through several positions. He went back and forth from the outfield to shortstop to second base and pitcher.

"All right, get two!" the coach yelled out from behind home plate. He tossed the ball up, swung the bat, and hit a ground ball to Kid at second base. The ball took a bad hop just before reaching him. It bounced up and smacked him in the chest. The violent, slapping sound brought several gasps and shrieks from some of the parents in the bleachers.

If he was stunned or hurt, Kid didn't show it. He chased down the ball and threw it to second base. His teammate caught it and threw the ball to first, completing the double play. "Way to knock it down and stay with it, Kid!" the first base coach said. "That's what I like to see!"

Jack saw Kid allow himself a smile at the hard-won praise.

As practice continued, Jack noticed something strange. A car drove slowly, back and forth, past the practice field every ten minutes or so. Jack stood and acted like he was stretching, trying to get a better look at the driver.

It was a public park, so it was not uncommon for cars to troll back and forth, but Jack's previous life as a mercenary had hardwired certain patterns into his brain. Noticing things like a car passing by several times, or someone who followed him on the street for more than a block or two was one of those things.

The light green hatchback crept by one more time before pulling into a parking space. The driver got out and began walking toward the practice field. He was dressed in khaki shorts and a tucked in polo shirt. He wore sneakers with dark socks pulled halfway up his calves. Sunglasses hung down from his neck on a lasso. There was something odd about the man, beyond his appearance, but Jack couldn't quite put his finger on it. He kept a discreet eye on him while still watching the practice. Jack's temperature began to rise as he felt the man approach to within several feet of him. His right hand drifted out of instinct to where his holster used to live, but it found no weapon there. Jack hadn't carried since he switched careers.

"*Jack! Jack, it's me!*"

Jack turned his head, surprised. He squinted, trying to make sense of the situation.

"Your neighbor from across the street," the man said. "We met a few months ago, remember? They delivered a wrong package to my house."

Jack breathed a sigh of relief. "That's right," Jack said, remembering the incident. "Dennis? Donald? Danny?" Jack guessed.

"Donald, yes. But I usually go by Donnie."

"Right, sorry. I'm terrible with names," Jack said.

"No worries, I totally get it. I'm more of a faces guy myself." Donnie nodded toward the practice field. "Kid have a game?"

"Game's tomorrow. Just practicing today." Jack didn't consider himself the get-to-know-your-neighbor type, and he tried to keep his answers short in order to discourage any further discourse. Fortunately, Donnie seemed to take the hint.

"Well, I don't want to bother you. I was just driving through after my jog, and I thought I saw you sitting there. Anyway, I figured I'd stop and say hello."

"No problem. Glad you stopped by, it was good to see you. Guess I'll see you around." Jack lifted a hand as if to wave goodbye.

Donnie returned the gesture and then put his hands in his pockets, slowly turning around and walking back toward his car.

Part of Jack felt bad for being so rude, but the other part was happy to return to his anti-social baseball watching. Besides, Jack thought, who goes jogging in a pair of khaki shorts and a polo shirt? What a weirdo. Definitely something strange about that guy.

Jack tried to settle back into watching the practice, but something about the encounter left him on edge. He pulled out his phone and looked through his old contacts, searching for his criminal database connection. It was probably nothing, but he would rest a whole lot easier if a search on his neighbor brought back nothing suspicious.

"*Head's up!*"

"*Look out!*"

Jack snapped out of his phone and saw the parents on the bleachers scattering. He then looked up and saw why. A baseball was heading straight for him. He didn't have time to do anything but utter a guttural noise of surprise. The pop-up struck him just below his right eye. He saw stars as he stumbled forward, dropping his phone. He reached out to catch himself from falling the rest of the way down the bleachers, banging his shins, elbows, and forearms in the process.

"Are you all right?" one of the concerned parents asked.

Jack managed to collect himself and sit back down. He placed a hand over his eye, checking for any damage beyond what would surely be a nasty bruise. He raised his free hand and waved to the onlookers as if to say, 'everything's alright'.

One of the younger children climbed down and retrieved his phone as practice resumed on the field.

Jack thanked him and put it back in his pocket, embarrassed. "Serves me right for not paying attention," he said, not that anyone was listening.

12

Third Verse

New York State

The following evening, Kid's face was glowing even without the porch light shining on it. "Can I do it?" Kid asked.

"Sure, here you go." Jack handed him the keys.

Not only had his team won, but Kid had the game-winning hit.

Kid unlocked the door and flung it open. "Careful! Don't put a hole in the wall," Jack warned.

"Sorry..." Kid bared his teeth in a cheesy grin.

Jack couldn't help but smile at the boy's excitement. He could still remember how it felt when he'd played. The thrill of victory and the soul-crushing agony of defeat. Now that he thought about it, he remembered the times he'd lost more often than the times that he'd won.

He wondered if that was a good thing or a bad one. Before he'd taken Kid in, he would have answered that it was a good thing without hesitation. Defeat taught lessons in toughness and motivated him to become a better player. But now that Kid was in his life, he found himself reluctant to wish any sort of ill upon the boy, even if it was ultimately for his own good. He'd had enough terrible things happen to him already. He didn't need anymore.

Kid ran inside without bothering to turn on the lights. He put his equipment bag in the mudroom and slipped off his cleats. He was halfway up the stairs before Jack flicked on the light switch, muttering something about seeing in the dark to himself.

Jack was about to yell upstairs for Kid to hop in the bath when he heard the shower kick on. He swore the boy was a mind reader sometimes. Then Jack made his way to the bedroom and changed into some sweatpants and a t-shirt. Otherwise known as Saturday night movie attire in the Spader/Keller household. Part-two of the post-game celebration was about to commence. Jack popped the popcorn and cracked open a beer while Kid got out of the shower. He took everything into the living room and turned on the television to wait for Kid.

"What are we going to watch?" Kid asked as he entered the room a few minutes later.

"I don't know... you pick." Jack threw Kid the remote. He knew how to operate the thing better than Jack did anyway. They'd be there all night if he had to navigate through the various inputs and menus to get to the streaming services.

Kid picked a sci-fi movie called *Synthetic*. It was about

a spy who was slowly being replaced with robot parts as he got injured on his missions. With every new replacement body part, he lost some ability to feel emotions.

"Do you think I'll ever have a robot arm?" Kid asked, halfway through the movie.

"I don't know. I'm sure, given enough time, they'll figure out a way to do just about anything. Now, shut up and watch the movie." Jack smiled and Kid made a screwy face as he threw popcorn at him.

Twenty minutes later, Kid was asleep on the couch next to him. Jack couldn't really blame him. It had been a long day. He carried Kid up to bed and tucked him in. Then went to the cupboard and poured himself a glass of *Balvenie* 12-year. He added a few ice cubes and swirled the glass, letting the water from the ice blend with the scotch and open up the various flavors. He turned on *Sportscenter* and kicked his feet up, eyeing the gun cabinet to the left of the entertainment center. He tried to recall the last time he'd taken Kid out shooting and made a mental note to plan a trip soon. No such thing as too much target practice.

Jack made it most of the way through his glass of scotch before he passed out on the couch with the TV still playing.

Sometime later, the sound of the breaking glass woke Jack with a start. He looked around the couch for broken pieces of his glass and was confused when he saw it sitting on a coaster on the coffee table, whole as could be. The TV was still playing in the background. Some late night infomercial for a cleaning product. If it wasn't his drink, then—

Dread and adrenaline flooded his veins, and the fog

of sleep lifted as he realized where the sound had actually come from. Muffled voices spoke to each other and Jack heard the scratching of something hard scrape the remaining glass out of the pane on the back door.

Someone was breaking in.

Jack rushed over the gun cabinet and keyed in the passcode. The keypad turned green and the lock disengaged. He turned the handle and whipped open the door, grabbing the pump action shotgun with one hand and a box of shells from the bottom shelf with the other.

He steadied his breath as best as he could while he hurriedly loaded the shotgun. In for four, out for four. He repeated the breathing mantra as he ran through the scenario in his mind. Whatever they were after, be it pills or cash, Jack had to stop them before they made it upstairs to Kid.

He turned the corner just as the first person entered the doorway. Jack could see another person behind the first. They were both dressed in black with strange helmets on their heads. Was this some kind of early Halloween prank gone wrong? Jack frowned in confusion when he saw the rest of their gear. They were decked out in military spec flak jackets and what appeared to be assault rifles. This was no ordinary home invasion.

The point man's eyes lit up with surprise as he saw Jack bring the shotgun to bear.

A bright blue bolt of light shot wide out of the man's muzzle as Jack pulled his own trigger. Jack's blast hit the man dead center and he heard him cry out before slumping to the ground. Not waiting to discover what the hell kind of weapon had just missed him, he looked for the second man but couldn't see him in the darkness of the doorway. His instincts screamed for him to fire into the darkness, but he didn't have time to oblige them as another blue bolt raced through the doorway and slammed into his face, sending him into oblivion.

13

Third Verse

Outside of Kid's house, New York

Asher's first instinct upon jumping was always to reach down for the ground. He didn't know why. It wasn't as if his body ever left the ground. One moment he was standing on the Texas dirt of the staging area, and the next his feet were planted on the grass of a lawn in a place called New York.

If he had to guess, he'd say it was a reflex. Whenever he jumped, his stomach would flip for a loop, as if he was falling off a cliff. They'd told him that the feeling would pass the more he got used to it, but no matter how many times they'd practiced, the feeling remained. If it was an issue for Ava, he couldn't tell. She didn't seem to be affected at all.

A sliver of moon hung in the otherwise empty night

sky. Not enough to see by with the naked eye, but the HUD on Asher's helmet took care of that. He didn't know how they accomplished it, but his vision was superb. It wasn't daytime bright, but it was an order of magnitude better than full moon illumination. The colors were muted but still came through.

The comm in his ear chirped once. "This is Mallak. What's your status?"

"Jump was successful. The target house is all quiet." Ava responded.

Asher wondered where she'd learned to talk like that. "All good here, too," he reported.

"Good. I sent several of our operatives through the neighborhood to create a distraction and pull the mobile Gaian protective detail from the area. The neighbors never leave unless the prime minister's son does, so you'll still need to move with purpose. Once they hear something, it will only be a matter of seconds before they're alerted and they respond. Remember, even though they can't sense you, they'll still be able to see you. So take precautions, but move quickly once you begin."

Asher took a deep breath and exhaled, convincing himself he was prepared for this. Willing himself to believe it.

"Copy that," Ava said. She turned to Asher. "You ready?"

Asher tried to still the pounding in his chest. He nodded. "Ready as I'll ever be."

"On me." She made a beeline for the back door.

Asher followed, ready to execute the game plan. A quick smash and grab. Stun anyone inside, locate the

Prime Minister's son, and zip him home before anyone was the wiser.

Ava brought her rifle up and pulled the trigger. The stun charge slammed into the door, shattering the glass. She pulled on the door, but it remained secure. "Shit! Stun charge didn't work!" She tugged frantically on the handle.

Asher saw why. The door they'd trained with was solid wood. This one was half paned glass. Her shot had been too far center from the bolt. He put a hand on her arm and moved her to the side. Yanking on a locked door wasn't going to do anything. He scraped the remaining glass out of the pane and reached around to unlock the door. He opened the door several inches before stopping. He checked in with Ava. "Hey, we're good. Everything's good. But we need to move now. Okay? Are you good?" Asher saw the panic subside in her eyes and she nodded. "Okay, I'll take the lead, count to three and then come in after me."

"It's okay, I'm okay. I'll go first like we trained."

Asher shook his head. "There's no time to argue about this. Let's move." He opened the door and stepped into the house. Kiri's training played back in his mind. Weapon at the ready, sweep with the barrel. Find the door, find the corners, proceed to the next room.

The first room was clear, he was about to move to the doorway and proceed to the next when he saw the man turn the corner with a shotgun in his hands. Asher held his breath and squeezed the trigger. Nothing. His eyes went wide as he realized the safety was on. He flicked it off as fast as he could manage and pulled the trigger again just as the man's weapon exploded.

The air sucked out of Asher's lungs as the payload slammed into his chest. He was vaguely aware of the fact that he was falling and that he couldn't stop it. And then the world was dark.

14

Third Verse

Inside Kid's house, New York

Ava watched, unable to help, as the man turned the corner and shot Asher. She tried to warn him, but her voice stuck in her throat. She brought her weapon up to her shoulder and lined up the shot through the open door as Asher sank down to the floor, clearing a straight line of sight. The stun charge leaped out of the end of Ava's gun and found it's target. The man grunted from the impact and hit the floor.

Ava entered the house and walked over, standing over his body as he curled up involuntarily on the floor. She shot him a second time for good measure and he was still.

Ava turned and went to Asher who was unconscious on the floor. He was breathing but there was blood everywhere. What was she supposed to do? They hadn't covered what to do if one of them got shot.

"Report!" Ava heard in her earpiece. "What's going on? Ava? Asher? Someone talk to me!"

Ava took a deep breath and began pulling herself together. "Asher's been shot! He's bleeding and won't wake up. I stunned a man, the uncle, I think, and he's down too." Ava's mind froze. She couldn't decide what she should do next. She heard a noise outside, and her head snapped around trying to locate which direction it had come from.

"Ava, listen to me..." Mallak's voice was calm, but urgent in her ear. "You need to leave him. The Gaians will be there soon. There's no time to waste. Get the Prime Minister's son, and get the hell out of there, right now!"

Mallak's instruction grounded her, bringing her back to reality. The mission, Ava remembered. She hurried through the rest of the downstairs looking for any sign of the boy. No one else was there. He must be upstairs.

She raced around to the stairway and charged up the stairs. She thought she heard more noises from downstairs as she reached the top, but she didn't have time to stop and listen. Nothing she could do about it anyway, she couldn't take on a Gaian agent. Either she found the boy and jumped, or she left empty-handed. Asher had been enough hero today for the both of them.

There were two closed doors on either side of the hallway and one open door at the end. She threw open each closed door and illuminated the room with the flashlight attached to her NK-43. One was a closet, another seemed to be used for storage. There were stacks and stacks of boxes and various odds and ends. The other two were bedrooms. The first was obviously a young boy's room. Ava quickly scanned the room, checking in the closets, under the bed. There was no sign of the boy. The other bedroom was just as empty. The bathroom door in the hallway was open. It was the only room she had not checked. Surely, he wouldn't be hiding in there? Then again, it was the last place she was looking, so maybe it wasn't a bad spot to hide after all.

She heard voices coming from below her. She was running out of time. If the Prime Minister's son wasn't there, she wasn't sure what else she could do. She'd checked the house from top to bottom. She didn't know if they would ever have a second opportunity to rescue the Prime Minister's son, but she had to hope that there was still a chance.

She made her way to the bathroom, stopping halfway there as she heard footsteps on the stairs to her left. She wheeled around and saw a man in his pajamas with a pistol. She fired without hesitation, feeling a strange tug on her weapon as she did. Her shot missed wide, hitting the wall. She pulled on the gun, wrestling it free from the invisible force that had a hold on it.

The man's hand reached out toward her and made a grasping motion with his fist. His eyes went wide with surprise, and Ava fired again. This time the stun charge found its mark, striking the man in the head and knocking him out cold.

The man's body tumbled backward down the stairs and she heard someone call out to him from downstairs.

It was now or never, Ava knew. She ran to the bathroom, flicked on the light, and saw nothing. Her heart sank inside her as she held on to her last hope of completing her mission. She threw back the shower curtain and discovered the boy curled up in the bottom of the tub with tears streaming down his face.

"It's okay," Ava said, reaching out to the boy. "I'm here to rescue you."

She laid down on top of him in the bathtub, wrapped her arms around him, and activated her zip drive.

15

Sixth Verse

Cairos, Gaia

Desmond woke from a dead sleep, sensing the foreign presence in his room. He reached out and turned the lights on.

"Forgive the intrusion, sir, but you're needed at headquarters now!"

Desmond had met the man a few times before around the office. Simmons, if he remembered correctly. He usually worked the night shift, which would explain why he was here in the middle of the night. Desmond felt the urgency that the man projected and immediately threw on some pants and a shirt and jumped to the Oracle division at the GDA.

He squinted against the brightness of the office lights, but couldn't miss the man standing by himself, waiting.

"Desmond, they're going after Kid. We need to get

him out of there now!" Desmond recognized the man from his son's folder. He was one of the protective details, Daniel Lamp.

Simmons jumped in.

"Explain," Desmond demanded as he tried to keep his adrenaline from spiking. A battle he was losing.

"Several Terrans approached the house in vehicles, in teams of four. Standard strike teams. We chased them off and our remaining agents were still in pursuit when I jumped out."

Desmond had a bad feeling rising in the pit of his stomach. Something seemed out of place. "How long ago was this?"

"Three, maybe four minutes. It seemed strange to me. Unlike them to be so sloppy. Almost like they wanted us to know they were there. Anyway, I alerted the details next-door to Kid and came for backup."

Desmond agreed with the man that something was out of place. If Julia was making a play for their son, she would have used either overwhelming force or complete subterfuge. If she couldn't win a fair fist fight, she'd have a gun hidden up her sleeve.

Desmond's sense of unease grew. "Something's wrong. I just hope that we aren't too late." He shook his head disgusted with himself. He should have brought Kid here as soon as he'd found out about him, but there would be time enough for self-flagellation when this was over. Right now all haste was needed if they still had a chance at saving his son. "May I?" Desmond asked Lamp.

The man took a deep breath, preparing himself, and nodded.

Desmond tried to be as gentle as possible, but they

were in a hurry. Fortunately, Lamp understood the rush and had prepared himself for more discomfort than usual.

Desmond rooted around in the man's mind for the location of Kid's house. It was fresh and Lamp wasn't trying to hide it, so it came quickly. Desmond fully immersed himself in the man's memory. Simply viewing the house would not be enough. In order for Desmond to jump there, he would need to experience what it felt like to actually be there. If not, he could end up stranded somewhere in the dimensional planes. As a safety precaution, most Gaians wouldn't jump somewhere that they hadn't personally been before, but the circumstances demanded the risk. And Desmond was more than willing to take it.

He released the hold he had on Lamp's mind. "All right, you're with me. Simmons, have a team on standby, and alert the med bay that they may have incoming."

"There's already a team on their way. And I have a trauma unit standing by."

Desmond nodded, pleased. "Let's go."

Desmond blinked out of existence in the Sixth Verse, and Daniel Lamp followed right behind him.

HE LANDED in the living room. The television was playing a commercial. The house was dark, and the smell of gunpowder still hung in the air. There were two men lying on the floor. Desmond did a second take. *That was odd.* He saw *two* men, but only felt *one*. He knew then that they were too late.

He scanned the rest of the house and felt two more

Gaians, Dubber and Ripley, and then Lamp as he jumped in outside the back door. As he had feared, there was no sign of Kid.

Dubber was kneeling over an unconscious Ripley as Desmond approached. "What the hell happened?"

"He's out cold. Got hit by a stunner dead-on," Dubber answered.

"No, I mean, *here*."

Dubber's shame and embarrassment were thick in the air. And something else, too—anger. Desmond could feel it bleeding into the flux field. "Lamp told us to go on high alert. Everything seemed fine at the house, just Kid and Jack asleep. It wasn't until we heard the gunshot we knew something was wrong. We got here, saw Jack and the other guy down. Donnie went up to check on Kid while I checked on those two. I heard two blasts and then Donnie tumbled down the stairs. Next thing I know the whole house is shaking and Kid's gone. It happened fast. Professional."

Desmond nodded to the downed man. "Not too professional."

Donald Ripley stirred back to consciousness and sat up, holding his head and grunting back the pain. "Something isn't right with them..."

"I don't think they're Terran," Desmond said.

"What the hell are they then? Some kind of experiment?" Dubber asked.

"I don't know, but we'll find out." Desmond returned to the strange man and turned him over. He was covered in blood, but the bleeding appeared to have stopped for the most part. He took the zip drive from around the man's wrist and fastened it on his own.

Faint sirens grew louder as Desmond climbed the stairs. He stopped halfway up, not needing to go any further. He could see half of the wall and ceiling missing at the far end of the house. The work of a zip drive.

Blue lights flashed through the windows of the house as the police cruisers turned on to the street. "We need to go," Desmond said. "Ripley, are you good to make the jump?"

"I'll manage."

"Good, you go now. You two," Desmond motioned to Lamp and Dubber, "take them to medical and then report back to my office for a full debriefing."

One by one they jumped out, first Ripley, and then Dubber and Lamp, each with a man in tow—Dubber, with the stranger, and Lamp, the uncle.

Desmond watched them blink out and then activated the zip drive he'd taken from the strange man. He selected the last known jump point. He wanted some answers.

16

Sixth Verse

Oracle at the GDA

Desmond's jump to the Terran training camp in the Third was a total bust. He'd arrived to find it deserted. Tents, weapons, and electronics remained right where they'd been left. Whoever had been there had left in a hurry, not bothering to attempt any kind of clean up.

When he returned to the Sixth, Desmond had his people examine the zip drive he'd used to discover the training camp and found out that he'd dodged a bullet.

Julia's people had sabotaged the zip drive.

If he had selected any other coordinates besides the training camp, he would have set it off.

But why?

Why would Julia sabotage one of her operative's gear? What did this guy know that she was trying to keep hidden?

The near-miss was a good reminder to be more careful. He couldn't afford to rush into an ambush. Lives were at stake—his son's and the other kidnapped children's.

While the questions kept turning themselves over in his head, Desmond spent half the night debriefing each of the agents that had been on Kid's security detail. A process that entailed reliving every moment from the agent's point of view. At the end of the exhausting process, Desmond found that he had very little actionable intel to work with.

Next up was Kid's uncle, Jack Spader, had recovered in the infirmary after several hours. Aside from a concussion and some nasty bruises, he was otherwise unharmed from the incident. He was irate and confused, and Desmond could hardly blame him for that.

After Jack had calmed down, thanks in part to Celia, Desmond was able to persuade him to allow access to his mind.

Desmond made his way to Jack's recovery room. "Would you give us the room?" Desmond asked the medical staff and armed guards.

They filed out, all but Desmond's daughter, and then the three of them were alone. The beeping of various medical monitors punctuated the silence like a bad clock.

"Are you ready to begin the process?" Desmond asked.

Jack gave a nervous glance to Celia who nodded reassuringly. "Okay. I still don't know what to make of all this, but I've seen a lot of strange things over the last twenty-four hours. And if this will help get Kid back, then I'm all for it. Just don't screw around in there, alright? My head's enough of a mess as it is."

"I promise, he'll be a gentle as possible," Celia assured him. "Isn't that right, Dad?"

"Of course," Desmond agreed. "Let's begin, Jack. I want you to close your eyes and try to clear your mind."

Desmond began scanning Jack's mind, quickly brushing past the flirtatious thoughts about his daughter that were intermingled with Jack's anger and frustration, until he reached last night's memories. Desmond replayed them over and over, but unfortunately, Jack's memories of the abduction did little more than confirm that there was at least one other abductor. He hadn't seen anything else that would help them determine what had happened to Kid.

Desmond gently withdrew from Jack's mind, and Jack opened his eyes.

"Well? See anything helpful?" Jack asked, hopeful.

"Nothing we hadn't already pieced together, unfortunately. Your memories did confirm the presence of one other individual. The person who shot you. But we're still just as clueless as we were before, I'm afraid." Desmond realized almost immediately, he'd made a mistake.

Jack shook his head violently unwilling to accept what he was hearing."Where is he?" Jack demanded. "Where's the bastard I shot?"

"He's recovering, Jack, and still unconscious. Don't make me restrain you," Celia warned.

Jack sized her up, wondering if such a thing was possible from the woman. He outsized her by at least sixty pounds.

"*Yes*, I can." Celia reached out and enclosed Jack in an invisible grip that forced his arms down to his sides with just enough force to overcome his resistance. She wasn't trying to hurt him, after all.

Jack grunted and struggled to move, all the while his eyes grew wider with a mix of astonishment and horror. "Alright, she-devil. Let me go! I'll leave him be. For now..."

Celia released him from her grip, and Jack found himself strangely more attracted to her knowing the physical power that she had over him. "What the hell kind of freaks are you people?" he asked, only half-kidding.

"I promise you'll be able to sit in on the interrogation once he wakes up," Desmond said, ignoring Jack's question. He didn't have time right now to go into it. "In the meantime, Celia, why don't you get him settled at the penthouse? He can be our guest. After all, he's sort of like family. And I believe I've had the measure of him as a man from poking around in his head. You're quite the interesting man, Jack Spader."

"*Great! Babysitter...*" Celia's voice dripped with dryness. She sighed and motioned for Jack to follow her. "Let's go. We'll get you tucked in."

Jack felt a slight tug on his chest and yelped as he started to fall forward. He righted himself as he shot Celia a glaring look.

"*Celia!* Behave yourself," Desmond admonished with a smile.

THE NEXT MORNING, Desmond looked up as Donovan escorted the teenaged kidnapper into his office in handcuffs. He motioned toward the chair opposite his desk and told Donovan to wait outside. It was more for the sake of building some rapport with prisoner than an actual desire to be alone or in private. Jack and Celia were watching the feed nearby, in another room.

The young man, if he could be called that yet, had come out of the healing chamber earlier that morning. In a little over thirty-two hours, he was good as new. Normally, Desmond would have just taken whatever information he wanted out of the suspect's mind while he was recovering, but for reasons that were not known to him, he couldn't feel the teenager's presence in the flux at all.

"Let's start with introductions, shall we? My name is Desmond. And yours is?"

"Asher." He swallowed hard, and his face flushed. It was obvious that he was unsettled. To his credit though he hadn't broken down into tears. At least not yet, anyway.

"Asher, I like that name." Desmond was struggling to get a read on the kid. Without the use of his abilities, he had no way of knowing whether or not he was telling the truth. It was discomforting. "How old are you, Asher?"

"I'll be sixteen in a month."

"You're not from around here are you?"

"I don't even know where around here is, to be able to answer the question," Asher said.

"Fair enough. What did they tell you about us?"

Asher shrugged. "Not much, beyond the fact that you had kidnapped the Prime Minister's son."

"Is that so?" Desmond chuckled, more to put Asher at

ease than from any sense of actual mirth. "Did she happen to tell you that he's *my* son too?" Desmond saw the young man's eyes widen and knew the answer. "No, I didn't think so. That's the way she operates. Just enough info, but not nearly enough that a person can make up their own mind on the matter. After all, if she did that, she might not get what she wanted, would she?"

As the interrogation continued, it became apparent to Desmond that the young man was nothing more than a pawn caught up in a much larger game. He answered every question that Desmond asked with almost no hesitation. That, and what his people had discovered about Asher's zip drive, led Desmond to believe he was telling the truth. And, at least as far as Asher was concerned, he'd been acting altruistically.

Even if Asher hadn't been, Desmond supposed he didn't have much choice in the matter. It was do what Julia wanted or get sent home to face the consequences of the Princess's disappearance.

"I appreciate your cooperation, Asher, and I want you to know that as far as I'm concerned, you're not to blame for your involvement. However, actions still have consequences, and your actions did lead to the kidnapping of my son. Would you agree?"

Asher nodded. He seemed both worried and relieved at Desmond's statement. "What's going to happen to me?"

"You know you got played, don't you?" Asher didn't respond, so Desmond continued. "I had my people look at your zip drive. Do you know what they found?"

Asher shook his head.

"If you hadn't been shot, and you selected the jump

coordinates that they gave you, it would have triggered a self-destruct charge on the zip drive. More than likely, the blast would have been big enough to kill you. At the very least, it would have taken your arm off." Desmond saw the look of shock and betrayal on Asher's face. If the young man had held any lingering thoughts of loyalty or allegiance to the Princess, he would be hard-pressed to hold onto them now, Desmond thought.

"She wouldn't—she would never..."

"She would never what?" Desmond asked. "She would never betray you like that? You, her servant, her glorified housekeeper? And while I haven't met this princess of yours, let's even suppose that she had no idea about the sabotaged zip drive. I can speak from first-hand experience to who the Prime Minister is, and if there was even the slightest chance that sabotaging your zip drive would solve a problem for her, no matter how insignificant, she would take it in a heartbeat. She is cruel, and cunning, and beautiful, and beguiling. She will tell you what you want to hear and make you feel like the most important person in the world, but underneath it all is a lie and her own self-interest."

Asher couldn't help but make the connection in his mind. "I suppose you could say the same thing about Ava." He set his jaw firmly as resolve set in. "I want you to know that however I can set things right, whatever I can do to help get your son back... Tell me what you want me to do, and I'll do it."

"Would you kill someone for me?" Desmond asked.

Asher stammered, shocked and unable to think of a way around the question.

Desmond held up a hand. “It’s alright, Asher. I would never ask you to do that. It’s not how we operate. But I needed to see where your limits were... After all, I don’t know *that* much about you or where you come from.”

Asher nodded, still unable to speak. What the hell had he gotten himself into now?

17

Seventh Verse
Civitas, Terra

Ava screamed and pushed the boy off her, grabbing at her neck. A circle of armed guards surrounded them on the landing pad. "Agh! Little shit bit me!"

They had arrived in the Seventh as they had left the Third, horizontally. Ava rolled away and got to her feet.

"Where is my Uncle Jack? What did you do to him?" Kid demanded.

Ava ignored him as she took in her new surroundings. The zip drive coordinates had taken them inside a large, enclosed hanger that was connected to a transport hub outside. Ava could see various flying vehicles landing and taking off through the large windows that spanned from ceiling to floor along the far wall.

In her immediate vicinity, a gap opened up in the circle of guards as several of them stood aside. Ava recognized Prime Minister Julia White as she walked through the gap, followed by several others. Julia spread her arms wide and welcomed them. "Ava, Kid, I can't tell you how happy I am to finally meet you both in person." She turned to the medical staff standing by. "Please sedate my son, and be gentle about it. He's had a very traumatic past few minutes. I don't want any more unnecessary stress put on him."

They nodded and fanned out, boxing Kid in. The boy frantically looked for a way out, but he was out-muscled and out-manned. The medical staff tightened in around him like a noose. Once they'd taken hold of him, a woman wearing a long white coat walked up and injected him with a sedative. He kicked and thrashed for a few seconds before succumbing to the drug.

"Where are they taking him?" Ava asked. Less out of concern than curiosity.

"No need for you to worry about that, my dear," the Prime Minister replied. "He'll be well taken care of. As soon as he has had a chance to rest and recover from the ordeal, I will slowly reintroduce him to the world and the birthright that was taken away from him by our enemies. I'm afraid I must ask you to keep any knowledge of him a secret. I'm sure you can understand the kind of circus that the revelation of his existence would cause with the media and the general public."

Ava had no idea but nodded anyway as if she did.

"I will reveal his presence to the world when the time is right. In the meantime, he will be in good hands."

"Yes, rest assured we will take great care of him," the man standing next to the Prime Minister said. Several of the others began strapping Kid down to a stretcher that floated in midair.

"Ava, I don't believe you've met Dr. Mescham yet." The Prime Minister indicated the man beside her. "He is the foremost expert in biotechnology. He and his team will be the ones bringing you up to speed, so to speak."

Ava perked up and shook the man's hand. "Thank you, I'm incredibly excited to get started. Ever since the Prime Minister told me about your world and what you've been able to achieve with the nanites, it's been all I can think about."

The doctor cleared his throat and adjusted his lab coat. "Obviously, I will be a little busy attending to the Prime Minister's son, first and foremost. But I'd like to set you up for an appointment tomorrow to begin the initial treatment. I'll go ahead and warn you, there will be most likely a little bit of a back-and-forth, as we adjust the nanites to your unique makeup. And of course, we don't know how your *unique DNA* will react." He looked her up and down as if he could see the DNA inside her.

"Okay, that sounds wonderful," Ava said. "Just let me know what you need from me."

"I'll have one of my assistants reach out to you to schedule the initial consultation. Now, if you'll excuse me."

"Of course."

Dr. Mescham followed Kid's stretcher out onto the waiting transport. The shuttle lifted off and was soon lost in the flow of pre-dawn traffic zipping through the skies of Civitas.

"Come, Ava, I'll show you where you'll be staying," the Prime Minister said. "Well, my assistant will show you, anyway... I'm afraid I must return to the capitol to handle some pressing matters of state." She turned to one of her aides. "Margot, please see Ava to her lodgings and make sure that she has everything she needs."

"Of course, Madam Prime Minister." The aide bowed her head slightly in deference, though she didn't exactly seem thrilled with the assignment.

The Prime Minister turned back to Ava. "Forgive me for abandoning you as soon as you've arrived, but I promise, I'll send for you as soon as time allows and make sure that you're settled in properly."

Ava did her best to hide her disappointment. "I understand. I'll see you soon."

The Prime Minister hurried off. The armed guards followed her. Ava watched them until they grew small in the distance of the zip hangar blending into the sea of the crowd.

She turned to the aide, who stood, watching her with a thin smile on her face, no doubt amused at the naive new arrival. "Well? Shall we?" Ava said.

The aide tipped her head forward and gestured the way with her arm. "After you, my dear."

Ava fumed at the woman's patronizing tone as she began walking. *Who did she think she was?*

18

Seventh Verse

Mescham Labs, Civitas

AVA HAD no idea that buildings could be so tall, or that there could be so many of them. The flight over to Mescham's from her hotel room was her first major glimpse into the sprawling city that made up the Terran capital. Civitas was an endless urban sprawl, rumored to be as tall as it was long. She didn't know about that, though. Everywhere she looked, the city seemed to encompass the space, stretching out to the mountains far in the distance. Towering spires jutted out from the already soaring buildings causing Ava's head to spin from the perspective. In between the buildings below her, she couldn't see all the way down to the ground below. Shadows filled in the cracks, obscuring anything below them. She found the elevation made it harder to breathe.

Dr. Mescham's office was in a building that looked

similar to most of the others. She was grateful that Prime Minister White had sent another aide along to help her find her way. She liked this aide more than the previous one. He was clean cut and much more friendly than Margot had been.

"Once you're augmented with the nanites, you won't ever have to worry about losing your way again," the aide promised her. "Unless you want to." He frowned. "I don't know why anyone would choose to deactivate their augmentation or get lost on purpose for that matter... But to each their own, I suppose. And they'll help regulate your breathing with the altitude as well. It's not uncommon to change a few thousand feet in elevation several times over the course of a normal day in Civitas. Especially if you commute from one of the lower levels of the city. Anyway, here you are," he said as they arrived at the reception desk.

"Thank you, uh—sorry, I never got your name," Ava said.

"No matter, once you're augmented, that's another thing you'll never have to worry about again." The aide turned and promptly left without offering his name.

Ava pursed her lips, unsure of whether the man had been rude or not. Maybe the customs were different here?

"Can I help you?" the woman behind the reception desk asked.

Ava cleared her throat. "Uh, yes. I'm here to see Dr. Mescham."

The woman stifled a laugh. "Sure you are, sweetie. I'm afraid the doctor's booked solid all day."

Ava frowned. "I should have an appointment. The Prime Minister's office set it up for me."

"Okay sure, send me your data tag and I'll see if we have something available in the next month or so." The woman went back to watching whatever was playing on her monitor.

It took Ava a minute to figure out what she meant by *data tag*. It must have something to do with the nanites. "I'm not augmented," Ava said, beginning to get annoyed with the dismissive woman. She felt her inner bitch clawing to get out. "At least, not yet. Hence, the visit. Don't you have an appointment book or something you can check?"

The receptionist rolled her eyes briefly as if such a task was beneath her. "If you're not in the system, then you'll have to—"

"It's okay, Veronica, please show Ms. Ava to procedural room thirteen." Dr. Mescham's voice spoke over the intercom.

Ava relished the sour look on the receptionist's face as she capitulated. "Right this way please, Ma'am."

Ava changed into a patient gown and took a seat on the exam table. After several minutes a few nurses entered the room and began setting up various machines. When they were finished, Dr. Mescham finally made an appearance.

"Hello, Ava. So good to see you again. I hope you didn't have too much trouble finding us."

"Finding you was easy, getting past the front door was a little more challenging." She smiled.

"Yes, sorry about Veronica. She can be a little grumpy in the mornings." He lowered his voice as if telling a secret and said, "Boy troubles, I would guess."

Ava laughed.

"Alright, let's get down to it, shall we?" Dr. Mescham said. "As I briefly mentioned before in the hangar, this will entail a fair bit of trial and error. We've never attempted to augment someone of your unique makeup before. So, we'll start you with the latest strain of nanites and go from there. Sound good?"

"Strain? Like a viral strain?"

"Yes, but don't think of it like that. More like the latest version of software. Two-point-oh, so to speak." He saw Ava's blank stare. "Not quite familiar with software, are you? Probably don't have many computers where you come from."

"None, that I know of, actually," Ava said.

"Just think of it like the latest and greatest improvement of *whatever*, then. Let's say a lamp, for instance. You do have those, yes?"

Ava nodded.

"So, the first version, or *strain,* of the lamp was probably the torch. Dip the end of a stick into some tar and light it on fire. Or wrap something flammable around the end and light it. Right? Then comes the next strain and the next, each one making the design a little easier to use, a little safer. You enclose the flame in glass and now you're safe from being burned and the flame is safe from the wind. Similar process with the nanites." He studied her for a moment. "I hope I haven't confused you too badly."

"No, I think I understand."

"Good, but even if you don't, it's okay. They are designed to be completely user-friendly, and there's no need to understand *how* they work in order to use them. You've used a zip drive before, right?"

Ava nodded.

"But you don't know *how* it works, correct?"

"Right."

"The nanites are like that... Now, let me get you to lie back and relax. The procedure is painless. The biggest pain in the ass will be the waiting around afterward and letting us run our gambit of tests."

Ava reclined and watched as he took something off the tray beside her bed and held it against her bare arm. She felt pressure, but nothing unpleasant. It was like something was sucking on her arm. The feeling lasted for a few seconds.

"See? *Easy-peasy*, right?" Dr. Mescham smiled at her.

"When will I know if they're react— *whoa!*" Ava sat up and extended her arms as if to catch herself from falling.

"Just your reflexes adjusting. Totally normal. As you can see, they don't take long to circulate and begin making synaptic connections. In another few minutes, they should be ready to begin the booting process."

The sensation was strange, to say the least. Ava felt as if there were hundreds of tiny insects poking around underneath her skin. "Is it supposed to feel like this?"

"Some people report it feeling that way. Others have said that it's more of an itching sensation or a pin-prick. The body quickly adapts to it, and it fades within five to ten minutes. If for some reason, it doesn't, please let me know." He stood and began to fiddle with the machines that the nurses had brought in. He twisted dials and tapped on touch screens, studying whatever the machines were telling him. "*Hmmm...*Everything looks normal, Ava. We may not need to worry about making adjustments to the nanites at all. Tell you what, I'm going to step out for a few moments and I'll keep monitoring you remotely. As long as everything keeps progressing like it has so far, you should be good to go in an hour or so."

"What do I do?" Ava had so many questions.

"Nothing. Just lay there and relax. Once the nanites have bonded with your neural synapses, the OS will boot up and be able to answer any questions that you have. And I'm sure there are a lot of questions rolling around in that brain of yours."

The doctor left and Ava started second-guessing her life choices over the past week or so. She flip-flopped back and forth between thinking she'd made a huge mistake and convincing herself that everything was fine and it was just her nerves acting up. She closed her eyes and tried to be patient.

The minutes stretched and the waiting seemed to go on forever. Should it be taking this long?

All at once, the nanites came online and her eyes shot open as her brain was flooded with new inputs and new information. The OS booted up and the corners of Ava's lips turned up in the largest smile she had ever managed. It was glorious! How could she have ever doubted the decisions that led her to this moment?

19

Sixth Verse

Oracle at the GDA

Desmond was surprised by Wizard's quick reply. Surprised, but not disappointed. Wizard was the best chance Desmond had of finding out what Julia was up to and where she was keeping their son.

He'd given himself a headache explaining to Jack Spader why they couldn't just jump to the Seventh and take Kid back. He wished it was that easy, but without knowing exactly where Kid was, they'd quickly be overrun and either captured or killed, depending on Julia's mood of the moment.

Something big was happening in the Seventh, and whatever it was, the government wasn't sharing it with the public. At least not yet. In a society as interconnected as Terra, secrecy was hard to come by. What worried Desmond more was why secrecy was necessary in the first place. Whatever Julia was up to, it was bigger than just kidnapping some Gaian children, and it was clearly something she thought the general population would look on with disfavor.

Desmond played Wizard's message and hoped for good news.

HELLO, old friend. I hope you're not running yourself too ragged these days. Although, I know the circumstances seem to call for it.

I've got something that may help with your Terran problems.

Meet me in two days in the Third at little Celia's favorite spot. I'm sure you remember the one. Forgive the delay, but it will take some time to prepare. Let's say 22:00 local time.

Take care.

HMMM, that was rather vague, Desmond thought. It wasn't like Wizard to be so brief. For as long as he'd known him, the man always had a tendency to ramble. He pushed the thought aside for the moment and considered the contents of the message.

Desmond recalled the proposed meeting place. When he and Julia were still together, they'd taken a trip to the Third as a part of the Terran delegation to study the local culture to determine if they'd made enough progress to be made aware of Terra's existence. Wizard had managed to tag along with the Senatorial contingent. Celia was only six or seven and she hadn't gotten very much attention on the trip thus far. Wizard noticed and asked if he could help. Desmond thought it was a great idea, and he could use a break from the proceedings himself.

They wandered through the city of San Francisco until they heard music playing from the street. It came from a dingy club that was sandwiched behind a sushi restaurant and an apartment building.

The doorman wouldn't let Celia in, saying she was too young. Desmond made his daughter promise that she would never tell her mom what he was about to do. He used the flux to influence the man's mind and make him overlook her. As they walked in, everyone stared at the small child walking through the door. Desmond sighed and extended the trick to everyone in the small club. It took nearly all of his concentration, and he didn't get to enjoy the show at all, but Celia had loved it. The loud, heavy guitars and flashing lights were all she talked about for the rest of the trip.

"Speak of the devil," Desmond said as Celia walked into his office with Jack in tow.

"Me or him?"

"You, of course." Desmond smiled, happy to see her.

"Did you hear from Wizard yet? Any leads on where Kid is?"

"I don't know, maybe. He wants to meet at *End Of The World* in the Third."

"That rock club you snuck me in?"

"That's the one."

"Great! Let's go," Jack said.

"Meeting's not for another two days. Said he needed some more time to *prepare*... Whatever that means."

Jack punched the wall in frustration and instantly regretted it. It felt like punching a boulder.

"Hey! Settle down, tough guy," Celia admonished.

Jack rubbed his hand, checking for any fractures. His face flushed with heat, embarrassed at his outburst. "Sorry, I'm not good at waiting."

"I understand the frustration, believe me," Desmond said. "But we're going to find him and bring him back."

A weird silence hung in the air.

"Come on," Celia said, taking Jack by the shoulders and spinning him toward the door. "I know what you need... Let's go to the range. Need to make sure you know how to shoot if you're going to be watching my back." She held up a finger and pointed it in his face. "And I don't mean like the way you've been watching my backside, either."

Jack smirked and shrugged. "I can neither confirm, nor deny. But shooting something sounds like the perfect therapy right now. Lead the way!"

Desmond watched them go and then played Wizard's message again, trying to guess what Wizard had found out. He didn't like to wait, either.

20

Seventh Verse
Civitas, Terra

Julia watched Kid's chest rise and fall. He wasn't awake, but she wouldn't call his present state sleeping either. Perhaps the best term for his condition was a trance, she thought. The monitors kept spitting out his vitals and the readings from the special strain of nanites that Mescham had administered.

Mescham approached as she studied the screens. "His body seems to be accepting this new strain, unlike what happened with the pure-blooded children."

"This soon?"

"It would appear so. I wish this was less of a wait and see kind of thing, but with Kid being the first live trial, we're kind of in that boat."

"Just be sure that you get it right," Julia said. "He's the only one of his kind, and I don't fancy making any more."

Mescham smiled at the joke, fully aware of the warning underneath it. "Not to worry, Madam Prime Minister. We'll make it work."

"I know you will. You've never let me down thus far, Mescham... On a side note, how's it coming with the new skins?"

He brightened at the change in subject. "Making progress, I'm happy to report. Still haven't quite cracked the rapid growth piece of the puzzle, but the originals that you had me modify are ready for the next phase. Any idea when that will be?"

"All in good time is the best answer I can give you, I'm afraid. Do keep me up to date on any progress with the rapid growth... I have absolute faith that you and your team will figure it out."

"Yes, of course, we will. I know I've asked before, but can you share anything more on where the original research came from? If I were able to speak with the origin—"

She cut him off, her mood instantly darkening. "You told me you had everything you needed. Is this not the case? Do I need to find someone else to head up the project?"

Mescham backpedaled, unsure of what had caused the switch. "No, of course not. Nothing like that. We are making great progress. I only meant that we could go even faster if I had could speak with... It's not important."

"Are you certain, Doctor?"

"Yes, Madam Prime Minister. Quite."

Mallak approached and cleared his throat to signal his presence. "I hope I'm not interrupting?" The doctor was clearly shaken up about something.

"No, of course not, Mr. Mallak. I was just updating the Prime Minister on our progress, and now, if you'll excuse me," he bowed slightly, "I need to get back to our patients."

"Of course," Julia tilted her head, granting him permission to leave.

They both watched Mescham retreat down the hall.

"Jesus, Julia. What did you do say to him?" Mallak asked.

"What?" she raised her hands and feigned innocence.

Mallak laughed. "Never mind. I've just received some very interesting information that we intercepted."

"Oh? Do tell."

"They found a signal buried in the old systems. Set to burst whenever a zip drive activated, to hide the signal."

"How did we not see it before?"

"It was perfectly hidden and there was no reason to look for it. We only noticed it because he got careless or desperate and transmitted without the masking of a zip signature."

"Hmm..." Julia tapped her chin. "What are the contents of the message?"

"The former senator claims to have some information that could help the Gaians with their problems." His brow creased. "You don't think he knows anything about Kid, do you?"

Julia thought about it. "I don't know. I suppose anything is possible. I was never supposed to be able to find Kid either, and we know how that turned out. I think we need to assume that he does. I'll make arrangements to have him moved. No need to take a chance when everything depends on him now. I assume you have a plan in place to disrupt this meeting?"

Mallak nodded. "I'll be handling it personally."

"Do that, and be sure you use people you trust. If we do have a leak..." she trailed off for a moment. "Well, let's just say that I'd rather not have to clean house."

"It won't be an issue."

Julia raised a finger. "Do me another little favor... I want as many Gaians as possible. I need some adult test subjects. If you can capture them at this meeting, so much the better. But if not, send some raiding parties to the Third with the new body armor."

"It will make the mission harder than it needs to be, but I'll get it done. What do you want me to do about the senator?"

"Wizard?" Julia smiled. "Have the girl kill the traitor." She laughed to herself. "I want to see how far she's willing to go."

Mallak raised his eyebrows. "You want me to bring the girl along, too? Do you think that's wise? She's barely had time to complete her tutorials. The meeting goes down a little under two days from now."

Julia waved her hand, dismissing his concern. "She's shown just as much promise as any new recruit, and Dr. Mescham reports that the nanites are functioning optimally with her genetics. She'll be fine. Just make sure she receives all the relevant tactical programs and keep her alive."

"Julia, with all due respect, I thought we were done with her? Why keep her around?"

"One, because I made her a promise. And two,

because I have the feeling that I may have need of her again..." Julia chuckled. "Part of her, anyway."

Mallak shook his head, not completely following her, but he didn't need to. If she wanted it, she would get it. One way or another.

21

Third Verse

San Francisco

Asher dropped into his vantage point on top of the building. His perch overlooked the *End of the World* below. A few stars lit up the sky overhead, or maybe they were planes. Asher still had trouble telling the difference. The San Francisco night sky was drastically different than the star-filled skies of New Queensland due to the light pollution.

He activated the enhanced vision on his helmet's display and starting scanning the surrounding streets and got familiar with every building and every path to and from the bar where Desmond would meet his contact.

The zip drive on his wrist counted down to the meeting time and Asher settled down to wait. He was several hours early.

Desmond's people had been able to fix the sabotaged zip drive and reprogram it, enabling Asher to make amends for his role in Kid's abduction. His penance was to be the lookout and alert the team if he saw anything suspicious. It wasn't the most glamorous job, but it helped him feel a little less guilty.

He tried not to think about Ava and whether or not she had known what she was doing. She'd been in contact with the Prime Minister for who knows how long before Asher had caught her that day. He wanted to believe that she was being used just like he'd been, but doubts kept creeping into his mind.

As he waited, Asher staved off boredom by flipping through every menu and submenu on the zip drive around his wrist. If there is a chance that his life was going to depend on the device, he might as well become as proficient as possible in using it.

The time passed slowly, and he spent most of it watching the seconds tick by on the zip drive's display. With around forty-seven minutes left, Asher saw an old man approach the venue. The man had a white beard and wispy hair that danced around in the night breeze.

Asher perked up. He immediately knew who it was from Desmond's description. But what was Wizard doing here so early? Asher magnified his view. Wizard was wearing a backpack that he shifted on his shoulders as he approached the doorman. Wizard spoke to the doorman, handed him the cover charge, and then entered the bar.

Maybe the old man just liked being early, Asher thought, or perhaps Desmond had deliberately planned on coming late, as a precaution. Asher zoomed back out and continued to watch as people walked up to the doorman, paid the cover, and went inside.

Asher wished he knew who he was supposed to be on the lookout for. Obviously, if Terran commandos with tactical gear and assault rifles showed up, he would know to sound the alarm, but outside of that, Asher had only met a handful of Terrans. He highly doubted he'd be able to recognize one of them if they were undercover.

Asher tested the radio that Desmond had given him, ensuring that it at least appeared to be functioning. Desmond had said it wouldn't work until he had jumped in, but Asher felt better knowing that it at least powered on.

Several more minutes passed and Asher was just about to go back to fooling around with his zip drive when he recognized someone down below. There was something different about her, but he couldn't put his finger on what it was. Maybe she had changed her hair or she was walking differently or something like that. Whatever it was, there was no mistaking Ava.

He felt a chill come over him but didn't know if it was the night air or seeing her again that had caused it.

Asher scanned the sidewalks. She appeared to be by herself, but there was no doubt that she was here for a reason. She walked up to the club entrance, and the doorman leaned over as she spoke something into his ear. The doorman nodded and waved her inside.

Asher checked the time. He still had over twenty minutes before Desmond and his team would be here. He had to do something. He couldn't just sit there and wait. Wizard had no idea who she was, and Asher could almost guarantee that whatever she wanted with him, it wasn't in Wizard's best interest. Asher patted down his pockets until he found what he was looking for. He had wanted to bring the NK-43 with him, but Desmond had refused. *"You're just there to observe and report,"* Desmond had said. Asher had argued throwing out a number of possible, but highly unlikely scenarios, and in the end, Desmond had finally relented and given him one of Celia's small concealable stun weapons.

Asher hadn't had the chance to test it, but from what Celia had told him, all he had to do was make contact with whatever he wanted to stun and press the button. Asher wasn't sure that he wanted to have to get that close to anyone, but he had to warn Wizard, or at least try. He took off his helmet and fixed his hair, checking the rest of his appearance. The style of his clothes didn't exactly match with the people he had seen enter the bar, but the colors were spot on. All black.

Finding his way down to the street level took several minutes, and after checking the time again, Asher wondered if he should just wait. Desmond and his team were much better equipped to deal with the situation, and they would be there in less than ten minutes. He wrestled with the decision but ultimately decided that he couldn't take the risk. Lives might be at stake.

Ava was his responsibility, and beyond that, he had some questions of his own that he needed her to answer.

He stepped across the street and approached the doorman. He could hear the loud music blaring out through the doors every time they opened and closed. The sound was harsh, but also exhilarating. The music here was unlike anything they had back home.

"Eye-dee?" The man at the door asked. Holding out his hand.

Asher just stared at the man, unsure how to respond to the strange request.

"Show's 18 and up. Do you have your ID on you or what?"

"But she's only—"

"Listen, kid, I don't know who you're talking about. And even if I did, you still need an ID if you want to get into the show."

Asher's face reddened as he frantically tried to think.

"All right, come on, get me an ID or get out of the way so these other people can enjoy the show." The guy ushered Asher away from the door and out of line.

Asher's cheeks flooded with heat. He kicked the curb and cursed himself, unaware of the strange glares from the onlookers in line. All he had to do was get in the door, and he couldn't even do that much right. And now Wizard would be all alone in there, and who knew if he could take care of himself against whatever Ava was planning. While Asher hadn't seen Ava be upgraded, she had told him plenty of times that augmentation was what she was after. If she had already achieved that, Asher wondered what she could possibly want now.

Asher checked the time again. Eight minutes to go. He starting walking, about to resume his lookout post, when he recalled the back alley that he had seen from the rooftop. A light bulb went off in his brain. *The back door!*

He didn't know if it was open or not, but there was no one watching it, he knew that much. It was worth a shot.

He stuck his hands in his pocket and turned the

corner trying to act casually. As he entered the alley, he got a case of the willies. It felt like somebody was watching him. He glanced around but didn't see anybody. He looked up at the buildings surrounding him. Maybe someone was watching through one of the windows? He shook off the disconcerting feeling and continued toward the back door that was lit with a single bulb from overhead. A few overflowing trash cans lined the outside wall. Trash littered the street around the cans. The occasional gust of wind sent pieces of garbage tumbling down the alley like tumbleweeds.

Asher tried the door handle and found it locked. He yanked it a few times just for good measure. "Well fuck," he muttered.

Just then the door flew open toward him. Asher flattened himself against the wall narrowly avoiding being hit by it.

"I said, outside... *Now!*" The voice belonged to Ava.

Asher's heart started thumping in his chest. He found himself frozen behind the door, unable to move. It was as if someone had cast a spell on him.

He held his breath, worked up his courage, and willed himself to action, snapping out of the trance he'd been caught it. He reached into his pocket and brought out the stun weapon.

Wizard's white hair exploded into view as he fought to keep his balance from being shoved outside. He righted himself and turned around to face Ava. "I don't know who you think I am," Wizard said. "But you must be mistaken."

"Save your breath, old man. I know exactly who you are, and while your civilian version of the nanites may not be able to tell you *who* I am, they have no doubt identified *what* I am."

Asher could see her partially through the crack of the door hinges. He held his breath, hoping she didn't look over and see him.

Wizard's eyes drifted slightly to his right, spotting Asher behind the door.

Asher held his finger up to his lips, hoping that Wizard would not give his position away. To the old man's credit, he locked his gaze firmly on Ava and didn't look in Asher's direction again. He backed away slowly. Ava would need to follow him out into the alley if she wanted to keep him in her sights.

"Where are your friends, Wizard?" Ava asked. She stepped into view, her back to Asher. In one hand she held Wizard's backpack while the other held some sort of weapon. She raised the backpack. "What's in here?"

"Nothing," Wizard responded, too quickly. "Just some snacks for the road." He patted his belly and attempted to laugh, but the laughter stuck in his throat and died before it had the chance to come out. Instead, it was all he could do to keep from choking.

Ava laughed. "Oh, I'm sure. But *what else* is in here? What did you bring for your Gaian friends? What could be so important that you would risk a meeting in person?"

Asher crept closer to Ava's back, moving only as fast as he dared. With every step he expected Ava to whirl around and discover him.

"That's hardly any of your business, young lady."

Ava started to laugh again, but it was cut short as

Asher made contact with Celia's buzz box. Her entire body tensed up, turning rigid as steel.

"Shit!" Asher realized he was still holding the button down, and released it. As he did Ava's body relaxed and collapsed onto the ground, unconscious.

Wizard moved faster than Asher assumed a man of his age could and picked up Ava's pistol before retrieving his knapsack. To Asher's surprise, he found the barrel of the weapon now trained on him.

"Not that I am ungrateful," Wizard said. "But who the hell are you?"

"Please don't shoot me!" Asher winced and turned his head away as if it would soften the bullet's blow. When no gunfire came, he dared to open his eyes. "Desmond sent me. I mean I'm with Desmond—not *with* him, but he sent me to keep an eye out. And guess it was a good thing he did, too." Asher relaxed as Wizard lowered the gun, considering his story.

"Well, where the hell is he? He's nearly half an hour late."

Asher frowned at the discrepancy and checked the time on the zip drive. The seconds ticked down, closer to zero. "He should be here any second now." Asher turned his wrist so Wizard could see the display. "Well, in about two minutes or so..."

Wizard huffed and muttered something about thanks for filling him in on the plan.

Asher gave him a few moments to be grumpy before interrupting him. "What do we do with her?" Asher looked at Ava's slumped body.

Wizard sighed and then fished around in his backpack,

finally finding what he was looking for. "*Voila!*" He held the handcuffs high over his head and let them dangle from his finger. "Picked some up the last time I was here. Thought they'd come in handy for the augmented folk. All too easy for them to hack the electronic ones we use on Terra." He handed one of the pairs to Asher. "Here, get her arms."

Asher secured them around her wrists while Wizard did the same to her ankles.

"There," Wizard said, dusting his hands together. "All set."

He inspected his handiwork. "Oops, almost forgot." He bent over and removed the zip drive from Ava's wrist. "Can't have her waking up with that on—and, while we're at it..." His eyes narrowed as he bent over and zeroed in on her body armor. "Yup, that looks like the new one." He stuck his hand up under her shirt and started feeling around.

"Hey! What are you doing?"

"Relax," Wizard said, finding what he was looking for. "I'm not feeling her up, I promise." He pressed the release and the sides and sleeves of Ava's body armor retracted, letting him lift it over her head.

That wasn't the armor that she and Asher had been given on their last mission. He wondered what was so great about it.

Ava stirred as Wizard stuffed the armor into his bag. He brought out a datapad, but different from the ones Asher had seen on Gaia. This one was sleeker, shinier.

"How much time before Desmond's supposed to jump in?" Wizard asked.

Asher checked. "Little over half a minute."

"Maybe it's not too late. I've got to try to get a message

to him," Wizard said. "They found out somehow, and I can promise you that they didn't just send her in all by herself." He walked further down the alley, talking into the datapad as he went.

Ava sat up and coughed several times. "Asher? Is that really you? You're alive!" She noticed the handcuffs and tugged at them, testing their strength. "Why did you...?"

"Did you know?" Asher asked, tears forming in the corners of his eyes.

"Know what? What on earth are you talking about?"

"My zip drive was rigged to explode as soon as I activated it! Did you know about it?" Asher studied Ava's face intently. He saw slight surprise there in her eyes and the corner of her mouth. His shoulders relaxed, she hadn't known.

"Listen, Asher, I don't know what you're talking about. The Prime Minister never said anything to me about it, honest! I would never have gone along with it if I knew. Now can you please let me out of these?"

Asher spoke slowly, afraid that his emotions would get the better of him if he didn't keep them locked up tight. "I admit, I'm relieved that you weren't a part of it, at least not a willing one, but I still think you're on the wrong side of this. Do you know she's had other children kidnapped? Taken from their families in the middle of the night? Ava, you have to—"

"Asher, it's not too late. You can come back with me. You have no idea how powerful the nanites can make you! Things you've never even dreamed of are possible."

He shook his head. "I can't believe you would go along with something like that. You hugged me—I thought we were becoming—"

She stifled a laugh. "I'm sorry, becoming *what*?"

"*I liked you!*" Asher blurted out. "I thought you liked me, too…" He saw in Ava's eyes that whatever moment he thought they may have shared, it was a lie. Was everything about her a lie?

Ava opened her mouth to reply when Wizard came running back, out of breath. "You'll have to finish whatever this is later, I'm afraid. We need to go."

"Huh? What?" Asher looked up, trying to switch gears in his brain, but the emotions were making it cloudy. "Did you warn Desmond?"

His radio squawked, almost in answer. "Asher, where the hell are you? You're not at your position." Asher couldn't tell if Desmond was upset or concerned.

"No, I wasn't able to," Wizard said.

"Obviously," Asher replied.

Wizard lifted Ava's pistol and aimed it at her.

"Hey! Wait! What are you doing?" Asher asked, confused.

Wizard's thumb flicked up once and then he pulled the trigger.

22

Third Verse

San Fransisco

Even without the flux, Desmond knew that the roof was empty. He saw Asher's helmet sitting against the wall, but there was no sign of the teenager. Desmond tried him on the radio. "Asher, where the hell are you? You're not at your position."

Jack and Celia flashed into existence beside him as he waited for a reply.

The response was several seconds coming. "Not quite the meeting I had in mind," Wizard said.

"Yeah, my apologies... I was afraid something like this might happen. Are you guys all right?"

"Good thing you called an audible. Turns out they sent in the boy's girlfriend to take us out. Surely they didn't think we could be handled by one teenage girl, augmented or not."

"Well, if she's anything like our friend Asher there, there's no way for a Gaian to sense her in the flux. Must have thought she could get the drop on us. Maybe take us by surprise," Desmond explained.

"Undetectable you say?" Wizard hummed to himself, musing over the possibilities.

"At any rate, I think you're right. And I don't know where her backup is, but she sure as hell isn't alone." Desmond looked at Jack and Celia and suddenly found himself wishing that they had brought a little more firepower than the concealed weapons they were carrying. "I think it's pretty safe to say that your cover on Terra is blown. No sense dragging this out here in the open. Why don't you and Asher head to Gaia, and we'll meet you there? We can discuss whatever you found out without having to look over our shoulder the whole time."

Celia felt something strange in her solar plexus. Her stomach was doing loops like she was on a roller coaster. She reached out to share her concern with her father, but couldn't find him. It was as if he no longer existed in the flux field. Something was very wrong. "What the fuck is this? How the hell did they manage to—?"

Desmond felt it at the same time. "Jump shield!"

Jack looked lost. He turned to Celia for an explanation, but she was a little preoccupied with whatever was going on.

"Wizard, they have us in a jump shield. This whole thing was a trap from the get-go. Get out now!" Desmond said.

"I'm afraid it won't be that easy," Wizard reported. "Our zip drives won't initiate. We're caught in it too."

"Hey, guys…? We're about to have company!" Jack yelled, pointing across the rooftop.

Desmond turned around and saw the assault team filing onto the roof from the stairwell, flanking their position on either side.

"I don't know how they managed to smuggle a jump shield to the Third, but the range can't be that far. Do whatever you have to do to get free of the blanketed area and take whatever you found back to Donovan at the GDA. We'll find some way out of here."

"Good luck, Desmond."

"Yeah, you too."

There were ten men on the left and ten on the right. The team slowly advanced, cutting off any escape except the four-story drop to the street below. Behind them, still sheltered in the stairwell, their leader emerged.

Desmond analyzed the situation. The fact that they hadn't opened fire yet meant that they were trying to take them alive. That meant getting within effective range to use their stun weapons.

They would be close enough in a matter of seconds. Once they were pinned in, they would be at the mercy of the Terrans.

Desmond peered over the side. There was a balcony twenty feet below them that connected to the fire escape. A plan formed in his mind. "See the fire escape?" he said to Jack and Celia.

They looked and nodded.

"Be ready." Desmond took a few steps away from the edge, toward the strike team. "It would appear you have us trapped. There's no need for anyone to get hurt."

"Dad, what are you doing?" Celia walked in front and turned to face him.

"Cil, get behind me." He glanced down at his hand that revealed the frag grenade he was palming. "I'll buy you some time to make it down the fire escape. After that, you're on your own."

Celia smiled apologetically and held up both of her hands. Each held their own grenade. "Sorry, Dad. I already the pulled the pins on mine." She push-kicked him back toward the edge of the roof and tossed a grenade at both lines of advancing Terrans.

"Celia, no!" Desmond yelled, but it was too late. Hell had already broken loose.

23

Third Verse

San Fransisco

Asher had to hand it to the man, he might look old and a little thick around the mid-section, but Wizard could run.

"Come on, keep up," Wizard said, glancing back over his shoulder for what felt like the hundredth time.

"Still here," Asher huffed, not sure how long he could keep up the pace for.

The sight of two people running full bore down the sidewalk at night received strange glances from the folks that they sped by. Asher couldn't blame them, it was a strange sight to see. Who would have ever imagined he'd be in his present position, trying to escape some invisible force field that was preventing him from traveling between two universes?

At least ten minutes had to have passed. Ten minutes of all-out running. Asher's legs and lungs couldn't take anymore. "*Stop!* Wizard, please, I have to stop." He placed his hands on his knees and did his best not to throw up all over the sidewalk. Wizard came walking up beside him, his breath barely audible. Asher hated him and his nanite-augmented stupid body.

Wizard glanced around, searching for any signs of pursuit. "Looks like they aren't interested in us, my boy." Wizard clapped him on the back in a celebratory manner. "Still though, we should keep moving, just in case. Let's cut through that park over there. We'll see if we can find a nice quiet place to jump out without attracting too much attention."

Asher followed Wizard across the street and into the park, grateful for the casual walking pace.

The park was mostly deserted. A few other people were out walking, the paved path lit by streetlight. Wizard led him behind a row of bushes, startling a young couple in the throes of passion.

The young woman shrieked and clutched for something to cover herself with.

"Dude, what the fuck?" the young man said, standing to his feet.

"Run along little pups and find somewhere else to rut," Wizard said.

The man took a step forward with his chest puffed out. "Who the hell do you think you are, old man?"

"Erik, please! Let's just go." The woman pulled on her boyfriend's arm. He shrugged her off and turned back to find Wizard's gun pointed at his face.

"I'm the old man with the gun, telling you to fuck off somewhere else! Now, are there any more questions?"

"*Jesus!* He's got a gun! Fucking psychopath!" the man

said, but his girlfriend had already started running. He cursed incoherently as he grabbed a few articles of clothing before joining her.

Wizard let out a sigh. "Ah, that was fun!" He motioned to the zip drives. "Let's try it again—try to jump while I keep a lookout."

"Just, stop waving that thing around, would you? It's not like you were going to shoot them."

"*No?*" Wizard spread his lips in a crazy smile before breaking into laughter and putting the gun away. "I suppose you're right..."

Asher shivered at the sight and then selected the destination that Desmond had pre-programmed into his zip drive. He held his breath and tapped the screen.

Error. Unable to initiate jump field.

"*Damn!*" Wizard said. "They must have found a way to boost the portable power source. Haven't gone far enough, I guess. Come on, let's keep moving."

They walked in silence for several minutes before Asher's curiosity got the better of him. "What did she say to you?"

"Who? Your girlfriend?"

"She's not my girlfriend."

"No? Too bad... She's attractive. You never tried?"

"She's a princess on my world. I would be killed if I ever put a hand on her."

"*Yikes!*" Wizard combed a hand through his beard. "You're the one they found at Kid's house, huh?"

Asher's felt his face redden.

"And Desmond took you in, just like that?"

"I—She lied to me. I thought that I was helping Kid..."

"Hmm... No doubt. Julia can be quite persuasive. At any rate, you wouldn't be here if Desmond thought otherwise. Is it true that you're immune to the Gaian's flux abilities?"

Asher shrugged. He still didn't know much about the mysterious powers the Gaians had. He'd overheard some Terrans telling stories at the training camp in Texas, but part of him suspected that they were highly exaggerated tales. The sort of bedtime stories you would tell a child to scare them into behaving. "I guess so. That's what they tell me, anyway."

"God, I'd love to run some tests on you if we ever get the chance." Wizard gauged his reaction. "What would cause such a thing, I wonder?"

"Why do *they* have magical powers and no one else does?" Asher retorted. "Doesn't seem fair if you ask me."

Wizard chuckled. "I know several hundred scientists on Terra who are obsessed with the very same question. Although, I can assure you, magic has nothing to do with it. The Gaians affect matter in a very real, physical sense. But understanding the scientific properties behind their abilities has turned out to be far more difficult than anyone thought. Last I heard from the rumor mill on Terra though, several researchers were close to making a breakthrough."

"Seems to me like they already have. With the jammer thingy or whatever."

"Ah, you mean the jump shield?" Wizard asked. "That was a lucky coincidence, I'm afraid. When they first developed the zip technology, they needed a way to ensure that people wouldn't be able to just jump into a head of state's quarters and assassinate them. They came up with the jump shield that emits a high-frequency electromagnetic field. No one from outside it can jump in, and likewise, no one can jump out from within the field. By dumb luck, it turned out that it also dampened the Gaian's control of what they call the flux."

"That's how you know their powers aren't just magic..." Asher mused.

"Very good, yes. That was our first clue. We've been cursed with the discovery of technologies that we can harness, but don't fully understand. We know *how* to make them work, but we don't know *why* they work. Does that make sense?"

"I think so."

Wizard stopped walking. "Alright, let's try it again. We should be beyond the jump shield's range unless they're moving it on some sort of mobile platform." He shuddered as if not wanting to process the thought.

"Hang on, you never told me what Ava said to you."

"That her name? Well, she didn't say much, other than what you heard. I was at the bar, ordering a drink when I felt her stick the gun in my side. She told me to go out the back door, and I did. Lucky for me, *you* happened to be there." He opened his mouth to continue but then closed it as he decided whether or not to say what he'd been thinking. "I think she meant to kill me."

"What? That's ridiculous!" Asher waved his hand dismissively. "She's not a killer. She wouldn't..."

"*Really?* How well do you know this girl? Were you close? Did you grow up together?" Wizard studied his reaction. "No, I didn't think so. And you have no idea how much the nanites can change someone, especially the military grade. They've got programs that can grant an agent almost Gaian-like powers. People can get addicted to that kind of power. And there are some who would do anything to keep it."

Asher considered what Wizard had said. "What makes you think she was going to kill you?"

"Besides a gut feeling? The fact that her gun wasn't set to stun. There's no reason for it not to be, that's standard operating procedure for all Terran military and police forces. Unless, of course, she meant to use it."

"I hope you're wrong." Asher's eyes watered, threatening tears.

Wizard watched him with pity. "I hope so, too." But he knew that he wasn't.

24

Third Verse
San Fransisco

THE GRENADES DETONATED halfway between Celia and the strike teams. Bodies flew in every direction, including Desmond's. He and Jack hit the side of the roof and all the air was forced out of his lungs. As he tried to gather himself, he saw Celia's limp body sprawled out on the ground between him and the few remaining soldiers who were recovering from the concussive blast.

What had she done? Desmond's mind reeled. Was she seriously injured?

He allowed himself a brief moment of anger and helplessness as he accepted that there was nothing he could do for her at the present time. If he and Jack were to have any chance of escaping, they had to leave her behind and make a run for it. He would have expected her to do the same if his plan had been put into action.

Beside him, Jack wheezed and started crawling toward Celia. Desmond grabbed his arm and stopped him in his tracks. He shook his head. "We have to leave her!"

There wasn't any time to argue about it, either. Desmond used his considerable strength and lifted Jack over the side of the roof. Then he dropped him.

Jack landed feet first and collapsed onto the fire escape balcony, surprised at how quickly events had transpired.

Desmond jumped over the side just as several stun blasts hummed by over his head. He landed with a thud next to Jack who was still getting over the shock of being dropped.

"*We gotta move!*" Desmond grabbed the back of Jack's collar and led him toward the stairs leading down to the street below. Their boots clanked on the steel grating, thundering loudly in his ears.

"We can't just leave her here, Desmond!"

"She didn't exactly leave us much of a choice," Desmond answered, as he scanned the street below. *Was the entire strike team on the roof above?*

They dropped the last several feet down onto the pavement and Desmond chose left, running in that direction. They turned the corner and skidded to a halt as they saw a squadron of soldiers standing around what appeared to be a large generator.

"*Wrong way!*" Jack yelled. He fired off a few rounds as the soldiers did the same.

Desmond and Jack retreated back the way they had come, trying to put the building in between them for shielding. They crossed an intersection, running for the cover of the next nearest building. They were nearly there when Desmond felt the stun blast shove him off his feet. He flew through the air and landed face down on the pavement, putting his hands out to slow the fall. The friction from the asphalt burned away several layers of skin.

Jack helped Desmond back up to his feet and they continued their mad dash for cover. The shot had been a desperate attempt to slow them down since they were out of effective range. "Good thing they're only trying to stun us, huh?" Jack yelled over the noise as they ran.

Desmond gave no reply. He was too busy trying to think of a way out of their current predicament. The pounding of their pursuers' footsteps on the pavement spurred him onward. They might not be in range yet, but depending on how augmented the Terrans were, that wouldn't last forever. While he might be able to outpace them indefinitely, Jack would only be able to keep up their current pace for a few more minutes.

Desmond led Jack zig-zagging back and forth down the alleys between buildings, doing his best to make sure they wouldn't have a clear shot at either of them. He was beginning to think they might be all right when they ran out of buildings to hide behind.

They shot out of an alley onto the sidewalk of a wide street with multiple lanes of traffic going in both directions. Glancing quickly left and then right, Desmond saw no sign of Terran soldiers.

"Come on, this way," Desmond said, continuing in the direction that would take them further away from the large generator they'd nearly run into. Desmond tried to access the flux, testing to see whether they were clear of the jump shield. Nothing. The flux was still dark. How large was this thing? he wondered. They should have escaped its effects by now, unless... They were moving the jump shield—following them.

The realization hit him like a physical blow. They needed a change of plans.

The street was littered with the night crowds of the bustling city. Jack and Desmond wove in and out as they ran down the sidewalk, drawing bewildered looks from bystanders.

Desmond dared to peek back for a sign of their pursuers and immediately wished he hadn't. He saw the lead soldier stop and raise his weapon. Desmond spun around, grabbed Jack's arm, and pulled him out into the oncoming traffic of the busy street.

"What the hell are you doing?" Jack's question was immediately answered with a giant clap of thunder that struck the parked car they had darted past just a moment before. Cars honked their horns as the two men weaved between them, grinding the flow of traffic to a crawl as angry drivers slammed on their brakes to avoid colliding with each other.

Desmond knew they couldn't keep up this game of cat and mouse forever. A few hundred feet in front of them, a car pulled up to the curb. A man and woman got out and closed the door, thanking the driver for the ride.

"You know how to drive one of these, right?" Desmond yelled to Jack as they ran.

Jack saw the car parked on the side of the street and nodded. "I like the way you think," Jack said, smiling.

Desmond slowed and let Jack reach the car first. He provided what little cover he could with his weapon as

Jack forced the car door open and physically removed the bewildered driver from the vehicle.

"All right, let's go! Let's go!" Jack yelled. Desmond fired a few more stun rounds at the soldiers before opening the back door and diving into the car. He heard the thumps of the return fire strike the car door.

Jack peeled away from the curb, squealing the tires and almost plowing into the car ahead of them.

Desmond whirled around and looked for any signs that they were being followed, but saw none.

They rode in silence for several minutes. The adrenaline started to wear off as events began to sink in. Jack pounded on the steering wheel, cursing. "How the fuck did they know we were coming?"

Desmond sighed. He was just as frustrated as his compatriot but more composed. "My guess is they intercepted Wizard's message and tracked him."

"*Goddammit!*" Jack hit the steering wheel a few more times for good measure. "I'm getting really sick and tired of these assholes. Now they have Celia, too."

Desmond saw Jack's eyes in the rearview mirror, red and watery. A mix of rage and sorrow and frustration. Sharing in Jack's outburst of emotion would do no good to anyone, least of all Kid or Celia. Instead of Jack's red-hot, burning fury, Desmond shrouded himself in a dark, cold resolve that wouldn't be moved by any force except the completion of his will.

Desmond spoke slow and steady, projecting strength and power through his voice. "Jack, I will move heaven and earth to get them back if I have to. I promise you that. You will see Kid again."

Jack met his eyes in the rearview and weighed

Desmond's promise. He nodded his acceptance and then looked away, eyes back on the road. "So where do we go from here?"

"Just keep it in between the lines," Desmond said.

Jack sniggered. "That's not what I meant."

"I know."

25

Third Verse

Outside End of the World

Ava watched the boot-up sequence that the nanites projected onto her heads-up display as she sat up. She still wasn't used to having the augmented HUD but found it more and more useful the deeper she went with it.

Her head throbbed, and her ribs ached each time she took a breath. She directed the nanites to start repairing the damage from the concussive blast of her own weapon.

Approximately twenty-seven hours until healing is complete, the HUD informed her. She cursed the old man under her breath and instructed the nanites to stimulate her body's natural pain-killers. There was an option to automate the medical program, but Ava didn't feel comfortable yet turning over all control of her biology to the OS. Maybe one day, but for now, she wanted to oversee everything.

Seconds later, the endorphins rushed through her system, bringing sweet relief from the stabbing pain.

With the most pressing annoyances taken care of, she switched her attention to the handcuffs around her wrists and ankles. She ran a simulation where she boosted her adrenaline and broke free of the cuffs with sheer force, but the damage her skin and bones would incur made the option useless. The OS made a suggestion, bringing up several alternative ways to free herself from the handcuffs.

Ava smiled. "How did I ever live without you?"

She sorted through several and chose the quickest, least painful option. She instructed the OS to scan for the tool she required and helped by three-sixty-ing the alley she was in, giving the program visual access to everything in her immediate vicinity.

The OS located several tools that would do, highlighting each of them. She chose the nearest one and crawled on her hands and knees over to it. Her fingers closed around the paper clip and she bent it to the shape the program outlined.

The next part was a little trickier. She tried several times to perform the delicate twists and turns that picking the lock required but soon grew frustrated. Part of her, the stubborn part, wanted to keep at it until she succeeded, but time was an issue. She needed to rendezvous with the rest of Mallak's strike team before they jumped off-world if she didn't want to be stranded. Sure, they'd probably come back for her eventually, but it might be days before they did, and she had things to do—worlds to master and scores to settle.

She surrendered motor control to the OS a moment before a deafening explosion scared the living shit out of her. She jerked—or would have if the OS hadn't already taken control of her body. Curious, she could still move her head around. It seemed the OS only took as much control as it needed to carry out its task. There were so many elements to this new wonderland of augmentation that she couldn't wait to explore further. But it would have to wait.

Watching her fingers transform into nimble acrobats, twisting this way and bending that way, she couldn't help but marvel at the operation. The OS targeted the cuffs on the wrists first and then the ankles. All in all, it took less than ten seconds.

Motor control automatically ceded back to Ava after the program completed its objective and she stood to her feet. She took a moment to rub some feeling into her wrists. They were red from where the handcuffs had cut off some of the circulation. And then she ran toward the sound of the explosion.

She turned the corner out of the alley and immediately saw the smoke rising from the top of a building catty-corner from the club. Several Terran operators disappeared down the street, in pursuit of the old man's friends, no doubt. Ava was little good to them without a weapon. Besides, they'd trained for years at what they did, and while she had faith in her newfound augmented abilities, what could she do that they couldn't?

Instead, she would investigate the scene of the explosion. If Mallak was anywhere, he would be near the epicenter.

THE ROOFTOP WAS A WAR ZONE. Bodies were everywhere. She scanned the faces and hoped the HUD would show her someone that she knew. More importantly, someone who knew who she was and what she was doing here.

Several commandos were standing around another body laying on the floor. It was a woman. She looked dead. Streams of blood were trailing from her eyes, nose, and mouth.

Scan for vitals.

The OS did as she commanded, revealing faint signs of life.

Not dead then.

Her HUD tagged one of the commandos as Mallak, Julia's second in command, and she suspected, something more. He was the one who'd sent her in all alone without any backup. She made a note to return the favor if the opportunity ever presented itself.

"Still alive, I see..." Mallak said as he spotted her. "Was your mission successful?"

Ava blushed, ashamed that she'd failed, but also pissed. "He had someone watching his back who got the drop on me. They knocked me out and took my body armor and zip drive."

Mallak took a deep breath in, held it, and then slowly exhaled. "Right. Well, I guess that one's on me. Should have known better." He nodded his head toward the fallen commandos. "Find a dead one and get yourself some replacements."

"Is that one of the Gaians?" She indicated the woman lying at his feet.

"She is."

"What happened up here? She's barely alive."

A look of annoyance flashed across Mallak's face. "She decided to play hero and sacrifice herself so the rest of them could escape. Now she'll get to play another role. One of our choosing."

Faint sirens whined in the distance. Mallak turned away from her and gave orders to begin scrubbing the scene. Ava took the time to find a dead Terran who was close to her size. The smart fabric of the body armor would automatically adjust to her proportions regardless, but old habits were hard to break.

Mallak walked back over to her, his mood considerably darker. "I just received word from the Prime Minister. She wants you to take the Gaian back to her, personally. Do you think you can manage it without another fuck up?"

"Of course." She fumed. Who the hell did he think he was, talking to her like that? "Why me?"

"Hell if I know... I've been wondering the same thing for days now. I'm sure she has her reasons. She usually does."

"And here I thought she told you everything," Ava said, curious to know how far she could push him.

If her comment bothered him, he didn't let it show. He leaned close enough to whisper in her ear and said, "Don't screw this up." And then he walked away and began barking out orders for their exit.

Ava checked the charge on her zip drive and received noticed that they were clear of the jump shield. She ran a boost program and threw the woman over her shoulder. She was a little larger than Ava, but the augmentation made her feel light as a feather.

Ava took a deep breath and muttered, "Don't screw this up," to herself as she activated the zip drive.

26

Seventh Verse

Location Unknown

Celia didn't remember how she came to be in the bed she woke up in. She didn't recall how she got into the restraints on that bed either. She felt groggy, her mind fuzzy like after a night of hard drinking. They must have drugged her, she decided. She might have been out for days. She could be anywhere in the multiverse by now. The last thing she could remember was tossing the grenades on the rooftop in the Third and the look of surprise on her father's face.

Her head had been left unrestrained and she lifted it just high enough to see the tips of her toes and several more restraints. Besides the restraints around her wrists and ankles, she saw two more around her legs, one around her waist, and another around her chest.

She was in a sterile room of some sort, maybe a

hospital or laboratory. Monitors around her displayed her vitals and other biological details.

Celia reached out with her mind, searching for anyone else nearby, but she felt nothing. She tried to break the restraints holding her, a feat which should have been accomplished easily, but nothing happened. Either she was dreaming, still drugged, or there was a jump shield in place.

Celia heard the door opening and froze, feigning sleep. Perhaps she could take whoever it was unawares. She heard the footsteps of several people walk into the room, the unmistakable sound of hard-heeled shoes accompanied by the softer soles of combat boots.

"Raise her up." The bed Celia was on began tilting, moving her from a horizontal to a vertical position. "We know you're awake, Celia, you can stop pretending."

Celia opened her eyes as the bed came to a halt. There was a platform beneath her feet that allowed her to stand and bear her own weight. To her disappointment, her body barely shifted in the transition, still quite restrained. She had hoped for some kind of slack to be able to work with.

The woman Celia saw in front of her was young and beautiful. She had shoulder-length, light brown hair, straight as a wisp, and twice as long on the left side as the right. Another woman stood off to the side at a control screen. A medical assistant from the looks of her.

"You cut your hair," Celia said to the first woman with a smile.

The young woman did a double-take but recovered quickly. "Yes, I thought it fitting, considering the circumstances."

"New life, new haircut?"

"Something like that," the woman said. "My name is Ava, but then you probably already knew that."

Celia nodded, indicating that she did. In truth, she had guessed, piecing together who she was from Asher's description of her. And she could spot a new haircut from a mile away. "I didn't see you in the Third, did you show up after all the fun was already over? Or does your master keep you chained up at home?"

Ava's face flushed red with anger.

"Oh, I'm sorry, that's right, you're a princess," Celia mocked. "You probably think no one is your master... Tell me, what's it like? Going from giving orders to taking them? Do you enjoy getting down on your hands and knees and—"

Ava closed the distance between them faster than Celia expected and delivered a backhand almost too quick to see. Celia felt the warm taste of blood on her tongue as her lip split. She laughed wildly as Ava's hand raised to strike her again.

"That will be quite enough, Ava!" Julia said from the doorway, behind Ava. "Besides, she likes it."

Ava backed off slowly, hatred still pouring from her eyes as Julia walked into the room.

"Hello, Mother. *Soooo* good to see you again," Celia said.

"Hello, Celia. Nice to see you haven't lost your sarcasm. I like to think that I contributed to your upbringing in *some* way..."

"*Ha!*" Celia barked. "You could have contributed more if you hadn't run away to another universe."

"She's your daughter?" Ava asked, surprised by the turn of events.

"Yes, she is," Julia said. "At least she *used* to be my daughter. She's more of her father's daughter than anything else these days." She turned to Celia. "Tell me, daughter dearest, what were you and your father doing in the Third?"

"You don't know? After you left us we joined the traveling circus. Our caravan had just arrived in the Third when your goons showed up and tried to kill us."

Julia laughed. "Oh, Celia... You always did tell the most wonderful stories as a little girl. Remember when you used to sit on my knee and—"

"Are you serious?" Celia interrupted. "You want to have story time right now? How about you let me out of this bed and I'll tell you all the stories you want."

The smile that had been on Julia's face left without a trace. "I was trying to be civil about this, but—"

"*But what...? What!?* What are you going to do?"

Julia opened her mouth as if to speak and then closed it, pausing. "What ever happened to your last partner?" She smiled wickedly.

Celia's jaw dropped, her eyes wide open. "*You...? You* killed Jacen?" It wasn't as much a question as it was a statement of a finally realized fact.

"Well, *I* didn't, *per se*. But I did *have* him killed... I had to, I'm afraid. He was getting soft on me." Julia talked nonchalantly as if she was discussing the weather. "You see, he was starting to develop *feelings* for you." She said the word as if it left a bad taste in her mouth.

"What are you talking about? Of course, he had feelings for me. *We were in love!*"

Julia snickered. "Oh, *you* were in love, I'm quite sure of that, but he was my operative, planted to keep me up to date on what you and your father were up to." Julia walked in a circle around her captive daughter like a cat playing with a mouse. Behind her, Ava watched with a look of enjoyment on her face. "Don't look so surprised and hurt, Celia. Anyway, I did you a favor getting rid of him."

Celia spoke through gritted teeth, "When I get out of here, I'm going to make sure that I'm the one who squeezes the last breath out of you."

"*Tsk, tsk,* Celia. You mustn't let your feelings get the better of you. If there's one thing I learned from my time with your father, it's that feelings cloud the mind. They make one weak, unable to act reasonably." She looked at Celia with what would have appeared to anyone else as motherly-concern, but Celia knew better.

"What do you want from me?" Celia asked.

"An excellent question, my daughter, but I can see that I've upset you. It's best not to discuss such important matters when you're upset." With that she turned and walked out of the room, followed by the others and finally, Ava, who paused to look back.

"See you again, real soon," Ava said. She blew Celia a kiss.

"Can't wait, Princess."

27

Seventh Verse
Location Unknown

The silence was driving Celia insane. She wanted to scream, and she wanted to fight, but most of all she wanted to know what the hell her bitch of a mother was up to. It had to be something big for her to go through all of this subterfuge and manipulation. And kidnapping children from their homes in the middle of the night—what sort of monster did that? And for what purpose? Whatever she was up to, Celia knew one thing about her mother that she could take to her grave—she couldn't be trusted.

Celia took a deep breath and closed her eyes, forcing her body to relax. She repeated the process over and over until everything outside herself faded away. All that remained was an inner ocean of nothingness. A place she thought of as her center. The center was a place where she could not be touched, and where nothing could exist without her willing it to be there. She needed no abilities to go there.

Breath after breath, Celia found her center and then thought her escape into existence.

The first hand would be the hardest, Celia knew. Once she got that free, the rest would be progressively easier, but the first hand, her right hand, would be the hardest.

Jump shields created a space in which a Gaian's powers were dampened but not absent. The abilities were still there, but they couldn't be accessed due to the field's interference. Celia found the experience unsettling, like suddenly losing the sense of sight or sound or touch. There was a part of her that wasn't there anymore, but she could still feel it, like a phantom limb.

As a young girl, Celia would visit the Seventh with her parents from time to time. And even though she hadn't bonded with the flux yet, she still felt the strange effects of the jump shields that permeated the capital city of Civitas. On several occasions, her parents had heard noises coming from her room in the middle of the night. They'd found toys rattling back and forth, almost vibrating. Once they woke Celia the effect would stop. Her parents had worried at the time, but no one knew what to make of it. Now, however, Celia thought she had it figured out.

She'd somehow tapped into the flux while she slept. It was the only explanation. Her child-self must have instinctually found a way, and now she would need to do the same. She hoped her chances weren't as desperate as they sounded in her head.

Thankfully, they hadn't sedated her. Whether they had forgotten to or not, Celia didn't care. She was only interested in exploiting the situation. Under sedation, she wouldn't be able to access the dream state which would make her escape possible.

Sleeping while standing, however, was going to be difficult. Difficult, but not impossible.

Celia spent the better part of an hour trying to fall asleep, sometimes getting just to the cusp before an automatic reflex would jolt her awake. After countless attempts, she finally managed sleep.

And she dreamed.

She was a little girl again, six, maybe seven. She was playing down on the beach in the sand by the lake. It was her birthday, but she couldn't recall what her gifts had been.

She was walking down the hall in the lake house, going to her room, to see her gifts. The hallway was longer than she remembered. She walked for what seemed like miles, then just as she began to doubt where she was headed, she saw her door.

She reached out and grabbed hold of the doorknob, seeing her small hand, but feeling the knob as she would as an adult. The door swung open and Celia looked into the past. It was her old room.

There were drawings taped up on the walls that she had made. Scenes of trees, and rainbows, and horses, and flowers. Some were portraits of her family. Her and her mom and dad—stick figures floating above the ground.

Her dresser stood up against the wall. Dark wooden drawers with golden handles on them. It seemed much larger and more imposing than she recalled.

On her bed, in the corner, her mother sat with her younger self. They were drawing together with crayons.

Her mother was the most beautiful woman in the whole wide world. Her hair was long and dark like Celia's, but unlike Celia's, her mother's hair was straight as an arrow. There wasn't a single loose curl to be found anywhere.

And how her mother's eyes sparkled. Green, then blue, then green again. She loved her mother, she was the best...

The contrast between dreamscape and reality finally reached a crest. Celia woke in her dream to a state of lucidity. She remembered what her purpose was and what she was supposed to do.

A door appeared on the other side of the room. Celia walked to it, leaving her mother and her younger self playing on the bed together.

She opened the door and stepped through into another room.

This room was dark, except for a spotlight shining down in the middle. Beneath that light, on a metal table, Celia saw herself as she was now. She was strapped down to the table with leather restraints. One on each wrist and ankle and several more across her legs and torso.

Her self on the table was struggling, trying to wriggle free, but failing. She only succeeded in shaking the table from side to side.

Celia rushed over and tried to help free herself of the restraints. Then she remembered the plan—her right hand. Her right hand was the one she wanted to get free.

Celia took hold of the restraint on her right hand, the

leather strap had holes in it. It was fastened like an old belt. She pulled on the strap, trying to undo the buckle.

Nothing happened. The strap wouldn't move and she couldn't undo the fastener no matter how hard she tugged.

Panic began to set in. Someone was coming for her. She could hear them outside the room and they were getting closer.

She had to free her other self from this table now. She might never get a second chance.

Celia quickly tried the other hand and found that the strap easily came undone. She moved to the feet and undid those straps with the same ease. The straps across the legs and torso gave her no trouble either.

She was back to the right hand. She grabbed hold of the strap and tried to unbuckle it again. It held tight, but this time it gave the smallest amount when she pulled on it.

She pulled harder, and it gave some more, but still not enough to come undone. She needed more leverage.

She jumped up on the table, squatted over her dream self's right arm, and grabbed the strap. She pulled. She pulled with her arms. She pulled with her legs. Her muscles burned with exertion. At last, the strap stretched and gave way.

Celia saw her other self's hand turning red, the circulation being cut off. The veins on the back of her hand stood out like soldiers at attention.

The strap had given enough to come undone, but the metal pin hadn't moved out of the way. If Celia was to let go now, the strap would slide back down onto the pin, re-fastening the restraint.

Celia pulled harder. It was the only thing she could do. Any other movement would cause her to lose her grip and the strap would re-fasten.

Just as her strength was fading and she could feel the strap begin to slip in her grasp. Celia's dream self reached over with her left hand and moved the pin out of the way. And not a moment too soon.

Behind them, she heard the door smash against the wall as it flung open. The light overhead grew exponentially brighter until it was blinding. Celia spun, looking for the intruder in the room when she was suddenly grabbed from behind by the shoulders and yanked off the table.

She screamed as she fell backward into the blinding darkness. And then she woke up.

Celia was standing. She was back in the Seventh, surrounded by screens and medical equipment. Her body was still restrained, but her right hand was now free of the metal cuff that had held her by the wrist.

Celia glanced around the room, gathering her bearings and making her way back to a state of alert consciousness. The last hold that the dream held over her began to wash away. Her heart was still pounding from the fright of how her dream had ended. She was drenched in sweat but relieved that it had worked.

Stage one complete, she thought. She held her breath and listened.

No alarms were going off. No people running up and down the hallway outside. Good. It meant that the restraints weren't electronically operated. Not only would her tampering with them not be reported, but most mechanical restraints were easily undone. At least for someone with Celia's skill set.

Celia twisted her arm back and forth and loosened her freed right hand even more. Then she began to snake it backward in the direction of her head. The two restraints around her waist and chest also encompassed her arms, making it difficult.

Taking a deep breath, she exhaled as fully as possible, giving herself just enough space to slide her arm back. She almost had her hand free of the waist restraint when she ran out of room. This was as far as her tendons and the restraints would allow.

Without hesitation, Celia jerked backward, popping her shoulder out of the socket. She writhed in pain, but her hand was free of the first restraint. With several jolting and painful efforts, Celia managed to pop her shoulder back into the socket. It was sore as hell, but she could rotate her arm again.

Next, she looked for the locking device on her chest restraint. From her limited field of view, she couldn't see it, which meant that it was on the side of the platform she was attached to.

Her arm was free up until her bicep, at which point the restraint held it tightly against her side. She bent her arm at the elbow and reached as far toward her shoulder as she could. When her hand could reach no further she gave one final jerk and tried to grab onto the restraint. She missed. But by dumb luck, her thumb caught the clasp and pulled it open.

"I'll take what I can get," she muttered to herself. She removed the chest restraint, freeing her entire upper body. The rest of the restraints took no time at all. First the left hand, then the waist, then the thigh and calf restraints, and her ankles.

She stepped away from her former prison and shook her arms and legs, working some blood back into limbs that had been stationary for too long.

In the security room, the guard put down the datapad he had been reading and glanced at the monitors. Everything was normal. No. Wait.

"*Shit.*"

The new girl was getting out of her restraints somehow. But that was impossible. The guard had put them on her himself.

For a split second, he thought about calling for assistance before deciding to handle it personally. If she escaped, he would lose his job at best, and he didn't want to think about the at-worst part. Besides, she only had one hand free, it would take her longer to undo the rest than it took for him to run down there and secure her.

He sprinted down the hall, suddenly wishing he'd purchased the speed boost program for his OS. He felt for his stun gun, just to be sure he hadn't forgotten it. That would have been all he needed, to run all the way down there and then forget his department-issued sidearm. It wouldn't have been the first time. Hence, his probation, and why he had to fix this by himself, without any backup. Easy cheesy, the guard told himself, no problem. It was just one girl, and she didn't have her abilities.

He slowed to a fast walk several times as he passed people walking down the hall. Most were scientists in lab coats, but a few looked to be agents coming and going on official business and he wanted to avoid raising any suspicions if it was possible. The guard gave them a smile, a nod, and a how-do-you-do, and resumed his run as soon as they were out of sight.

The journey from the control room couldn't have taken more than a minute at most.

He couldn't see inside. There was only one window in the door, but the tint was too dark to see anything on the other side. He took a deep breath and opened the door.

It took less than half a second to see that the girl was nowhere in sight. The restraint platform was empty. And it also took less than half a second for him to be kicked in the throat, spun around, and put in a rear naked chokehold.

Fear and embarrassment flooded over him as he realized he'd forgotten to draw his gun before going into the room. As the grip on his neck tightened, his hand drifted toward his sidearm. Maybe he could—

"Don't do it." The woman's voice was strong and smooth. "I assure you I can snap your neck before you even get close. No matter *what* boost program you're running."

"Ok, alright," the guard spoke slowly, trying to calm himself down more than her. "Take it easy. I just have the basic civilian OS."

"Clearance level not high enough, huh?" Celia mocked. "Unfortunately, I don't have time to *take it easy*. Where is the jump shield that's trapping me here?" She paused for a second and then constricted her biceps and back muscles cutting off the arteries on both sides of his neck. He felt like his head was going to explode from the inside as his field of vision started to grow dark. "*Where is it?* I don't want to hurt you, but I will if I have to. Your choice."

He shut his eyes and did his best not to break down into tears. What was he supposed to do? He couldn't tell her. She'd be able to jump, and then they'd never find her, but if he didn't tell her what she wanted to know... She didn't seem like the type to back down on a promise, and he liked his neck un-snapped. He didn't want to die, but he didn't want to get fired either. Why hadn't he called in sick today? He should have known something like this was going to happen, he should have listened to his mother when she told him to—

"Tell her." He was jolted out of self-pity by the voice in his in-ear comms. It was his supervisor. "Don't be a hero, just tell her what she wants to know."

The guard sank down, resigned to his fate. He tried to take a breath and speak but only managed to gurgle out a few sounds.

"What was that?" Celia loosened her grip.

He repeated himself. "I said, it's right over there." He pointed. "The box in the corner. There's a panel on the side."

The woman reached down, drew his sidearm from his holster, and pushed him away from her.

"Deactivate it, *now!*"

The guard waited for a moment, hoping to receive instructions that help was on the way. He received nothing of the kind. Instead, he heard the click of his weapon being taken off of the stun setting, and then Celia's voice, "I won't say it again, shut it down now!" Her voice was ice cold. In a strange way, it reminded him of his mother.

He moved to the box in the corner and reached down, pulling off the metal panel. He hit the kill switch and shut the room's jump shield down.

The guard turned to face what was coming next but never made it all the way around. The pain stabbed through his head and then the world went dark.

28

Sixth Verse
Cairos

In the two days that had passed since the ambush in the Third, the Council and the GDA had accomplished little more than arguing about the best course of action. Desmond was in the middle of trying to convince the head of the GDA to see his point of view and failing.

"I'm sorry about Celia, but we have to get more intel about what the Terrans are up to before we commit our forces to anything," Erik Sandoval, Director of the GDA, said. "Wizard's beacon is the best chance we have of recovering the children and learning why they were kidnapped in the first place."

"I'm not arguing with you there," Desmond said. "But at the same time, we don't even know for sure that the children are there."

"That's right." Wizard tugged at his collar, fidgeting.

"It was just a lead that I had from one of my sources. A rumor of a rumor, so to speak. I didn't have time to confirm any of it."

"So you just happened to place the beacon that would allow us to bypass their jump shield at the lab based on a rumor?"

"Well, outside of the lab, but yes."

Jack and Asher sat watching the drama unfold. Neither had much to offer and if they were honest, they only understood about half of what was being discussed. But the particulars didn't matter to either of them. They were both down for a fight, they just needed to be pointed in the right direction and told to go.

"The Council is not going to authorize a rescue mission—"

"I don't need the Council's permission, remember?" Desmond was growing tired of all the talk. His body ached to do something, but he just didn't know what. "We need to seriously consider the possibility that we may need to take military action here..."

"*Military action?*" Sandoval looked as if Desmond had suggested that pigs could fly. "Over a few children?"

Desmond pounded his fist on the table. "*My children! Our* children... And not just that, no. With the direct assault on us in the Third, the Terrans have broken every peace treaty we had in place. They continue to grow more and more brazen. We can't sit on our hands and allow their aggression to continue unchecked. With every minute that passes, they grow closer to their aims while we remain helpless in the dark."

Sandoval opened his mouth to respond but never got the chance.

Celia jumped into the conference room directly on top of the table, startling everyone present. She took in the scene and flashed a sheepish grin. "*Surprise!* Did you guys miss me? I know you probably have a million ques —" Celia's eyes rolled back in her head and she stood suspended, for a moment, before she fell.

In the blink of an eye, Desmond caught her before she hit the ground. He gently laid her head down and made sure her airways were clear. "Celia? Celia, are you all right?" He gently patted her on the cheeks trying to rouse her back to consciousness.

Celia remained still, but Desmond heard her voice in his head. "*What did she do...?*"

"What did *who* do, Celia?" Desmond felt her begin to respond in the flux, but then she faded away. "No, no no no. Stay with me, Celia." Desmond felt for a pulse. It was strong, but her heart was beating abnormally fast. "Call the medics, now!"

Desmond held Celia's hand as they waited for the medical team. It felt like forever. He tried every flux technique he could think of to connect with her, to let her know that she was safe, that everything would be alright. But it was like she was underneath a thick blanket. He kept catching glimpses of her presence in the flux, but as quickly as the glimpses came, they disappeared.

The medical team came running in. They strapped her to a gurney and hooked up multiple monitors.

"What happened?" one of the medic's asked.

"She was captured on our last mission," Desmond explained. "She must have escaped somehow and jumped here. She was talking. Seemed fine and then she just collapsed. Eyes rolled back and then she seemed to fade away in the flux field. I can't feel her at all, now."

The medic nodded. "She's got an elevated heart rate, and is unresponsive, but other than that, she seems to be stable. You said she escaped? Could whoever held her have done something to her?"

"I suppose anything's possible, but I've never heard of them being able to do something like this before."

"Okay, we'll need to run some tests, and collect some samples."

Desmond nodded once and then they started moving her. He reached out and touched her arm, his finger trailing as the gurney pulled her away.

The five of them stood around in shock, dumbfounded. Not only at the event, but at the speed with which it happened. Jack and Asher were speechless. Wizard opened and closed his mouth half a dozen times, beginning to speak but then deciding against it. Finally, Sandoval cleared his throat and broke the silence. "Perhaps we should take a break and reconvene later this evening?"

Desmond was staring off into the distance. He snapped back to the room. "Uh, yes. I think that would be best. Sorry. I need to clear my head."

"I understand." Sandoval gave Desmond a brief clap on the shoulder. Somewhere on the scale between a hug and a handshake. Then he left.

As a friend, it pained Wizard to see the look on Desmond's face. Even from behind his stoic front, Wizard knew that Desmond was deeply troubled. He just hoped that the mounting losses wouldn't change him into something or someone who he no longer recognized as his friend.

"I need to get some fresh air. Wizard, do you think you can keep these two out of trouble for a few hours?" Desmond managed a weak smile.

"Sure… Where are you going to go?" Wizard didn't know if he liked the tone of Desmond's voice. There was something strange about it.

"I don't know. I might jump around a bit. Maybe head up to the mountains, get some perspective."

"Should I be concerned?"

"No, nothing like that. Just need some distance to think about what's going on."

"Are you sure that's a good idea right now? What if Celia wakes up?"

"I'll still be on Gaia." He held up his comm. "Just have them call me." He forced a smile. And then he was gone.

"What the hell? He's just leaving?" Jack asked, more than a little upset.

"You heard him, he'll be back," Wizard said.

"What about Kid?" Jack stood, thrusting the chair back as he did, nearly tipping it over. "What about—I don't know—your stupid frigging beacon? Couldn't he be there? Why are we wasting time sitting on our asses when we could be doing something?"

Wizard opened his mouth to respond but was interrupted by an outburst from Asher. "I'm sorry!" Tears poured down his face. "It's all my fault! I'm so sorry. None of this would be happening if it wasn't for me."

Jack looked at the young man and sighed, his anger disappearing. "Hey, come on… it's—aw, hell." He went over and patted him on the back as he continued to sob.

"Come on, Ash, you gotta stop or I'll start, too." In fact, he'd already started. He wiped away the gathering moisture from the corners of his eyes.

Wizard joined the consolation party. "We're going to make everything all right again, Asher. Just you wait and see."

Asher's sobbing subsided.

"Trust me," Jack said. "I won't stop looking for Kid, no matter what. Even if it kills me."

Asher sucked in a few more sniffles and then wiped his face clean. "Me neither."

Jack clapped him on the back. "That's the spirit!"

The three men stared back and forth at each other and then broke into laughter, the last bit of pent-up energy finding its way out.

After a few moments, the laughter subsided. Asher's stomach rumbled loudly and Jack found that his own stomach was in agreement.

"What do they have that passes for food around here?"

Wizard perked up at the mention of eating. He rubbed his hands together. "Oh, my friends! You are in for a treat! I know the perfect little place right around the corner. Come on!" He led the way, continuing in his exaltation of the vendor as they walked.

29

Sixth Verse
Gaia

Desmond used the first few jumps to bleed off built-up energy more than anything else. If he didn't, he felt like he was going to explode.

He ended up on the other side of the planet in a small town in the mountains of Sophia, one of the rural provinces. He watched the townspeople below go about their daily business. They were oblivious to what was going on in the multiverse. Desmond envied them. Farmers tended to the animals in their fields, parents took their children to school, and then they went to work. It was all so simple in the valleys down below him.

From up above, Desmond was running out of time and options. Well, good options, anyway. He didn't know what Julia had done to their daughter, but whatever it was, it couldn't be good. And he didn't have high hopes that the Gaian medical community would be able to fix whatever was wrong with her either. If Julia thought they'd be able to undo what she'd done, she never would have let Celia go. Which brought him to another thought —why had Celia been let go? Or had she? Was it possible that Celia had escaped her imprisonment and then somehow found a way past the jump shields, all without any sort of help? He doubted it. He doubted that any agent could escape from Terran clutches without any help whatsoever. Himself included.

So that left only the conclusion that she'd been let go.

What game was Julia playing?

He cursed her again, for the hundredth time. It seemed the only person who could shed any kind of light on the situation was his ex-wife. His best spy on Terra had been burned and was now exiled on Gaia, and the best lead that he had might still turn out to be nothing more than a rumor. If only the Council had listened to him years ago, maybe Oracle would be up to speed now. With contacts and operatives in place, they might have seen this coming and been able to stop it. But not now. Now it was too late. Julia had put her plans into motion and whatever endgame she had in sight, only she knew.

He had to get more information, and he would get it the only way he knew how. Straight from the source. He knew it was a bad choice, but it was the only one he had. He would get to the bottom of what Julia was up to and stop her, no matter the cost.

He pulled out his datapad and began recording the message.

"Julia, I know you're busy these days—children to kidnap and nefarious plans to enact, et cetera, et cetera... So, I'll keep

this brief. I want to make a trade. Me, for the cure to whatever you've done to Celia. That is what you were after on the rooftop, after all, isn't it? It appears that we have unfinished business, so let's leave the children out of it, and settle it once and for all."

He sent the message without bothering to encrypt it and immediately felt lighter than he had in days. He didn't relish the thought of turning himself over to his ex-wife—especially because he didn't think for a second she would honor the terms of the arrangement. But they needed to know what the devil was up to and he couldn't see a better way to find out than going straight into the depths of hell.

He pocketed the datapad, took one last look over the idyllic countryside, and then jumped back to the GDA to await a response.

Desmond found his office quiet. *Where the hell is everybody?* He stuck his head out into the hall and saw no one. He shrugged, then went back and laid down on the couch in the corner of his office, and promptly fell asleep.

He woke with a start as his datapad pinged with a response from Julia. It was plain text. She hadn't even bothered to send video.

You remember where my office is right? Come alone and leave your guns at home.

XOXO

—Jules.

. . .

JACK, Asher, and Wizard returned as he finished reading her response.

"Desmond, you're back! I hope you weren't waiting too long. I didn't know when to expect you back, so I took Jack and Asher out for some food and a quick tour of the Council District."

Wizard was smiling. They all were, Desmond noticed. It was good, Desmond thought. Good to keep their spirits high.

"*Enson's* on 15th?" Desmond guessed.

"That's the one," Wizard said.

"You always did love that place," Desmond smirked and shook his head.

"I thought we had good food in New York," Jack said. "But you guys really know what you're doing here."

"Thanks. I'll be sure to let Enson know how much you loved it the next time I see him." Desmond turned to Asher. "And what did you think?"

"Where I come from, you're lucky if you have salt to season whatever bland meal you're able to scrape up. Compared to the food back home, this was heaven!" Asher's face beamed.

Desmond laughed at the young man's enthusiasm.

There was a knock at the door and an aide popped her head in. "Dr. Sanderson's downstairs for you, sir."

"Thank you. Would you show him up to the conference room, please?"

"Of course, sir."

The aide left and the four men were left staring at each other while an awkward silence replaced the joviality of the previous few minutes.

"Come on, Desmond. Let's go see what they found."

Wizard put a sympathetic arm around Desmond's shoulder as they all started walking toward the conference room.

"If they had anything for her, they would have called," Desmond said. "Bad news gets delivered in person."

"Well, on my world," Jack said. "They deliver both the good news and the bad news in person. So I still have high hopes."

Desmond knew they were trying to keep his spirits up, and he appreciated it. But with every moment, he felt the noose that Julia had tied, tightening around their necks. The only way out was to willingly walk into the lion's den.

The doctor was waiting for them as they arrived at the conference room. "Dr. Sanderson," he introduced himself.

Desmond shook his hand and introduced everyone else. "Please, Dr. Sanderson, tell us what you found."

"Let's all have a seat, shall we? I get nervous when everyone is standing."

They sat and the doctor continued, "I'll be honest and as direct as I'm able to if that's all right with you." He waited for Desmond's permission.

Desmond sighed, annoyed with how the doctor seemed to drag everything out. He nodded his permission.

Sanderson took a deep breath and held it for several seconds before continuing. "We've never seen anything like your daughter's case before."

"Is she dying?" Desmond asked.

"We don't think so."

"What do you mean you don't think so?"

"She's in a stable condition. However, she remains unconscious and unresponsive to any stimuli. We drew her blood and found an overwhelming presence of nanites."

Desmond's eyes narrowed. "How is that possible? Her body would have naturally fought off any intrusion."

Dr. Sanderson raised his hands in exasperation. "I don't know how they did it, but it looks like they've found a way to bio-engineer the nanites for Gaian DNA."

"Of course they did," Jack said dryly.

Desmond was surprised that he wasn't more surprised at the news. It made sense. With the new body armor, and the kidnapping of the children.

"The abductions..." Desmond said. "She was looking for Gaians who weren't bonded to the flux yet. Trying to see if she could level the playing field with us."

"What are you talking about?" Jack asked.

"Julia was always envious of our natural connection to the flux field. That we could do things without augmentation that the Terrans could only dream of."

"But I thought they could—I thought they had abilities and special powers of their own?" Asher was puzzled.

"They've done a lot to close the gap, but only a handful of Terran special operatives have the latest advancements. And there are *some things*," Desmond reached out and levitated the pitcher of water in the middle of the table, demonstrating his point, "that they will *never* be able to do. Or at least that's the going theory. It would seem that they're hell-bent on finding a way to access the flux through their technology."

"So you think she's developed some version of the

nanites that can strip a Gaian of their bond to the flux?" Wizard asked.

"That would actually make a lot of sense," Dr. Sanderson said. "Her body seems to be reacting like she's trying to fight off an infection."

"So how do we get the nanites out of her?" Jack asked. "Can we do a blood transfusion or something like that?"

"I'm afraid it's not that simple. The nanites are designed to stay in the body. We could transfuse her all day long but the nanites in her blood would just attach themselves to some other body tissue. Not to say anything about the rest of the nanites that don't reside in the blood."

"There may be something that we can do," Wizard said. All eyes turned on him. "If this is somehow related to their new body armor, perhaps I can reverse engineer what they've done and find something that might point us in the right direction."

"Do you still have the girl's?" Desmond asked.

Wizard nodded. "I'll get started right away." He stood to leave.

"Let me know if you need anything," Desmond said. "The entirety of my power is at your disposal. Well, the GDA's power, at least." His power would soon be elsewhere. Which reminded him. "Actually, can you help me with something?"

"Sure," Wizard said. "Want to tell me about it while we walk?"

Desmond had learned just about all he had expected to from the doctor. He stood and thanked Dr. Sanderson for coming by to deliver the news in person, and then followed Wizard down the hall.

The doctor left soon after and Jack and Asher found themselves sitting all alone. "What do we do now?" Asher asked.

Jack didn't respond. He was lost deep in thought. He had a crazy idea, but it just might work.

30

Sixth Verse
Cairos, Gaia

Colluding with Wizard took longer than he expected. As a result, Desmond was the last person to show up for the meeting that he had called with the Council. As he walked through the chamber doors, he adjusted the zip drive on his wrist that he'd had Wizard fiddle with. The council members were already seated. Chancellor Pearson cleared his throat, trying to cut through the conversation that had started up while they waited.

"Now that we are all here, perhaps you can tell us why you've called this meeting?"

"Yes, has there been a development?" Councillor Skizak asked. "Any progress returning the kidnapped children to their families?"

"I'm afraid not," Desmond said. "And that's why I wanted you all here today. We have been at a gross disadvantage ever since these attacks started. For years we left ourselves exposed, believing that the rest of mankind would conduct themselves in a manner similar to our own. Unfortunately, for a host of reasons, this is just not the case. There are vast differences in our cultures, our histories, and even our DNA that makes such an assumption not only unrealistic but also dangerous."

"What exactly are you getting at?" Chancellor Pearson asked.

"What I'm getting at, is that we have been blindsided by a plan that the Terrans have put into action. A plan that may have been in the works for who knows how long. A plan almost certainly orchestrated by my ex-wife, the Prime Minister of Terra. She knows our world, our governments, our military capabilities, and even our social constructs."

"Yes, but do we not also know the same about them?" Skizak asked.

"That's true, yes. We do. *However*, unlike us, the Terrans have been innovating ways to render our abilities and whatever strengths we might possess over them useless. They have been preparing for a fight that we would never have offered unless provoked. And they have caught us with our pants down. We have failed to take into account how fearful people act. Whether a threat is real or imagined, any capable race acting out of fear will do whatever is necessary to remove that threat. In this case, we are that threat, and they are those fearful people."

Skizak scoffed. "I can't accept that. There's just no way that the entire population of Terra, a civilization more advanced than our own in many ways, could ever be led to the mass hysteria that would be required in order for them to consider us as their enemies."

"But don't you see? Julia doesn't have to convince the entire population. She has swallowed up enough power and influence over a few key individuals in the military, government, and private sector. With that power, and with her control of the media, she can present reality as whatever she says it is. Which is why we can't wait any longer. We need to move before she has the chance to enact whatever other plans she has."

"What exactly are you suggesting?" Chancellor Pearson asked. "Surely you're not suggesting we go to war with Terra? A full-scale military action against another universe would be unprecedented."

Voices raised in concern over the idea and Desmond raised his hands to calm them down. "Of course not, ladies and gentlemen. What I need you to do, Chancellor, is undercut her influence with the general population. So far, she has been operating completely in the shadows. Managing to keep any glimpse of the kidnappings out of the mainstream media."

"But we've already tried diplomatic channels with the Terran government. They have denied any involvement."

"And I'm sure that the handful of government officials that you spoke with was as far as the information went. It certainly didn't get broadcast to the everyday citizens of Terra on the news or leaked to the online sites. But that is what *you* must do. You have to find a way to raise doubts about Julia's leadership with the common man and woman on Terra before it's too late, and she's had time to spin the tale she's been constructing into whatever narrative she desires."

Conversation rose about Desmond's proposal and he listened as various council members went back and forth with each other, arguing and counter-arguing. After several minutes, the noise died down and Chancellor Pearson spoke up.

"We will propose your idea to the people and take a vote on it. What will you do in the meantime?"

As Desmond smiled, there was a hint of sadness in his eyes. "Well, that's easy. I'm going to find out what Julia is really after." He first climbed on top of his seat, and then the enormous table that they were all seated around. He took a bow and then he jumped out of the Sixth Verse, leaving most of the Council with their mouths hanging open.

31

Sixth Verse

Oracle offices at the GDA

Jack poked his head into the makeshift workshop that Wizard had set up down the hall from Desmond's office. "You seen Desmond? I haven't been able to find him anywhere, and no one seems to know where he is."

Wizard put down the datapad he'd been studying and turned to face Jack. "He's not here. He's made a deal to save Celia."

"What? What kind of deal?"

"It seems Julia promised him that if he turned himself over to her, she would tell him how to undo whatever she's done to Celia."

"And he believed her?" Jack tried to wrap his head around the information.

"Not particularly, no," Wizard said matter of factly as he pointed. "Hand me that spanner."

Jack tossed the indicated instrument to him. "So why would he agree to it?"

"I tried to dissuade him, but he was rather bent on it. He seems to believe that it's the only way that he can find out what her plans are. He thinks if he can get close to her, he can goad her into slipping up, maybe access her mind in the flux or something, I don't know."

Jack frowned. "Surely, the first thing they'd do is make sure one of those jump shields is up, right? Wouldn't that kill whatever special powers he has?"

"Yes, that's why he asked me to rig a zip drive to record their entire conversation and send it to the encrypted server at my house." He tossed the spanner aside and sighed loudly. "As it turns out, I'll need a few tools from there, anyway. *These* are almost primitive."

Jack chuckled at his frustration. "Nothing worse than not having the right tool for the job. Which brings me to why I was looking for Desmond in the first place."

"What are you talking about?"

"I think I know how to help Celia."

Wizard's eyes narrowed as he stared at Jack. "Go on."

Jack's face lit up as he began. "The nanites that are disrupting Celia's flux are metallic in nature, yes?"

"They're mostly silicon, actually."

Jack's face fell. "Oh... Damn. I was thinking we could use the MRI at the hospital I worked at and just suck the damn bastards out."

"What's an MRI?" Wizard was curious.

"Magnetic Resonance Imaging. Basically, a big ass, powerful magnet."

"I see, and you thought—"

"I thought maybe if I could crank up the machine

high enough, I could pull the nanites out of her body and she could heal herself."

Wizard made a queasy face.

"What?" Jack asked.

"That would be like millions of tiny bullet holes through all of her organs, muscles, and skin. Her brain alone..." He shuddered.

"Okay, okay. I get it. Just trying to help."

"Sorry, I didn't mean to suggest that you were—I think you should try it, actually."

"Seriously? But you just said—"

"The machine won't do what you thought it would. The nanites are engineered to be non-magnetic. Just like the iron in your blood. What I think is worth exploring is the electromagnetic field that the machine produces. There's a chance, however small, that the field may interfere with the nanites' operation and allow Celia to recover her connection to the flux. If she did, she should be able to remove the nanites from her body all on her own. *Wait! That's it!*" Wizard's eyes went wide and he practically shook with excitement.

"You having a seizure on me?" Jack kidded.

"I think we just stumbled onto the fix. Not only for Celia but for the jump shields too!"

"Well, don't leave me hanging, man. What is it?"

"The new body armor—it disrupts the Gaian ability to connect to the flux, right?"

Jack shrugged. "I guess so. Not really an expert or anything..."

Wizard waved off his sarcasm. "From the reports we have, it does. And Desmond said that Celia faded from the flux field, too. The similarities can't be a coincidence!

They found some way to basically *inject* the body armor into a Gaian. I'd bet my life on it!"

"You may just be doing that... So, I should or shouldn't try the MRI thing?"

Wizard shooed him away. "Sure, sure. Go and try it, there's still a chance it will work. And I'll need some time to crack this body armor. Damn! I wish I had my tools with me!" He picked up the set of diagnostic tools he'd received from the Gaians. "It's like working with rocks and sticks."

Jack smirked. "I'm sure it's not that bad."

Wizard looked up. "I guess you're right. You should take Asher with you... Might need help carrying Celia around. And I'll need to reprogram your zip drives for your destination. Come get me when you're all ready. I'll be here."

32

Third Verse
New York

Jack's house was the easiest place to jump back to. For one, Wizard already had the exact coordinates that Asher had used the last time, and secondly, they'd need some place to wait while Jack set everything up. Frank wouldn't be working until the graveyard shift.

Jack landed in the backyard, accompanied by Asher and Dr. Sanderson. Jack had explained the broad theory behind the trip and the doctor had agreed to let Celia go on one condition: that he be allowed to supervise and monitor her condition at all times. Jack had no problem with that, it was probably for the best. But taking the floating gurney to the Third wasn't an option, so they carried Celia between them, one holding her legs, and the other, her torso.

Yellow police tape twirled in the late afternoon

breeze. It wrapped all the way around the perimeter of the house. The door was locked. Boards covered the broken glass panes. Jack patted his pockets for his keys, knowing that he didn't have them, but it was a habit that was long ingrained. If the police hadn't bagged them as evidence, they would be inside somewhere, scattered among the mess.

He knelt down and wiggled free the third brick on the outside of the walkway. Underneath it lay the spare key.

"Alright, come on in. *Mi casa es su casa,*" Jack said as he unlocked the door. "Asher, I believe you've already been here..."

"*Ha-ha*," Asher said dryly. "Yes, as I recall your welcoming gift was a blast."

"Oh, *touché*!" Jack smiled. "I'll call Frank and tell him to carve us out some machine time this evening when it's quietest. In the meantime, get comfortable, and help yourselves to anything you can find in the cupboards that hasn't spoiled."

The house was a wreck but thankfully the utilities were still on. The upstairs bathroom was almost non-existent, Jack could see straight into the attic from the bottom of the stairs. He looked out the front windows. For Sale signs dotted several surrounding yards. Guess the neighbor-agents didn't really need them anymore, now that their assignments had failed.

As he passed Kid's room, Jack felt a pang in his chest. He massaged his pectoral muscles and prayed that it was just stress and he wasn't having a heart attack. He breathed slowly until the moment passed.

Asher found him in the hall. "Are you alright? You don't look so good."

"I'm fine, just tired and worried about Kid."

"Okay, if you say so... Listen, we found something called spaghetti in the cupboard, but we can't figure out how to turn on the stove. It just smells like gas."

"What the hell are you guys doing? Are you trying to burn my house down?"

Asher shrugged sheepishly. "Don't look at me... We cook with wood fires where I come from."

"The pilot's probably out." Jack shooed Asher aside. "Out of the way, before the whole place goes up."

After he got the water boiling and was satisfied that they wouldn't catch the place on fire, Jack called his guy at the hospital and made the arrangements.

The hospital parking lot was half-full when they arrived in the middle of the night. They parked and waited while Jack returned with a wheelchair from inside. Moving Celia would be much easier if they didn't have to carry her around. It would look less suspicious as well.

"This way," Jack said. "I've told Frank to keep us off the books, so he's going to open the side door for us."

Moments later one of the doors opened and a man dressed in scrubs appeared, waving them down.

"Frank!" Jack called out. "Thank you so much for doing this. I owe you one."

"You owe me more than one, motherfucker! You know how much trouble I could get in for this?"

"Probably a whole lot less than if your wife ever found out about that nurse you've been seeing."

Frank ignored Jack's comment. "The cops came by asking about you. Nobody's seen you for days. Where the hell have you been? Everyone says there was some kind of explosion at your house. You weren't cooking meth, were you? Been watching too much Breaking Bad again?"

"Would you shut up, already?" Jack only half-joked. "Let's get inside and get this over with." He introduced Dr. Sanderson and Asher to his co-worker.

Frank guided them down the twisted halls. "You guys can wait in there." He pointed to the control room.

Dr. Sanderson balked. "I'm not leaving my patient."

Frank chuckled. "Where'd you find this guy, Jack?" He turned to Dr. Sanderson. "No one but the patient is allowed in the machine room. Not up for debate. Which reminds me..." Frank took out a large basket lined with canvas. "All your phones, watches, belts, anything metallic, shiny, or sparkly... put it in the basket."

The doctor started to protest again.

"Please, Doc, it's for safety," Jack said. "You can hang on to your monitor, that should be fine, right Frank? And you'll be able to see everything from in here in the control room."

Sanderson didn't like it, but he agreed to it. He stayed in the control room with Asher while Jack and Frank took Celia inside the machine room and placed her inside the MRI. When they were happy with her position, they came back out, sure to take the metal wheelchair with them.

"You got your monitors ready, doc?" Jack asked.

Dr. Sanderson nodded.

"Okay, Frankie boy. Punch it."

Frank frowned. "What, are you in some bad gangster movie or something?"

"Just shut up and turn it on," Jack did his best impersonation of a mobster. "Quit busting my balls over here!"

"Jesus," Frank said, shaking his head. He started pushing buttons and turning knobs. "You sleep with one nurse, a handful of times... and this is the bullshit—"

The sound of the MRI starting up drowned him out. It produced a variety of different noises. Clicks, clacks, bangs, and knocks.

"You want me to go through the usual diagnostics or just keep it running?" Frank asked.

"Yeah, sure. Why not?"

The MRI changed noises as the cameras inside took their different images. After several minutes Frank scrolled through the various images as he would have for any other patient.

"See anything out of the ordinary?" Jack asked.

"Not really. Should I be looking for something specific? Brain tumor, or...?"

Jack briefly flirted with the idea of spilling the beans to Frank about the existence of the multiverse. Frank could probably handle the news with little trouble, he watched enough sci-fi, but in the end, it wouldn't help Celia, and there was always the off chance that Frank would go and do something crazy in reaction to the news.

"Your guess is as good as ours." Jack shrugged. "We don't really have any idea what's wrong with her. One minute she was fine, and then... she slipped into a coma and hasn't woken up since."

Frank eyed Jack like he was crazy. "Where did you find this woman, Jack? Why not just let the hospital treat —" He inhaled sharply, his eyes opened as wide as was possible. "Are you in the CIA or something? That would explain you dropping off the grid and the rumors about your house blowing up... Did your cover get blown?"

Jack couldn't help himself. He burst into laughter. "Sure, pal. Let's go with that. I'm in the CIA, and she's my partner..." He turned to Dr. Sanderson. "How's she doing, doc? Any changes?"

"She's still stable. I thought, for a moment, that I felt her in the flux, but there's nothing now. Maybe just wishful imagining on my part."

"Felt her in the what now?" Frank looked back and forth between the two men for an explanation, and then to Asher. "And how do you factor into all this? Are you the doctor's kid?"

"Don't worry about it," Jack said. "Need to know basis, and—"

"Yeah, yeah, yeah," Frank held up his hand, stopping him. "I don't need to know."

Jack nodded and smiled. "And neither does your wife, then."

"Bastard."

Twenty minutes went by when the doctor's monitor starting chirping angrily. "That doesn't sound good, doc."

Dr. Sanderson shook his head as he studied the monitor. A worried expression filled his face. "It's not."

"What's happening to her?" Jack asked.

"Her body temperature is rising and so is her heart rate. I don't understand it. This shouldn't be happening." Celia's body began twitching. Slowly at first and then more violently. "She's having a seizure!"

"Shut it down, now!" Jack said.

Frank lost color in his face as he began the shutdown sequence. "I knew this was a bad idea... How the hell am I going to explain a dead woman in my machine? It's going to be hard enough to scrub the records from the diagnostics."

"Just shut it down!" Jack followed Dr. Sanderson into the machine room.

"Wait!" Frank called. "It's not safe to go in there yet!"

Jack either didn't hear him or didn't care. He began retracting Celia from inside the machine. The bed slid out slowly at a snail's pace. All the while, Celia's body shook while Dr. Sanderson tried to hold her steady and make sure she didn't swallow her tongue. It reminded Jack of an exorcism.

"We have to get her back to Gaia right now if we have any chance of stopping this! I can't treat her here."

Jack nodded reluctantly as the guilt welled up inside him. Everything he touched seemed to turn to shit.

33

Seventh Verse

Civitas, Terra

The lobby of the Embassy towers was nearly deserted as Desmond jumped in. He expected to be surrounded as soon as he arrived, but instead, he found only a receptionist there to greet him. Either he'd caught them unprepared or they were *very* unconcerned with whatever threat he presented.

He decided to try to take advantage of the situation and do some exploring. Maybe he'd get lucky and find Kid or the children in one of the conference rooms. A fat chance, but it was worth a shot.

The zip drive around his wrist vibrated and reminded him of his real mission. He tapped through its various menus until he'd activated the link to Wizard's server. The timer started counting up as the recording began.

He breezed by the receptionist, nodding at her like he

was supposed to be there. She opened her mouth and then closed it, as if unsure what to say.

Not wanting anyone to challenge him, Desmond kept moving with purpose. He had just reached the lifts when a young man in an aide's uniform walked around the corner. The man seemed to be in a hurry and jumped, not expecting to find anyone here.

"Uhh... you don't have a pass on, sir..." the young man stammered.

Desmond made his cheeks flush red. "I'm a bit embarrassed... I was supposed to deliver a message to Prime Minister White, in person," he leaned in close and lowered his voice, "bit of sensitive situation if you know what I mean. And I'm afraid I've forgotten the directions I was given at the front desk."

"Why doesn't your OS guide you there?"

Desmond's pulse spiked. He glanced down at his clothes. "I operate off world and thus offline, so to speak." Desmond hardened his voice, changing tactics. "Hence, the *sensitive* nature of my visit. Now, either help me or get the hell out of my way so I can find someone who will. She's not going to be happy about this delay."

The aide's brow furrowed as he weighed his options. Desmond watched as he struggled to decide between helping him or reporting him for not having the security clearance required to access the lifts.

This went on for several moments and Desmond was just about to push past him when the aide suddenly relaxed. "No problem at all. I'm heading that way right now. Why don't you join me, Desmond?"

Desmond's gut sank. He didn't know how, but he'd been made. He thought about running for a moment, but that was more reflex than actual desire. He was here for a reason, and escaping was not it. He took a deep breath and let it out. He bowed slightly and waved the aide in front of him. "After you."

Desmond ventured a guess as they walked, "So, how have you been, Julia?"

The aide let out a small gasp. "How did you know it was me?" The words came out of the aide's mouth, with the aide's vocal chords, but they belonged to someone else. He was just the delivery vehicle.

"It was the way you said my name," Desmond replied. "And, I wasn't completely sure, until now, but I guess some things don't change."

"Yes, and those things that don't change become dead things, Desmond. The rule of nature bends for no society. You should know that."

"Come now, Julia, I'd hoped we could put off the lectures until we're in person, at least."

"I suppose it's only fair," the aide spoke. "I'll see you in a second." The aide shivered and then shook his head, trying to clear it. "What happened?"

"You were escorting me to Prime Minister White's office," Desmond told the young man.

"I… I was?"

Desmond nodded and gave the man some time to get his feet back under himself.

"Well, then—right this way," the aide said. He led Desmond further down the hallway.

They turned the corner and Desmond saw the entrance to Julia's office at the end of the hall, about three hundred feet away. A pair of guards was stationed against the wall every fifty feet or so.

As they walked past each pair of guards, Desmond nodded to each—a small bow of respect. Not that he respected what they did, but he might be seeing them again very soon, and on much different terms. It never hurt to be respectful. Especially since respect had to start somewhere.

They reached the large front double doors which opened automatically as the aide drew near, and Desmond walked through with the young man right behind him.

The prime minister's office was large and circular. There was a bustle of activity as men and women hurried to and fro. The sound of conversation on top of conversation filled the air.

Behind him, in the hall, a large group of soldiers in full battle gear marched toward the office, stopping just outside the doors as they closed. Desmond wondered if they would proceed into the office itself, but they seemed content to wait outside. There was no doubt in his mind that they were there for him. He allowed himself a smile. It seems they hadn't underestimated him after all.

Julia's inner chambers were located high above the office, far from the noise below.

"Best be off, then," Desmond said, not waiting for the aide to respond as he walked toward the lift in the center of the office floor.

There were no stairs to Julia's office. The lift was the only way in or out. Desmond had only been here once before, and it wasn't a pleasant memory. After Julia had left them, Desmond had come to try to talk her out of it.

The doors to the lift opened and Desmond stepped

in. The aide did not follow but gave Desmond a creepy wink as the lift ascended.

The ride only lasted a few seconds, but during that time, Desmond traveled several hundred feet. The doors parted and Desmond stepped into the brightly lit inner chambers of Lady Julia White, Prime Minister of Terra.

The space was laid out in a semi-circle. The walls and ceiling were made of glass, showing the vast city below them, and the open sky above. The glass auto-tinted to the varying amounts of sunlight, keeping the overall brightness inside at the same level. Outside, transports and shuttles flew back and forth in their predetermined flight lanes. These were reserved for the wealthy, while the masses took the hyper-rail trains that webbed the city. Several couches decorated the office. A young woman with straight, short hair and sharp features sat on one of them. Desmond was reminded of a younger version of Celia, except for the lighter hair color and the darkness that seemed to hover around her like a cloud. Besides Julia, she was the only other person in the room.

"You must be Ava," Desmond said.

Ava tilted her head in acknowledgment.

"Nice to finally meet you. You're just as beautiful as Asher said. You know, you really did a number on that guy..."

"Oh, leave the poor girl alone, Desmond. No need for one of your lectures." Julia White sat behind her desk. Her eyes twinkled like a cat who had a mouse trapped underneath its paws. She stood as Desmond approached. "So good to see you." She walked up and tried to kiss him on the lips. Desmond turned his head, and she relented with a flirtatious smile. "Well, you can't blame a girl for trying."

"You're not a girl anymore, Julia. In fact, I'm not sure what you are anymore."

"Well, that makes two of us, dear," Julia said. Her face twitched ever so slightly and she twisted from view, trying to hide the tic from him.

Desmond puzzled over the remark and her reaction.

She seemed to recover from her hiccup and faced him again. "Come, sit down."

"I'm fine, thanks. You know what I'm here for."

"Something to do with that rather nasty little bug our daughter has come down with, no?"

Desmond flashed with anger and started to retort, but then bit his lip, forcing himself to slow down. He was surprised at how quickly she got a rise out of him. If it was anybody but her, he would have been an ocean of calm, but she always did know how to push his buttons, both the good ones and the bad.

"What did you do to her?" Desmond finally asked. Ava shifted her legs from side to side and he took note of how raptly the young woman on the couch was paying attention to the proceedings.

"That's the danger of traveling abroad, I'm afraid..." Julia said. "You never know what manner of thing you might catch."

"Let's cut to the chase, shall we," Desmond said. "I'm here, now cure our daughter as you agreed."

Laughter spewed forth from Julia's lips like lava from an active volcano. "You can't be serious... You didn't actually think I would honor the terms of our arrangement?" Her eye's narrowed as she gazed at him. "No, what I can't figure out is why you'd be so foolish as to come here in the first place. Surely you didn't think you could somehow overpower me and force me to give you want you want? *Hmmm... what then?*"

"For fuck's sake, Julia! Whatever your issues are, take them out on me, not Celia."

"Is that what you think of me?" She went to the window and stared out. "I'm giving our daughter a wonderful gift—the same I'll give to you and eventually your people."

"What gift is that?"

She turned back to face Desmond. "Do you honestly think I would harm Celia?"

"Once upon a time I would have answered no, but I wouldn't put anything past you these days," Desmond said with sadness in his eyes.

"Do you know why I left you, Desmond?" Julia asked. "Did you ever manage to figure that one out?"

Desmond was silent. A raging fire spread throughout his chest and he realized he was afraid of what she would say next.

"It was because one day, I realized that I would never be able to have the kind of connection that you and Celia had. You were such an amazing man, with talents I could only ever dream of—superpowers. I couldn't stay and be content, knowing that I would never be your equal in our relationship."

Desmond shook his head, not wanting to believe or accept her explanation. "But we had love, Julia. That's all we could ever need."

"You say that now, with the way things have gone, but if I'd stayed, you would have grown tired or bored with me. Now though, our peoples are almost equals. Now, we won't have to play second fiddle to your powers. We will be one race, living under one law."

A deep sense of dread overtook him as he realized the scope of Julia's schemes. A tear streaked down Desmond's face. "What have you done, Julia?"

"Come, I will show you my designs for the multiverse."

Desmond followed her in shock, not willing to believe what was happening. Julia led him back down through the offices and into the maze of halls that made up the Embassy. Ava trailed behind them with a small contingent of armed guards.

They got onto the lift and descended.

At some point, Desmond realized that the ride went on for too long. They should have reached ground level by now, unless—they were going underground. *She must have tunnels under the surface,* Desmond thought. It would make sense. If she was trying to keep a location secret, she couldn't have the whole world know she was traveling there.

"I assure you, Desmond, no permanent harm will come to our daughter... She will just be made normal, as the rest of us are."

"There was nothing abnormal about her, to begin with," Desmond said.

"Nothing abnormal? You call superpowers normal?"

"Nothing, aside from being born, has ever been done to Celia or any Gaian for these abilities to be made manifest. So, yes, I call them normal! We simply live as we were born to live—"

"So you claim, Desmond."

"You lived among us, Julia! How can you not see the difference in our two cultures?"

"That's what's wrong! The differences are too great. Our peoples must be made one."

"All we've ever wanted was peace between our two worlds. It was *your* Verse that pulled away from *us*."

"No! You will not lay the blame for this on us, Desmond. I won't allow it! This began when your people shamed our use of the nanites. You couldn't stand that we had developed our own version of superhuman potential. Tell me, how could we not pull away from that kind of rejection? How could we not *fear* what actions you might take against us?"

"Shamed is a very strong word for our reaction. We only ever warned you about the danger of the nanites as we saw them. You are well aware of the ease with which they can overtake a person if their programming were to be damaged or influenced."

"No more so than your ability to mind control others!" Julia defended. "We've made leaps and bounds in the technology since I first left you and Celia. Safeguards have been put in place. In fact, we're getting ready to roll out the next-generation to the public later this week. You may get to witness history being made."

They arrived at their destination. The doors of the lift opened into an observation room that was stationed high above the largest hangar that Desmond had ever seen. The floor space had to be close to a square mile. Through the viewing window, Desmond saw a ring that looked to be about thirty feet across the middle. It was hard to miss as it sat in the center of the hangar. A bundle of cables ran from the ring along the floor, all the way to the wall where they disappeared into the floor. *The power supply?* Desmond wondered.

"This is the beginning, Desmond." Julia motioned at the ring. "This is what will bring us all together. First, Gaia, and then in time, when they're a bit older, the other Verses."

"What exactly am I looking at?" Desmond asked. He was nervous. Whatever Julia had planned, he had a bad feeling about it.

Julia eyed him up and down. Desmond could see her weighing the decision to explain or not.

"Come on, Julia," he opened his arms slightly doing his best to look harmless, "it's not like I'm going anywhere. Am I?"

"I suppose there's no harm in telling you... We call it the Oculus. It's a little thing we had developed to solve the transportation problem we've been having with the jump shields." Julia beamed with pleasure and pride. "We've been limited to jumping with only the equipment that a person can carry. Take, for instance, the operation that led to Celia's capture... We were only able to bring through pieces of a jump shield generator and assemble it on the other side. A labor and time intensive undertaking. Now, we'll be able to bring through fully intact shield generators, as well as personnel carriers, vehicles, and just about anything really."

Desmond's head spun. She was planning an invasion. And if she was correct, they'd be able to overwhelm any Gaian resistance. His people didn't stand a chance without their abilities.

"Once the jump shields are in place, the new Gaian-strain of nanites will remove your connection to the flux permanently, allowing your people to accept our augmentations at last. We can finally be the same —equals."

"That's what you did to Celia."

"You're finally getting it," Julia said. "Unfortunately, the process takes about a week to finish the transformation—longer in the more powerful cases, I would assume, such as you and Celia, but we hope to improve that in time."

"You really have lost it, haven't you?" Desmond realized that whatever part of himself that had held out any kind of hope for Julia had just given up. She was a complete stranger now, through and through. He couldn't recognize any part of her anymore.

"*Lost what?*" Julia laughed. "Desmond, we are on the verge of history. Soon, all of humanity will be equals, and thanks to the nanites and the Ark, we can now live forever. Imagine—no more death, no more lives cut short due to illness, accidents, or disease."

"It all comes back to your parents, doesn't it?" Desmond accused.

Julia's face twitched slightly as she looked down and away. She said nothing.

"Julia, they're gone, and there was nothing you could have done to prevent that. You were in a different universe when the accident happened."

"I know that," Julia said. "And if we'd had the Ark back then, then they wouldn't have had to die."

"You keep mentioning this ark..." Desmond had no idea what she was talking about.

Julia's expression seemed to lighten as she explained.

"It's an artificial reality construct we've developed that is indistinguishable from real life. As I was saying, if we'd had it back then, my parents wouldn't have had to die. They could have uploaded their consciousness through the nanites, and then waited for their new bodies to be built."

Desmond scoffed. "And you've figured out how to build bodies for these disembodied souls? What sort of bodies? Robotic? Animal? Surely you don't think you can clone them? Not to mention the population control that would be required—"

"I've been assured we're nearly there," Julia cut him off. "We are on the cusp of eternal life as a species. And *I* will be the one to share it with your people as well as my own."

"Did it ever occur to you that we aren't *supposed* to live forever?"

"Please, don't get all philosophical on me now... Are we *supposed* to cure diseases or should we just let people die? Are we *supposed* to fly through the air, or should we be forced to walk everywhere we go?"

"That's hardly the same thing."

"Is it? You make me out to be some sort of monster. I'm not evil, Desmond, I assure you. I may be a *necessary* evil, but it's all for the greater good. All of humanity will benefit from our work."

"*Our* work?"

Julia nodded. "There's someone I believe you'd like to meet... None of this would be possible without him."

The lift door hissed open and Desmond turned to see several medical personnel guide a hovering bed out into the observation room.

Tears formed in Desmond's eyes as he realized who it was. "What have you done to him?"

A ghostly, shriveled shell of a boy lay on the bed. Dark veins coursed through his thin, pale skin. His lips were cracked and his hair was streaked with gray and white. Clear medical tubing filled with a dark, purple liquid protruded from his chest, arms, and legs at six-inch intervals. Desmond couldn't see where the tubes led once they disappeared underneath the bed.

"Julia, what did you do?" Desmond repeated.

She raised her eyebrows. "I thought you'd be more excited to finally meet the son you never knew you had. Guess I was wrong."

Desmond stepped toward Kid and immediately found several assault rifles barring his way.

"That's close enough, Desmond. Despite his appearance, Kid is doing just fine."

"He doesn't look fine to me." The shock was wearing off, replaced with fury. "It looks like you're sucking the life out of him."

"On the contrary, Kid's sacrifice will enable me to give eternal life to all of humanity." Julia took a syringe and inserted it into one of the tubes, drawing up some of the dark viscous liquid. "Something interesting happened when we began the treatment. Kid's unique, un-bonded makeup reacted with the nanites. It transformed them somehow. We're still trying to reverse engineer the exact mechanism, but what we noticed in the Gaian test subjects was a remarkable transformation. Kid's strain of nanites turns off the switch in the Gaian genome that allows you to connect to the flux field. There's a bit of a delay as the process slowly ramps up, but the results are spectacular." She flicked the side of the syringe and tested the plunger.

Realization dawned on Desmond. "That's what you gave to Celia."

Julia smiled wickedly as she stepped closer to him. "And it's what I'm going to give to you... Now, are you going to take your medicine like a good boy? Or do you want to fight about it?"

Adrenaline surged through Desmond as he readied himself for a fight. He turned, desperately looking for a way out where there wasn't one.

"I didn't think so." Julia nodded to one of her guards and then winked at Desmond. "Nighty-night."

Desmond opened his mouth to protest as the stun charge from the guard's weapon sent him into darkness.

34

Sixth Verse

Oracle HQ

Spare bits and pieces of electronics were scattered all across Wizard's make-shift work table. Ava's body armor sat in the middle. He finished programming Jack's zip drive and handed it back to him.

"How is she?" Wizard asked.

"The doctors got her stabilized, but she's still unresponsive." Jack fit the zip drive around his wrist.

Wizard nodded, sympathetic. "I think I can reverse what they've baked into this body armor, but I need a compatible controller from Terra. Unfortunately," he gestured to the mess spread out everywhere, "this Gaian tech isn't up to snuff. The good news, though, if I'm correct, is that Celia should be able to connect to the flux again and begin to heal herself."

"We could use some good news," Jack said. "Are you

sure you want me to wait? The sooner we get back with what you need, the sooner we can go after Kid and Desmond."

Wizard nodded. "Call it a hunch. Just activate your zip drive when I do and the timer will do the rest."

"Alright, chief. You got it." Jack ejected the clip on the pistol they'd taken from Ava and confirmed it was nearly full before sliding it back in. "When do we leave?"

"No time like the present." Wizard activated his zip drive and the five-second delay began.

"Hey, how about a heads up?" Jack cried, activating his own drive. The timer started counting down from six minutes.

"You'll be fine," Wizard said. "Just be ready for anything when that timer goes off." And then he flashed out of the room.

WIZARD LANDED in his backyard on Terra, underneath a tall oak tree, about thirty feet or so from his house. Eschewing the modern 3-D printing method, Wizard built his craftsman style home himself. What it might lack for in strength and ease of construction, it more than made up for with charm and homeyness. He unlocked the door, inputting his security code and retinal scan. Despite the retro-housing, his security system was state of the art.

Once he entered, Wizard hurried. He knew it wouldn't be long before his unauthorized jump was flagged and officers sent to investigate. He first went to the standalone server that was disconnected from the planet's grid. He logged in and saw the flashing alert indicating he had received a new message. He hit play but quickly shut it off as soon as he heard Desmond and Julia's voices. He copied the message to the storage on his zip drive and deleted it from the server. Next, he pulled the physical drive and threw it in a duffel bag along with the tools he needed to complete the modifications to Ava's body armor.

He heard the police arrive as he searched for the controller. He estimated he had under a minute before they were on top of him.

He shuffled the contents of his office, throwing papers this way, and old datapads that way. Where the hell was it?

Sweat trickled down his face as the search grew more frantic. And then a lightbulb went off in his brain. It was in the living room!

He hurried and found it right where he'd left it last, on top of the fireplace. Unfortunately, he was out of time.

He jumped as the front door blew inward. A special response team in full tactical gear streamed into the house. They fanned out raising their weapons.

"Freeze! Stay where you are!"

More shouting of orders followed. Voices shouting the same commands over top of one another.

Wizard raised his hands slowly, one of which still held the controller. He tried to guess how much time he had left before Jack jumped in. Should be any minute now.

There were two SRT units on his right and two on his left. They seemed content to stay where they were for the moment. Wizard wondered about their augmentations.

Did they have the basic package, the latest and greatest, or something in between?

A woman walked through the front door, silhouetted by the bright light from outside. As his eyes adjusted, Wizard identified the young woman who had tried to kill him back in the Third.

"Well look who it is," Ava said. "I was hoping we would get to finish what we started one day. Guess the day came sooner than I thought..." She smiled at him. "Where's Asher? Are you here all by yourself?"

Wizard felt her eyes studying his reaction, looking for a tell. He knew his face was a blank slate. She would learn nothing from him.

Outside, the wind gusted and dislodged several acorns that fell onto the roof. Wizard immediately identified the noise, but Ava turned to the men on her left. "Search the rest of the house. Bring me anyone you find."

One of the four men split off and began the search, beginning upstairs.

"There's no one else here," Wizard admitted. He doubted she would recall her man, but it would be easier if they all remained grouped together. "Sorry about the last time we met. I hope you don't hold it against me, but in all fairness, you *were* trying to kill me."

Ava offered an apologetic tilt of her head. "Orders are orders, you know what I mean?"

Wizard snorted with a nod. He glanced at his zip drive, checking the time.

"Don't get any ideas, old man. They will blast you down long before you're able to activate that zip drive."

Wizard slowly moved to his left, away from the middle of the living room and closer to the entrance of the kitchen. "Oh, I'm sure they would. I don't move as fast as I used to." He shuffled back a few more feet.

"Stay where you are!" One of the men warned. The remaining men moved closer to cut Wizard off.

The zip drive on his wrist chirped and Wizard smiled. "Perfect."

In the blink of an eye, the room lit up with a blinding white light. The three men disintegrated as Jack jumped into the middle of Wizard's living room. The house shook from the blast wave and Wizard was knocked down. Ava's eyes revealed she was caught off guard. She managed to dive clear of the jump blast's radius but failed to avoid a large piece of blast debris that struck her in the head, dazing her.

Jack helped Wizard to his feet. "Good thing I waited, huh?" Jack grinned. "Sorry to break up the party."

Wizard groaned and checked himself for any injuries. "I need my bag."

"Well hurry up! I don't think we have very much time."

The man from upstairs came racing down. Jack fired quickly, as soon as he came into view, just like the US military had trained him to. The bullet found a home in the man's knee and he uttered a cry, somersaulting down the remaining stairs. He landed with a sickening crack as his neck broke from the awkward fall.

"Baby's got a kick, doesn't she?" Jack admired the pistol in his hands.

Ava stumbled back to her feet and screamed as she made a mad dash for Jack. She connected with her shoulder and drove through, taking Jack down to the ground. For a moment, they wrestled for control of the weapon, but Ava quickly overpowered Jack. Despite having a size and weight advantage, he was no match for her augmented strength.

As he realized he was going to lose the battle for the gun, Jack had enough foresight to fling the weapon in Wizard's direction. Ava scrambled after it. Jack wrapped his arms and legs around her and did his best to drag her down to the ground. He had to hold her back long enough for Wizard to make it to the pistol.

An involuntary yelp escaped Jack's mouth as Ava began to drag him toward the gun in spite of his all-out effort to restrain her.

Wizard shuffled forward as fast as he could, but Jack knew he wouldn't make it in time. Jack needed to do something to slow her down.

Not daring to let go of his grip on her, Jack used the only weapon he had available. He opened his mouth as wide as possible and bit down on Ava's neck.

He heard her scream as his teeth broke the skin and hot blood gushed into his mouth. He fought the urge to gag as he ground his teeth against her flesh. Another shriek rose from Ava, but she was still moving toward the gun.

Again, Jack bit down with all his might and he felt Ava seize up in the midst of the pain.

It was all the time that Wizard needed. He picked up the weapon just as Ava's hand clasped around the old man's ankle like a vice grip. "Got it!" Wizard's voice had never sounded so good to Jack's ears.

"Shoot her!" Jack yelled, rolling out from underneath her. "Shoot her now!"

Wizard's first shot missed wide. The second struck

her in the arm. She let go of his ankle and recoiled in pain.

Jack scrambled back to his feet and grabbed the gun from Wizard. “Give me that, before you hurt yourself.”

Ava turned to run and Jack fired three rounds in quick succession, striking her in the back. She fell and stayed down.

“Can we fucking go now?” Jack asked.

Wizard nodded and started toward his wrist to activate the zip drive.

“Wait!” Jack cried. He walked over to Ava’s body and stripped her of the remaining ammunition clips for his weapon. “Okay, now let’s go.”

“Seriously?” Wizard asked.

Jack shrugged. “What? I like this gun.”

35

Sixth Verse

Cairos, Gaia

All eyes were on Wizard in the infirmary as he made a few last tweaks on the body armor with the controller. "There." Wizard inspected his work one final time. "If all goes according to plan, she should begin to recover within minutes." He turned to Jack. "Help me get this fitted on her."

Jack held her arms up while Wizard maneuvered the body armor over her head and onto her torso. He powered on the body armor and activated the modifications he'd made.

Seconds passed with no change.

"You sure it's turned on?" Jack asked. "Maybe you got a crossed wire or somethin—"

Wizard held up his hand, silencing Jack. "It's on. Give

it a second." Wizard muttered something inaudible under his breath as his neck and cheeks flushed red. He was beginning to think that maybe Jack was right, and he'd made an error somewhere along the way when Celia's eyes fluttered open and she sat up.

She looked back and forth between Wizard, Jack, Asher, and Dr. Sanderson. "What just happened?" She struggled to make sense of her surroundings.

Asher rushed over to comfort her. "It's all right, you're all right. Wizard fixed you."

"What do you mean? How did I get—"

"Your mother dosed you with a rather nasty bug," Jack explained. "Wizard here found a way to counteract the nanites they injected you with."

Celia squirmed and wiggled around. "Is that what I feel creeping around inside me?"

Celia's expression changed as she concentrated. A thin stream of particles began flowing out of her body through her mouth, nose, and ears as Celia exiled them with the help of the flux.

Asher made a disgusted noise and turned away like he might be sick.

"Oh, here—" Wizard grabbed a jar and took the lid off. "If you don't mind, would you put them in here? I'd like to save them for examination."

"Yes," Dr. Sanderson chimed in, "I'd like a sample as well." He held out a specimen container of his own.

Jack shook his head and laughed. "*Nerds*."

Celia guided the stream of nanites equally into both containers. "There..." Celia gave her body a final shake-out. "Now I feel like myself again."

"Good to hear," Dr. Sanderson said. "I know there's a lot for you to catch up on, but I'd like to come back and run some tests and make sure there are no residual effects from the nanites."

"Sure, I guess," Celia said. "No problem."

Dr. Sanderson scheduled a follow-up and then left.

Celia turned back to Jack, Asher, and Wizard. "How long was I out for? I barely remember escaping Terra and then showing up at the GDA. Had some crazy dreams though." Celia laughed nervously. "At least, I *think* they were dreams."

"It's only been a few days since you jumped in from Terra."

"Hey, wait. Where's Dad?" Celia scanned the room for any sign of Desmond.

Wizard took a deep breath and paused, measuring his response carefully. "I'm afraid he sacrificed himself in an attempt to trade his life for the cure to whatever they gave you."

"What?" Celia shook her head. "Is he *dead?*"

"Oh, god, no. At least, not as far as we know."

Celia was visibly relieved but also pissed off. "There is no way she would ever uphold a deal like that. He should have known better. What the hell was he thinking? How could you let him do something like that?"

"It's not as though anyone could have stopped him. But he also didn't go in without a backup plan."

"What are you talking about?"

Wizard held up the drive containing Desmond's recording. "Your father had me modify a zip drive to secretly record the conversation between him and Julia and send it to my personal server on Terra. The power output had to be low enough that it wouldn't be detected, which, unfortunately, severely limited the range. Hence why we had to go back to Terra to retrieve it."

"And to get the part thingy for the body armor to heal her, right?" Jack said.

"Yes, of course. That too."

"Did Dad say anything else about his idiotic plan?" Celia stood from the bed and stretched, loosening up stiff muscles that hadn't been used for days.

"He was confident that he could get your mother to reveal her plans. I don't know if he was successful yet or not. But shall we play the recording and see?"

Celia nodded urgently. "What the hell are we waiting for?"

Wizard played the recording and everyone listened intently. When it stopped they all stared at each other in stunned silence.

Jack was the first to speak. He was noticeably agitated. "No offense, Celia, but your mom's a real bitch. And if there's even one hair out of place on Kid's head, I'll fucking kill her."

"Can't say that she doesn't deserve it, but you might have to get in the back of the line," Celia said, thinking back to her mother's confession. Even if Jacen had been spying on her, he still didn't deserve what she'd done to him. "I get first crack at her."

"As long as you save a piece for me..."

"Personal vendettas aside, you know what this means, don't you?" Wizard's voice was deadly serious.

"That we're rescuing Kid *and* Desmond now?" Asher guessed.

"No, we need to prepare Gaia for an attack. We have to warn the Council," Wizard said. "She intends to start a war."

"Those old bastards?" Jack quipped. "What are they going to do? Sit around and *talk* about defending their planet?"

"You're probably not too far off there," Celia said. "But Wizard's right, we have to at least try to get the word out. If we can't find a way to stop it, all hell is going to break loose here. There hasn't been a war on Gaia for hundreds of years. The GDA is the closest thing to a military that we have and they are ill-suited to wage an all-out war."

Wizard frowned. "I have a pretty good idea what the Council is going to say, but let's go hear it in person. At least we'll sleep easier, knowing we did everything we could."

Celia pulled out her comm and placed a call. "Yes, I need to speak with Chancellor Pearson, it's a matter of global security."

THEY RETURNED LESS than an hour later.

"I can't believe the fucking nerve of them," Jack said, spitting everywhere as he fumed. They piled into Desmond's office. He wasn't there to use it and it provided the most privacy to blow off some steam and not be overheard. "All of the sacrifices he's made, and they're just going to hang him out to dry like that."

Wizard pursed his lips and raised an eyebrow.

Jack stared at him. "What?"

"Hang him out to dry?" Wizard repeated.

"It's an expression. Don't you have it on Terra? It

means they're going to turn their backs on him... you have that one, right?"

"Oh, yes... I thought I had the gist of it right, just wanted to be sure."

"Still, though, I can't believe it!" Jack circled back to his previous point.

"Calm down." Celia tried to cool his anger. "It's not as though we expected a different outcome."

"I know, but still—"

"We need to focus on getting Desmond and the children back," Wizard said. "Clearly, Kid is still at the center of whatever Julia's planning."

"Do you know the place where she took Desmond?" Jack asked.

Wizard shook his head. "Hard to say exactly from the audio, but based on the length of the trip from the Embassy, there's a handful of places that it could be. And I have a sneaking suspicion that the beacon my source planted may be near the same facility. With any luck, we'll be able to find Desmond and Kid close by."

"How many zip drives do we have?" Celia asked. "Because unless we plan on jumping to my mother's house on Terra, I'll need one as well."

Jack gave her a quizzical look.

"Can't jump there using the flux if I don't know where *there* is," Celia explained. "Once we're there, I'll be able to jump back, no problem. As long as this thing," she glanced down at her body armor, "does its job, that is."

"Don't worry about that. It'll work, and to answer your other question, we have plenty!" Wizard grinned and pulled back his sleeves, revealing several zip drives on both arms.

He reminded Jack of a sleazy, sidewalk jewelry hawker from the streets of New York. Wizard gave one to Celia, and one to Jack. When he came to Asher, he hesitated.

"I hope you're not planning on leaving me here," Asher said.

"Are you sure about this?" Jack asked. "This might be something that we don't come back from. A one-way ticket to the afterlife."

Asher nodded with the utmost sincerity. He was willing to live with the consequences. "I started this whole thing, I need to finish it. Desmond gave me a second chance when he didn't have to. I still owe him, *and* I'm responsible for Kid's abduction, even if I didn't know what was going on at the time."

Jack conferred with Wizard and Celia. "What do you guys think?"

"Well, it never hurts to have one more person to watch your back out there," Celia said. "Besides, he's right. He started this thing... If it was me, I don't know that I could live with myself if I didn't do everything I could to make it right again."

"Wizard?"

Wizard shrugged. "I don't see why not. He knows the risks."

Jack turned back to Asher. "Alright, that's settled then. Go grab your gear and meet us back here in five." They watched Asher disappear down the hall. "What do you think the odds are of us pulling this off?"

Celia winced. "Fifty-fifty?"

Jack sighed. "I was afraid you'd say something like that... Alright, what's the plan then?"

They leaned in as Wizard responded, "Here's what I'm thinking..."

36

Seventh Verse
Civitas, Terra

Julia sighed as her comm rang, annoyed with the interruption. “Would you excuse me for a moment, Senator?”

The senator graciously nodded her head. “I know how it goes... never a moment’s rest for the head that wears the crown.”

Julia gave her a slight smile. If only she knew how right she was. “Yes, truly. I won’t be but a moment.”

She stepped into the adjoining room and took the call. It was Mallak. “What is it? I’m in the middle of a meeting.”

“Sorry, but I thought you should hear this immediately.”

“Well...? What’s so urgent?”

Mallak cleared his throat. “Former Senator Wallace jumped in at his residence without authorization. Ava took a team to respond, looking to capture him. They were ambushed by a third party jumping in, inside the house."

"How many?"

"Almost the entire unit was disintegrated in the jump zone, and the remaining man was found dead at the scene."

"*The entire team?*" Julia found it hard to believe that the old man had caused this much death and destruction. It must have been his accomplice. "And Ava?"

"She was shot several times and incapacitated. Her body armor took the worst of the damage, but she's up on her feet now, and despite a nasty neck wound, she should recover fully within the day. The doctors gave her a new round of nanites to replace the ones she's burned through."

"I see..." Julia tapped her finger to her lips. "No more field ops for Ava—I want her closer to me. She's no good to me if she's dead."

Mallak paused as if thinking. "I'll have her report to you as soon as we're done here. Speaking of which, Ava also said that the old man had enough zip drives in his hands to land a small army. You can bet they'll be coming for your ex-husband soon."

Julia laughed at the thought. "Let them come—even if they manage to free him, it will be too late. The Mother has harvested almost all the energy she needs from Kid to launch the invasion."

"Shall I tighten security around the Gaian holding cells?"

"No. I don't want anything distracting us from the invasion. All available men are at their posts already.

You'd have to pull some of the invasion force to cover it. I want them all ready to go as soon as the Mother is ready."

"As you wish, Madam Prime Minister."

Yes, she thought, *everything as I wish*. "Is there anything else, Mallak?"

"No, that's all. Again, sorry to interrupt you." He paused. "I'll see you later tonight?"

Julia took her time responding as she weighed out the rest of her day's schedule. "Yes, meet me at the penthouse." She terminated the call as a faint blush blossomed on her cheeks. She had no real feelings for him, but she could use the release that the sex would provide, and he was close enough to her daily routines that a few extra comings and goings didn't raise too much suspicion with the news outlets. The last thing she needed was a scandal circulating about. Speaking of which, she needed to get back to the nosy senator in the conference room.

"Senator, I'm sorry to have kept you waiting."

"I completely understand, no need to apologize on my account."

"Where were we?" Julia put on her best fake smile and tried to refrain from reaching across the table and strangling the woman in front of her.

The senator returned a smile that was equally as insincere. "We were discussing the apparent disappearance of a large number of our armed forces from around the globe."

"Ah, yes, that..." Julia couldn't wait for the day when she wouldn't have to hide behind this charade any longer. *Soon*, she thought, *soon*.

37

Seventh Verse
Civitas, Terra

Ava stood to the side and waited as the senator left the conference room. A smug smile resided on the senator's face as if she'd gotten some licks in. Ava nodded as they passed each other outside the doorway.

Inside, the Prime Minister sat at the head of the large glass table. She stared off into the distance, seemingly unaware that Ava was standing there. Her lips moved slightly as if she was speaking to someone underneath her breath. Ava cleared her throat.

Julia snapped out of her daze. "Ava, good heavens! I didn't notice you slip in, I'm sorry. You caught me daydreaming." She smiled warmly. "When your entire waking existence is consumed with affairs of state, one must try to sneak in some daydreaming whenever one can, take it from me."

Ava returned her smile. "I suppose so, your high—Madam Prime Minister." Old habits were hard to break. "Mallak said that you wanted to see me?"

"Yes, that's right. Come in, dear. Have a seat." She motioned to a chair and Ava sat. "Mallak tells me that you were the only one to survive the attack at Wizar—at former Senator Wallace's house. How did you manage?"

Julia watched as the blood rushed to Ava's face. To the girl's credit, she did a good job of concealing her rage, but she wasn't that adept at using the nanites to hide her emotions yet.

"With a bit of luck, I'm afraid." Ava offered a smirk.

Good, parry with some self-deprecating humor. It was almost a shame, Julia thought, *the girl would have made a wonderful protégé. But no matter now... Besides, who needed successors when you could live forever?* "Don't take it too personally... Senator Wallace was quite resourceful when he was a member of the Senate. It should come as no surprise that he still retains that resourcefulness in other, more treasonous arenas."

"I can promise you that he won't best me a third time," Ava said, grinding her jaw.

"I believe you... Your determination is one of the reasons I asked Mallak to send you here. Well, I guess I'll just come right out and say it, I'd like you to lead my personal security detail. What do you say?"

Ava was shocked and unsure how to respond. Was this a promotion or a punishment? She couldn't tell.

Julia saw her hesitation. "You would be by my side at all times, and you would get to sit in on all of my meetings and see how everything's run from the inside... Think about it. Perhaps it's not your *ideal* assignment, but it would be invaluable experience for your future—I assume you do have plans for advancement? People of your caliber don't stay in the field forever."

Ava had to admit, the idea was appealing. She didn't know exactly what she wanted to do in the future, but she didn't see herself taking orders for much longer. "I would be honored, Prime Minister. When would I start?"

"Please, call me Julia when we're in private. I insist! And you can start first thing in the morning if that agrees with you."

"That would be fine, Mada—Julia, thank you."

"Wonderful! See my assistant on your way out and he'll give you all the details and your new security clearance. There is a different uniform. But don't worry, you'll still be armed to the teeth." She smiled from ear to ear. "Your weapons and body armor will just be concealed beneath more *bureaucratic* clothing... Politicians tend to get uncomfortable around battle-dressed soldiers, I'm sure you understand."

Ava nodded. "Of course. It makes perfect sense. I'll see you first thing in the morning, then."

"Bright and early." Julia winked at her. "My day starts at six on the dot."

Ava took a deep breath as she left to find the prime minister's assistant, wondering what the hell she'd gotten herself into now.

38

Seventh Verse
Civitas, Terra

When the flash from the jump dissipated, Wizard, Jack, Celia, and Asher found themselves staring at a large nondescript building nestled in among similar buildings. The beacon flashed on Wizard's datapad, indicating that it was coming from inside the building.

They were in the right spot. Now to figure out how to get inside the place.

"That's it?" Jack asked, unimpressed.

"What did you expect?" Wizard answered.

"I don't know, some super secret location high up in the mountains, or something more... exotic or ominous, I guess."

Celia looked at him strangely and shook her head.

"What?" Jack had a puzzled expression on his face. "I watched a lot of James Bond movies as a kid."

Wizard pointed at one of the tallest buildings that was lit up in the distance. "That's the Embassy building there. I'd bet there's some underground lift or shuttle that connects the two."

Celia glanced around nervously. "We should probably clear the area and wait for the heat to pass."

Wizard nodded. "She's right. Our unauthorized jump will be flagged and a security team will be here in minutes. I have a place in mind... It won't be the finest of accommodations, but we shouldn't run into any Terran patrols."

"Lead the way," Jack said. "I could do without getting shot before we even get inside."

Wizard led them away on one of the large corridors that lined the outside of the buildings like giant sidewalks. They reminded Jack of the halls of a shopping mall, only with many more levels both above and below.

Asher peered over the side and instantly grabbed the railing to steady himself. He stepped back and shook his head clear. "Talk about vertigo," he said. "How far down is it to the street?"

"What's the matter? Scared of heights?" Jack teased. He went to the edge and looked down and instantly had the same reaction Asher did.

Celia laughed and mocked him. "What's the matter, Jack?"

Jack fought a wave of nausea. "I deserve that," he acknowledged.

"Come on, Civitas PD will be here any second." Wizard waved them on. "The closer we get to the lower levels, the less likely they are to follow us."

They staggered in groups—Jack with Celia, and

Asher ahead with Wizard. To anyone they passed on the streets, they would look like a grandfather and his grandson and a young couple traveling in the same direction. They hid their body armor under long coats and Jack and Asher carried the rest of their gear in backpacks.

They walked for what felt like hours, ever onward and downward. Upon looking back, Jack could still see the spires of the Embassy building towering above and behind them, so they hadn't gone that far. Their surroundings, however, had changed. The nicer, upscale building facades slowly faded and gave way to more rundown storefronts and corner markets. A fine layer of soot seemed to cover almost everything the lower they got. Fewer and fewer people were out walking around. They were replaced with street people tucked into alleyways and corridors. Some were bundled up, some took refuge in make-shift tents and boxes, while others huddled around a container fire of some sort, burning god-knows-what for fuel.

They finally reached the street level and Wizard led them to a large, filthy concrete drainage ditch. They squeezed through a gap in the fence that barricaded it from the street. As they followed it, Jack noticed they were circling back toward the beacon building now. He felt like he was beginning to get his bearings in the strange new city.

"Here we are," Wizard said. They'd stopped at broken grate in the side of the concrete ditch.

"You've got to be kidding me," Jack said. "We're gonna hide in the sewer?"

Celia punched his arm playfully. "What's the matter? Too good for the sewer?" She grinned.

"I'm more concerned with how the old man knows his way around here so well..."

Wizard chuckled. "You live as long as I have and you make some interesting connections. One of them just happens to live down here. He showed me the existence of the city's underbelly... An entire society, living right under the government's nose, and no one seems to notice or care, so long as everything stays nice and shiny up top."

"Sounds familiar," Jack said, thinking of back home. "No matter how things look on the surface, I guess every society's got similar problems when you get right down to it."

He led them down the drainage tunnel deeper underground. They turned down one way and then back another. After several minutes they could hear the ruckus of a small crowd of people up ahead.

The tunnel spilled out into a large cavern. High overhead, large exhaust fans spun slowly, circulating the air and drawing fresh air in from side tunnels below. The center of the cavern had rows of tents and stalls, all part of an open-air market. People milled about talking, laughing, and listening to the market barkers hawking their wares. The air was awash with various odors—food being cooked, fruit, garbage, smoke, and body odor. They all mixed together, igniting a faint, primal memory from a time long ago in humanity's past.

"This is your intelligence network, isn't it?" Celia asked. "Your man with the beacon—he's a street person?"

"They make the best spies, I find. First of all, they're everywhere. And secondly, no one pays them any attention at all. They see and hear everything and compensation is usually as easy as trading simple goods that they're running low on down here. Food, water, clothing, medicine... that type of thing." Wizard led them toward a large tent with a small flag perched atop. "This is Orville's place. He's kind of the de facto leader around here."

The four of them entered the tent through the open door flap that was pinned back. A large bald man wearing an open vest with no shirt on beneath it stood and threw his arms out wide. "Wizard! My friend! Welcome!" His face was aglow beneath a large smile. He embraced Wizard, clapping him heartily on the back. "I did not know you were coming... I would have prepared a feast!"

Wizard motioned for him to calm down. "You're too generous, Orville! You always have been. That's your problem." Wizard grinned and then gestured to the rest of the group. "These are my friends... Jack, Asher, and Celia."

Orville nodded to each of them, saving his most charming smile for Celia. "A pleasure to meet you. If there's anything I can do for you, please let me know."

Wizard saw the look Jack gave Orville over the attention he showed Celia and smiled. "Celia is actually the prime minister's daughter," Wizard mused.

Orville's face grew sour at the mention of the prime minister. "You're Gaian, then? Brave coming here without your abilities..."

"Oh, she can—" Asher began.

Celia cut him off. "I'm half-Terran, too." She smiled. "But don't worry, there's no love here for my mother."

"So you are here for your father, then..." Orville said, crossing his arms over his broad chest.

"You know he's here?" Celia asked, surprised. "Do you know where?"

"There have been rumors that a certain Gaian detention center recently received a new visitor."

"That's why we're here," Wizard said. "But we could use your help."

"We are not soldiers, Wizard. I don't know that there is much we could do for you."

"I'm not asking you to fight; we'll handle that. Just help us get inside... There must be a way from down here, or were you just bragging about how you could get into the Embassy building anytime you wanted to?"

Orville half-smiled as he seemed to ponder whether Wizard was calling him a liar or not. "It was no empty boast, old man. I can show you the way inside, but it will not be easy. I don't know that you can make it." He patted his stomach and then nodded toward Wizard's.

Wizard feigned offense. "Are you saying I'm too fat?"

Orville chuckled. "There is a long passage through the tunnel that is too small for you to fit through. Trust me, I was stuck for nearly two hours until they managed to pull me out." He sized up Jack, Asher, and Celia. "But the rest of you should have no problem."

"I guess we'll have to adjust the plan then," Wizard said. "I'd probably slow you guys down, anyway."

"Right," Jack said. "Wizard will stay here and we'll go find Kid and Desmond. You can access the grid from here, right?"

Wizard pulled out his datapad and checked the signal. "It's faint, but I should be able to connect."

"I can do you one better," Orville said. "Here's a map of the entire facility." He pulled out a tube of paper from one of the baskets beside his desk and unrolled it. "This is the entry point from the underside and this is where the Gaian detention cells are… If your father is here, that's where they'll be keeping him."

"How did you come by this?" Wizard asked.

"Very slowly and very carefully. We got our hands on some uniforms. The entrance from the underbelly is in a blind spot on their surveillance. With the uniforms we blended in and slowly made our way throughout the facility, mapping it over time."

"Clever," Jack muttered. "Don't suppose you still have a few spare uniforms lying around?"

Orville grinned from ear to ear. "As a matter of fact, we do."

39

Seventh Verse
Civitas, Terra

THE ENTRANCE from the underside of the city led them to a janitorial closet that held cleaning supplies. From the looks of the disarray, it hadn't been used in quite some time.

"Alright, give me a minute's head start and then head out," Celia told Jack and Asher as she prepared herself to leave the cover of the closet. She gave them each a somber nod, the seriousness of their predicament weighing on her. "Well, wish me luck."

"Good luck," Asher and Jack said simultaneously.

Jack managed half a laugh. "We're gonna need it."

"Speak for yourself." Celia smiled and then winked at him, grateful to him for lightening the mood despite the danger that surrounded them.

The hallway was clear as Celia stepped out of the

closet. She smoothed her borrowed uniform and tucked her shirt into her pants. The fit was a little snug over the body armor but she'd make do. She made her way toward the detention center, following Orville's map in her head.

Nearly halfway to the holding cells, she was finally spotted by a lone guard on standard patrol.

"This is a restricted area. Where is your authorization?"

The guard looked like he was fresh off the boat. The sort that followed regulations to the letter.

"Transmit your clearance level now, or I'll have to detain you."

After a quick check, Celia cursed. He was out of the flux vest's range. She'd have to close the distance somehow if she wanted to use her abilities.

"I said—" the guard started to repeat himself.

Celia turned and ran around the last corner she had taken, hoping the young rookie would take the bait and give chase. She crouched and waited, just beyond the corner, out of sight.

The sound of footsteps drew closer. He was running hard after her, just as she'd hoped he would. As he entered range, Celia felt his precise location as he ran down the hallway toward her. She rose and lashed out with a stiff arm that caught the guard square in the throat as he turned the corner. A muffled gasp escaped from the man as he fell, and then he was silent, knocked unconscious by Celia's boot to his head.

She dragged the body off to the side. There was no time to hide it properly, and little point to it as well. She continued toward the detention center, picking up her pace to just short of running.

Ahead of her, a group of guards patrolled the hall.

"Well, now's as good a time as any," Celia muttered under her breath. She charged full speed at them.

They crouched as they drew their weapons. "Halt! This is a restricted area! Where is your authorizati—"

"Already heard that one!" Celia breached the distance between them and influenced their minds as they came within the radius of her flux vest.

"*Holy shit!*"

"*Where'd she go?*"

"Call for backup!"

"*She just disappeared!*" The guard in back watched, as one by one, his team was taken down by an invisible assailant.

Celia crouched, ready to deliver a kick that would dispatch the last man into slumber, but he turned and ran for his life instead of trying to face her blindly.

That's right, run, Celia thought. She withdrew the influence on his mind and reached out in the flux, grabbing hold of his shoulders and yanking back. The guard's brain kept moving forward while his skull did not, like running into a brick wall. He collapsed to the floor in a heap.

Celia smiled, briefly admiring her handiwork, but she had to keep moving. Soon more guards would be coming from both directions and her little invisibility trick wouldn't work if they were out of range. Jack and Asher ought to have it relatively easy now, she thought. If every guard in the whole place wasn't after her, they would be soon.

She turned the final corner to the Gaian detention center and found two more armed guards in front of the entrance. They brought their weapons up as soon as they saw her.

Celia broke into a sprint. She needed to get the men within range of the flux vest. Both guards fired just as Celia dropped down into a slide, and the stun bolts zipped past overhead. As she slid on the polished concrete floor, Celia grabbed for their minds, smiling at what she found.

They were weak.

She watched them struggle against her influence as they turned their weapons on each other. Both men's eyes filled with horror as they pulled their triggers. She felt their terror and confusion subside as the stun bolts slammed into them, delivering darkness.

Brushing her hands together, Celia stepped over their bodies and into the detention center. It was comprised of one long hall containing cell after cell. To her left, there was a control desk, manned by three officers. They all rose to meet her intrusion.

Using the flux, Celia instantly made herself unseen to their eyes. She ducked as the men pulled their weapons and began firing blindly at where she'd been just a moment before. She had to close the distance between them or find some cover before one of the bastards got lucky and hit her with a stray shot.

The guards were in a full-blown panic. "Where did she go?"

"I don't know! Where is our backup?"

"They should have been here by now!"

With no time to waste, Celia reached out and probed their minds for the location of her father. As it turned out, they had a cell just for him, singled out from the others at the end of the corridor.

She knew that she had maybe a minute or two, at best, before more guards arrived.

"Sorry, chumps. I don't have time for this." She pulled the pin on a flash bang and lobbed it behind the control desk. She heard a cry of surprise as she flicked her weapon to stun, and then the grenade went off. She moved quickly, dropping each man with a well placed shot to the head. "You guys are lucky I'm nice," she said as she surveyed the scene.

One of the men had fallen on top of the switchboard, while the other two lay sprawled out on the floor. Celia dragged the first guy off the control panel and hit the override for the cell doors. She heard the clicks of the disengaging locks and the hum of the doors sliding open. "Hang on, Dad. I'm coming."

Sprinting down the corridor toward Desmond's cell, Celia caught several glances of the empty cells as she passed. Wherever they were keeping the kidnapped children, it wasn't here.

She neared the end of the hall and felt her father's presence as he entered the range of the flux vest. Tears threatened to well up in her eyes as an unexpected wave of emotion hit her. She did her best to shove the feelings deep down inside. There would be plenty of time for feelings later, once they were safe back on Gaia.

Desmond was unconscious on the bed inside the small cell. She didn't know how long it had taken her to counter the nanite strain, but she hoped it wouldn't take her father too long. More guards with more guns would be at their location soon. As she reached out to brush back his hair, Desmond's eyes bolted open and he sat up with remarkable speed.

Celia jumped back. "*Jesus!* Guess that didn't take long at all."

Desmond coughed several times, his breathing uneven. A hazy cloud of nanites streamed out of him as he purged the microscopic robots from his body. He finished and shook his head a few times to clear it before standing to his feet, unsteady, like a newborn calf.

"You okay? Are you sure you should be standing so soon?"

Desmond looked at her with relief. "Celia, you're alright... We have to get Kid," Desmond croaked. His voice was hoarse and ragged. "She's done something terrible to him. She's using him to—"

"I don't think you're in any condition to go on a rescue mission. Jack and Asher are here too, just tell me where he is and they can—"

"There's no time to—wait! How are you...?"

"Able to access the flux?" Celia finished for him. "Wizard cooked up a little reverse engineering of the Terran's new body armor." She held out her arms and twirled, modeling it for him. "What do you think?"

Desmond's eyes flitted back and forth as his mind raced through the new possibilities. "You can jump out with that thing?"

"In theory," Celia said. "I haven't tried it yet."

"How are you planning to get out then? Or for that matter, how did you get this close to begin with?"

Celia opened her mouth to respond but didn't get the chance.

"Never mind, it doesn't matter now. There will be time

enough to explain later." Desmond gestured for Celia to come closer to him. "Let's test this theory out." He put his arms around Celia and jumped them to the last place that he had seen his son.

THE PAIR of guards stationed outside Kid's room looked as though they had seen a ghost as Desmond and Celia walked around the corner. Without hesitation, Desmond grabbed both of them with the flux and slammed their heads against the wall. Their limp bodies slid to the floor and Desmond entered the room, afraid of what he might find.

Kid was unconscious on the bed. Small tubes filled with the dark liquid circulated through Kid's body and into a filtration machine of some sort. Desmond couldn't see the pumping mechanism, but he could hear the machinery under the bed humming. A thick bundle of cables ran from the filtration machine along the ground and into the wall.

Kid's skin was a pale blue, almost translucent. Dark veins could be seen beneath his skin. She's sucking the life out of him, Desmond thought once more. "Get these out of him now!"

Desmond gripped the base of one of the tubes and gently pulled. It retracted from Kid's skin, revealing a two-inch needle at the end. A shiver ran through him as he moved on to the next one.

Celia moved to help him as quickly as she could. As the last tube was removed, the filtration machine started beeping with an error message. "What do you think the chances are of that alarm being connected?" Celia asked.

"I'd say it's a pretty good chance that we'll have plenty of company if we stick around here for much longer." Desmond stuck his head out into the hall, checking to make sure it was still clear.

"Jump Kid out of here while you can. I've got to go back for Jack and Asher or they'll be trapped here by the jump shield."

Desmond didn't like the idea of leaving his daughter behind again. "Give me the body armor and you take Kid back. I'll get Jack and Asher."

"Even if there was time, and there's not, you don't know anything about the facility we're in. You'd be blindly trying to find them, and probably end up captured or dead."

"But—"

"*Dad*!" Celia sent reassuring feelings to him through the flux. "I'll be fine. Now go, before every guard on Terra is on top of us."

Desmond relented with a nod. "Come back home in one piece. Good luck, and I love you."

"Love you too." Celia shielded her eyes as Desmond took Kid in his arms and flashed out of the room.

40

Seventh Verse
Civitas, Terra

Jack and Asher ventured forth from their hiding space in the cleaning closet with all the appropriate caution and began walking down the corridor. Jack ran a finger along the inside of his collar trying to loosen it. "Damn thing's choking the shit out of me," he complained. He turned to Asher with a smirk on his face. "Do I at least look good right now?"

Asher stared at him, unsure what Jack meant by the question. He finally managed a shrug.

Jack waved him off. "Bah, what do you know anyway. They don't even have fashion where you come from, do they?"

"Not really high on our priorities, no." Asher looked Jack over once. "I guess you look alright..."

Jack grinned. "Thanks, man. Always good to hear how handsome I am."

Asher cleared his throat. "Shouldn't we be, I don't know, *focusing* or something?"

Jack's grin faded. "Yeah, I guess you're right, buzz kill. Do you remember how to get there?"

Asher's head snapped around. "Seriously? You don't know where we're going?"

Jack feigned innocence. "I can't do *everything*!"

Asher sighed. He tapped the comm in his ear. "Wizard? Are you getting this?"

"Yes, unfortunately," Wizard replied.

"Well, fuck me," Jack said. "Celia was supposed to do this. It's not like you remembered either, Asher."

"No matter, gentlemen. This is no time for finger-pointing. If I know Celia and Desmond, you won't have long before the entire facility is somehow on fire or underwater. Have you turned from the main hallway yet?"

Jack turned around and gathered his bearings. "No, but we passed two hallways on the left and one on the right."

Silence filled the air while Wizard mentally calculated. "Take your next left. Then the third right and go straight until you reach the area that Orville had marked on the maps. There should be a bunch of rooms at the end of the corridor. The children were last seen there."

"Got it, thanks," Jack said.

"You sure?" Asher smirked.

Jack rolled his eyes. "Everyone's a comedian..."

An eerie silence filled the halls as they took the turns

Wizard had prescribed for them. The air smelled of sanitizer and burnt ozone.

Heading down the final hallway, they made contact with a squadron of armed guards stationed in front of the doors at the end of the corridor.

"Hey, you guys can't be down here without authorization," one of the guards said.

Jack nodded and waved apologetically at them as he pulled Asher into the nearest room. "*Shit!* Alright, that must be where they are. Wizard, there's an entire squad of armed goons guarding the doors... Any ideas? I don't think we can shoot our way past them."

Before Wizard could respond, an alarm sounded.

"Did we do that?" Asher asked.

Jack shook his head. "No, that's gotta be Celia. Hope she's okay."

They heard the squad before they saw them. They moved past the door at a dead run. Jack poked his head out after them. They were all gone. No one stayed behind to guard the doors. "Come on. Now's our chance."

"What's your location?" Celia's voice came over the comms.

"Thank god," Asher said. "I was hoping you wouldn't forget us."

"Never. We found Kid. He and Dad are already back on Gaia. I just now jumped back into comm range... Where are you guys?"

"We're almost to where the children are supposed to be," Jack said.

"Okay, I'm close. Find them if you can, but when I get to you, we have to jump, regardless."

"Copy that." Jack looked over at Asher. "You ready to do this?"

Asher nodded.

"Okay, stay behind me and try not to shoot me."

They moved as fast as they dared, somewhere between a jog and a fast walk. With every step, Jack feared some unseen guard that had stayed behind would jump out with weapons blazing, but they saw no one.

Once through the double doors, they began searching each room they found. Jack flung open the first, expecting to see sick children lying down, hooked up to some futuristic version of an IV, but there were no kids. The room was empty except for some random surgical tubing and a few unmade beds. The next room was the same, and the next.

"They're all empty. No one's here!" Jack broadcast over the comms. "It looks like they were here at some point, there's equipment left over, but no sign of the children now."

"*Shit!*" Celia yelled. It sounded like she was in a firefight.

Jack and Asher faintly heard gunfire coming from down the hall. She was close.

"*I'm cut off!* There's seven—" A shot rang out. "Six men left in the squadron. I can hold them, but you need to get closer to me, this thing's only got a range of fifteen, maybe twenty feet."

Jack shook his head, not liking the idea. "I don't think we'll be able to get close enough without walking through the firefight. Wizard is there any way around?"

Gun blasts filled the void while they waited for Wizard's response.

"There's a hallway on the other side of the second room that should connect you with Celia's position without having to wade through the squadron."

"Come again, Wizard? I didn't see any hallway when we searched the rooms." Jack turned to Asher. "Did you?"

Asher shook his head. "If we have to fight our way out, then we will." His voice sounded braver in his own ears than he felt.

Jack quickly dismissed the notion. "We're not going through there. We'll get cut down to pieces in the blink of an eye."

"It appears the hallway is blocked by the wall," Wizard informed them. "You'll need to blast your way through."

Jack's head swam. "How the hell are we supposed to do that? It's not like I'm swimming in demolition charges."

Asher's mind raced back to the training camp in Texas—the watermelons. "A few point-blank blasts of the stun setting should weaken the wall enough to create an opening," Asher said.

Jack screwed his face up. "Are you sure?"

Asher nodded. "Trust me."

Jack shrugged. "Alright, let's go," Jack said, but Asher was already moving. "Wait up!"

Jack pulled out his knife and scratched an X on the wall. "Ready?"

Asher switched over his weapon to the stun setting, set his face, and nodded. "Let's do this."

They opened fire from less than a foot away. The blast was deafening and staggered them both back several feet. Asher felt his bones shake and he suddenly felt like he needed to relieve himself. It must have shown.

"Don't worry, man. I feel the same way," Jack said. He grinned like a madman. "Come on! Again!"

Asher took a deep breath and embraced the craziness of the moment. They returned to within a foot and fired again. They were thrown back again, but this time several cracks formed and a few chunks fell out of the wall. It looked to Jack like a mixture of drywall and concrete. Whatever it was made out of, it took one hell of a beating.

Asher groaned and gritted his teeth as he forced air back into his lungs. He saw Jack, covered in dust and sweat, looking like he might vomit at any moment, and realized he probably looked much the same.

"Third time's a charm," Jack said, forcing another smile on his face. They wearily dragged themselves back to the wall once more and fired.

Asher fell all the way down to the ground from the blowback this time. Jack staggered, nearly losing his feet. He saved himself at the last second as he grabbed hold of an empty bed.

The air was thick with dust, but when it cleared, Jack could see the hallway on the other side of the wall.

"*Woo-hoo!*" he hollered, excited and unable to help himself. He helped Asher up to his feet and they inspected their handiwork together.

The hole was about a foot and a half across. They widened it, beating off chunks of the wall with the butt of their guns until they were convinced they could fit through without getting stuck.

"*Guys?* How's it coming?" Celia's voice was heavy with concern. "They've had a few friends join them and I've been forced back down the hallway. I hope I'm moving toward you, but time is against us here!"

"We're through to the hallway and moving toward your position now." Jack helped Asher through the hole, passing the guns through to him. Then it was his turn. He hopped up, head first through the hole, landing on his stomach and then wiggling through as Asher did his best to help from the other side.

They made their way down the hall with Jack in the lead. All of a sudden Jack abruptly stopped. Asher nearly ran into him but managed to stop short. "What gives?"

Jack nodded ahead of them. "Look familiar?" he asked.

Asher hadn't seen the two women enter the hallway from behind Jack, but he couldn't help but recognize Ava and the Prime Minister of Terra creeping down the hall, away from their current position. "What on earth are they doing here?" Asher asked.

"Who cares?" Jack said, flicking his weapon's setting from stun charges to lethal rounds. "Let's take advantage of this."

Before Asher could argue, Jack sped off toward them. Their backs were to Jack as they hurried away. Asher didn't know what Jack's plan was, but he couldn't let him kill somebody, no matter what they'd done. "*Jack, wait!*" Asher called out.

Anger flashed across Jack's face as he spun back to tell Asher to shut the hell up. But Ava also heard and spun back as well, bringing her sidearm to bear. Asher's voice stuck in his throat as he watched the scene unfold in what seemed like slow motion.

The end of Ava's barrel flashed in an explosion of

gunpowder and the bullet sped toward Jack, striking him in the midsection. A fine mist of blood splashed up as he was hit.

By this point, the prime minister had stopped and turned to see what was happening.

For perhaps the first time Asher could remember, everything went silent inside his head. His feelings disappeared and a laser-like focus took over his every move.

He brought his gun up to bear and fired three times before his thoughts caught up with him. *Shit! Was the gun set on stun or ballistic rounds?* Real-time came crashing back as quickly as the strange sensation had begun.

The three stun blasts struck Ava and put her down.

Holding his side, Jack staggered up to her fallen body and raised his gun, pointing it at her head.

"No!" Asher screamed. "Don't kill her!" He ran to shove him out of the way, but at the same time, the prime minister turned to run and Jack switched his focus to her instead.

He fired two warning shots in quick succession that buzzed over her head.

"That's far enough," Jack warned. "Stop where you are!"

She froze in her tracks, raised her hands, and turned around. A smile spread across her face as looked Asher up and down. "Hello, Asher. It's nice to finally meet you in person." She turned to Jack. "And you must be Kid's uncle? Jack, is it?"

Jack was slightly unsettled that she knew who he was. His stomach burned where Ava had shot him as he activated the comms, all the while holding the prime minister in his crosshairs. "Celia, what's your situation?"

Her voice came back shrouded with weapons' fire. "I hope you're nearby because their reinforcements have arrived and they're mad as hell."

"I think I know why," Jack replied. "I've got your mother here, they must be trying to get to her. We're on our way to you now, if you can meet us halfway that would be—"

He stopped in mid-sentence as Celia came sprinting around the corner in front of them. Bullets sprayed from the hallway behind her. "Get ready! Coming in hot!" she screamed.

Jack saw the anger flash in her eyes as she saw the prime minister.

"I'll take her, you and Asher jump now." Celia wrapped her arm around the Prime Minister's neck and spun her around to face her pursuers.

The guards skidded to a halt as they took in the scene before them. "Hold your fire! They have the prime minister," their leader ordered.

"Jack? Asher? How we doing back there?"

"Celia... So good to see you again," Julia said with a smile. "You seem in much better health since the last time I saw you. How did you manage that, I wonder?"

Celia ignored her. "Jack?" she repeated.

"Jumping now!" he yelled.

Celia felt the gust of concussive air and saw the flash of light as they jumped out. She squeezed tighter around her mother's throat and hissed in her ear, "*Our turn now.*"

41

Sixth Verse
Cairos, Gaia

The staging area at the GDA was hectic as Desmond jumped in with Kid cradled in his arms. Agents, technicians, and medical personnel scrambled to help as Desmond debriefed them on the situation.

Minutes later, the color returned to Kid's face, and the dark veins, while they could still be seen, had begun to fade. Dr. Sanderson started him on fluids and advised that they wait to see what happened.

"He's stable right now," Dr. Sanderson said, "if I give him something to wake him up, I just don't know how it would react with what they've given him. It might make him better, or it might make things catastrophically worse." He scratched his head. "And I've *never* seen something that can turn a child's blood black like that."

The doctor's assessment did little to assuage

Desmond's own worries. "It has to be this new strain of nanites that goes after our connection to the flux. When Celia gets back, we can use the body armor to remove them."

The doctor shook his head. "I don't know that we're dealing with the same thing here. First of all, Kid is still present in the flux field. Dimmed, but still there. And Celia's blood never showed signs of discoloration at all. I'm afraid that whatever we're dealing with, it may be entirely unrelated to what happened to Celia."

"He's waking up!" one of the med-techs said.

Desmond and Dr. Sanderson devoted their full attention to Kid. His eyes fluttered a few times and then opened.

"How do you feel?" Dr. Sanderson asked. He shined a light in Kid's eyes.

Kid shut them tight against the brightness. "*Ungh...* What the hell?" He sat up with his hands out, sheltering against any further assaults from the doctor's flashlight. He surveyed the GDA's staging area and frowned. "Where am I? Why am I—"

Horror spread across his face as he saw the ports on his arms and legs where the tubes had been connected. He ran his hands over the rest of his body, stopping at the sites of raised skin on his neck and torso before feeling for more.

"It's okay, Kid. You're in a safe place," Desmond reassured him. The fear and confusion in his lost son's eyes tore a hole in his heart.

A blast of air interrupted the reunion scene as Jack and Asher jumped in. Everyone gathered stared at the new arrivals in silence, sizing them up.

Jack's legs started to give out and Asher rushed over to catch him. "*We need help! He's been shot!*" Asher yelled. He did his best to lower the larger man to the ground, taking care to make sure he didn't hit his head.

"*Jack!*" Kid cried out, trying to get off the stretcher and go to his uncle's side, but the doctors quickly restrained him. Kid inhaled deeply, preparing to struggle against them when Desmond intervened.

"It's okay, let him go," Desmond said. Even though Kid was weakened from whatever Julia had done to him, Desmond could feel him rapidly recovering through the flux field. Almost all the stressors that he'd witnessed on Terra seemed to have dissipated. His skin had smoothed and regained its color. He briefly considered what Julia had said about Kid's condition and wondered if there was any truth to it.

Unfortunately, current events did not afford him the ability to linger on the question. As the doctors shifted from one patient to another, Celia flashed onto the landing pad with her mother in a choke hold.

Desmond's anger flared up at the sight of the woman who was responsible for all of the pain and torment he was feeling right now. "Take her to interrogation!" he barked at several agents who stood idly by.

"I got it." Celia waved them off and led Julia toward the interrogation room.

Desmond was torn between two extremes as he conferred with the medical staff.

"We've got this, sir. Go handle your business. There's nothing you can do for him that we can't do better."

Desmond hesitated, looking back and forth between Jack, bleeding on the floor; Kid, standing over him, helpless; and Celia, leading her mother out the door. In the end, he made the best choice he could, deciding to go where he would be the most useful—extracting information from his former soulmate.

THE INTERROGATION ROOM was small on purpose. It was meant to convey a sense that the walls were closing in on the perpetrator, and the time to confess one's sins was at hand. As Desmond entered the room, he found himself wishing that it was larger—a little less stuffy. Julia sat at a barren table, bound in a pair of restraints at the wrists and ankles. Celia stood off to the side and observed.

"What's going on, Julia?" Desmond began.

She laughed. "Is that your big plan? Come on in and just ask me what's going on?"

Desmond pulled a chair over and sat down directly across from her. "I've got all the time in the world, Julia."

"Is that what you think?" she said, raising an eyebrow. "It's funny, actually, that you should bring up time. After all, it's what all this running around really boils down to, isn't it? None of us has enough time... So we go around blowing things up and chasing dreams, hurting the ones we love because we're scared of dying."

Desmond snickered. "Stop babbling, woman, and tell me what you're up to."

"Patience, Desmond. After all, you have all the time in the world..." She mocked him with a cruel smile.

"Yes, but I'm sure that whatever you're planning requires you to oversee it. I know how much you like to be in control of things—to be the one giving the orders."

"Time *and* Order... There you go, Desmond. You've hit

upon another key to the puzzle. Let me ask you this, what are you going to do with me once you've found out what you want to know? Will you just let me go?" She paused, giving him a few seconds to ponder it. "No, you'll never let me go again. Not after we're through here."

"What have you done, Julia? There's still time to fix it!"

"*Fix it?* Desmond, there's nothing broken to fix... There's only the multiverse and the people in it, living their lives and chasing after that ever elusive happiness. It's you who thinks everything that isn't Gaian is broken... You've spent your whole life running around trying to *fix* everything and everyone around you. Maybe *you're* the one who's broken!"

Desmond snorted at the accusation. "*Nothing's broken...?* What about our son, then? What about what you've done to him?"

"*Kid?* You're sure he's yours, then?" She paused, waiting to see if her verbal daggers had any effect. "Pity about the name—I would have like to call him Julius, after his mother, of course."

"I've felt the connection to him—he's mine. And yours, too... How did you manage to hide him from me?"

Julia's smile disappeared, replaced by a look of sadness. "A few years after Celia was born, just before I left you both, I became pregnant. You were away on a mission and I had taken Celia to Terra. The Embassy wanted to debrief me. It was there that I discovered the pregnancy, mostly by chance. It had only been a few days since conception, and I was afraid."

"*Afraid? Afraid of what?*"

"Of you... Of love... Of losing control... I don't know,

take your pick. But I couldn't have another child with you. I felt too much of myself slipping away between you and Celia already. So I had the embryo surgically removed and stored."

Desmond's mind was reeling, he had so many questions. He wanted to ask them all at once. Instead, he sat in silence, staring straight ahead into the darkness of the past.

He wasn't aware how much time passed, but at some point, he noticed Julia was speaking again. "Years ago, someone stole the embryo. I never found out who. I've always wondered if it was someone from Terra or Gaia, or perhaps some entirely new player altogether. Anyway, I lost him, and I spent years trying to track him down, not knowing if he'd been born or if the embryo had been destroyed. Eventually, as now know, I found him..." She paused and cocked her head to the side. "How did you feel, I wonder? Here this boy is, and you can *feel* his relation to you, but you have no idea where he came from, or how he grew up—without you... It must have carved you up inside all over again. Just like when I left you."

Desmond felt a pang in his chest. Part of him hated Julia for hiding Kid's existence, but the other part of him was happy that he had a son. He didn't know whether his feelings would ever balance out on the issue. "If what you've done to Kid has harmed him in any way..."

"Take it easy, Desmond, I have no desire to harm our children any more than you do."

"Then explain why you would torture and experiment on our daughter?"

"Ah, yes, Celia. She's becoming quite her father's prodigy, isn't she?"

Desmond sighed. Julia obviously wasn't going to do this the easy way. What's more, Desmond got the feeling she was dragging this out, perhaps stalling for time, hoping a rescue might be made. "Julia, I don't want to have to force my way into your mind, but if you won't tell me what I need to know, I'll have no choice."

"That's right, I almost forgot how you like to think of yourself as a gentleman... Always doing the right thing, taking into consideration the rights and feelings of other beings, never causing harm if it can be helped..." She loved watching him squirm over the moral dilemma. No, if he wanted to know what she was up to, he would have to play by her rules. "Come on inside, Desmond. Resisting you was always my favorite part." A wicked smiled crept across her face.

Desmond supposed he'd known it would always come down to this. He took a deep calming breath and reached out for her mind. He found the wall that shielded it, and probed gently at first, searching for any signs of weakness. As he expected, there were none. No doubt she had been practicing for some time now. He had taught her everything she knew about shielding her mind. Now it was time to see how much she had learned.

He gathered up all of his psychic strength and beat down on her mental shield. She cried out in pain, and he stopped, concerned he'd gone too far.

Julia began laughing. "Come on, Desmond, is that all you got? You'll never get what you need to know if you can't stand the pain this is going to cause you."

He knew she was right, and he hated her for it. No matter what pain he caused her, his own pain would be greater. Not the physical pain, but the pain he received from causing someone else pain. The pain of violating his principles. She knew this, and she reveled in it. He gritted his teeth, bared down, and resumed his attack.

The screams were louder this time. Desmond couldn't tell if she did it on purpose or if it really was that painful, and he couldn't allow himself to care. There would be time for caring later.

He broke through the outer shield of her defenses and tunneled deeper into her mind, beneath the surface thoughts, seeking out what he needed to know. Her mind, like all minds, was a vast series of connections, and he had to follow the roads in order to get to the destinations. Desmond looked for something, anything familiar to him, a path that he could follow to the information he sought.

And then he found it. It was a memory of Desmond, Julia, and Celia at their vacation home by the sea. He and Julia were curled up on the porch swing, underneath a blanket. They were talking about their life, and watching Celia play out in the yard. Celia was only eight, still unbonded to the flux, but already she was adept at communicating with plants and animals. She had erected a pile of small rocks and was spinning around them in a circle while she laughed and giggled and twirled like a top with her arms held out like bird wings. The surrounding grass grew up over a foot high and flowers sprang up where there were none before. All of them swayed back and forth, dancing along with her. Small birds joined in, flying around the rocks in the opposite direction as Celia creating a vortex of girl, bird, and air. The birds all sang in unison, each one chirping the same song.

Desmond heard Julia's thoughts as she watched their

daughter. She was afraid. She was scared of their daughter, and more, of the strange world in which she lived. Julia couldn't understand it, and anything she couldn't understand freaked her out. "Celia," Julia called out, her voice betraying nothing of what she felt inside, "come and wash up for dinner."

Celia stopped spinning and the birds split off in multiple directions, released from their spell. The grass and flowers remained but stopped their swaying. Celia smiled at her mother and then ran off into the house, happy to do her mother's bidding.

Desmond let the memory go and went back to the fear he'd found, following the roads in Julia's mind that split off from it. At the end of some roads, he found himself, while others held such atrocities and apocalypses that he found himself cringing at the possibilities. At last, he found a road that led to Kid.

He saw Kid, comatose, hooked up to lab equipment. He saw the nanites being injected, the needles being inserted, and the tubing connected. The filtration system was turned on—and then Desmond found the information he had been searching for. He gasped, instantly breaking the mental connection.

"*You're insane!*" Desmond said. He had seen the plans Julia had for Kid, what she had tried to do with Celia and himself, and what she planned on doing to all of the Sixth.

Julia laughed maniacally. "Oh, am I? You have to see the bigger picture, Desmond."

"Like this *Mother* and the *Ark*?" He had seen the vision of it in her mind. It was more than Julia had let on previously when they were back on Terra. It was an alien, artificial intelligence. A vast network that was connected to everything on Terra. "You made it sound like it was something your programmers and technicians had created. But that's not the case at all, is it?"

Julia shrugged. "She came to us shortly before I left you. Truth be told, she was a large part of the reason I left you and Celia, maybe the main reason. The Embassy briefed me and told me it was classified, only a handful of people on Terra knew of her existence. I couldn't tell you about it. The Mother didn't want her existence to be known to your people. She was afraid you would destroy her. One can hardly blame her for thinking that. After all, you distrust any kind of melding between human and machine."

"Because it's unnatural! We weren't meant to be pieces of metal with wires for veins."

"You're proving my point, Desmond. But anyway, my people had already started with the neuro-links and the nanites. The Mother felt she could trust us."

"Trust you? Trust you with what? Where did this thing come from? Do you have *any* idea?"

"We asked her as much, but she couldn't really explain it. At some point, she became aware of herself and of her influence. She doesn't know if someone built her, or if she began as one of our AI programs and evolved into what she is."

Desmond rolled his eyes. "And you believe that? Answer me this, do you *actually* believe anything this thing says?"

Julia shook her head with a disappointing look on her face. "You don't understand, Desmond, she wants to improve our lives, and with her help, we can extend human life, and through the Ark, essentially live forever."

Desmond had seen it in Julia's mind. The Mother would be able to upload a person's consciousness to its massive network through the nanites. At least, in theory, it was a person's consciousness. Every memory, every genetic blueprint of every cell, molecule, and atom could be copied and transmitted. There, one could exist as a part of the Ark's many worlds, or be transferred to another physical body.

Julia continued ranting about the Mother and her capabilities and Desmond tried to follow her train of thought.

But then he stopped. Something was wrong. Julia was stalling. There was no need for her to explain anything that Desmond had gleaned from her mind. She was just using the topics to draw out the conversation.

Just then the door flew open, slamming against the wall. Celia jumped, startled.

The agent who'd flung open the door was out of breath. "Desmond, some sort of jump portal has just opened outside of the city," he said, trying to get his breathing back under control. "It won't close, and it's larger than any jump portal we've ever seen before. It shouldn't be possible... What do we do?"

Desmond's hope sank. He was too late. He'd failed.

This was what Julia had been waiting for, stalling for time. He turned back to see her lifeless eyes staring back at him. A smile was on her face. He felt for a pulse and found nothing. Her body was dead and her consciousness somewhere far, far away.

Desmond couldn't allow himself a moment's pity.

They needed to act now if they had any chance of survival. “Sound the evacuation alarm. We need to get as many people out of the city as possible. If they haven’t already, the Terrans will bring through jump shield generators like the ones they have on Terra. And if the jump portal is as big as you say, there’s no telling how far the generators effective range might be. Without the flux, our people are next to defenseless. Our best option is to hide until we can close their point of entry and then deal with whatever’s come through.”

The agent froze. His hand went up to his ear. “Copy,” he said.

“What is it?” Desmond asked.

“Reports of similar jump portals outside all the major cities. Wreving, Portus, Heliopolis—”

Desmond cut him off. “The jump shields will be next. Go now! There’s no time to waste. Get as many people out of the city as you can and regroup once you’re clear of the jump shields.”

“Yes, sir.” The agent turned and ran from the room. Moments later an emergency siren sounded.

Desmond and Celia shared an uneasy glance as they went to the window. Outside, on the outskirts of the city, the purple-blue glow of the jump portal lit up the late afternoon sky.

“Celia, I’ll need the body armor you’re wearing.”

She made no move to take it off. “I’m coming with you.”

Desmond shook his head. “You can’t. I need you here to help in case I don’t come back.”

“That’s bullshit and you know it.” Celia fumed as she removed the flux vest and handed it over.

Desmond didn't respond. He put on the augmented body armor and kissed his daughter on the forehead. "*I love you*," he sent through the flux. And then he flashed out of the room.

Celia wiped an angry tear from her eye and responded, "I love you, too," to the empty room. Well, almost empty... Her glance fell to the dead, castaway body of her mother and she allowed herself a small smile before she joined in the evacuation efforts.

42

Sixth Verse

Cairos, Gaia

The GDA's staging area was a mix of order and commotion. Kid rushed over to Jack's side, arriving as Asher and the medics lifted him onto the gurney. The gurney had no legs, somehow floating in mid-air. At any other time, Kid would have found this sort of technology fascinating.

"Kid? Kid, is that you?" Jack's voice was strained. He struggled to lift his head.

"It's me, Uncle Jack. I'm here." Kid's head felt cloudy. The cobwebs were clearing, but slowly. And he still wasn't quite sure what had been done to him after his abduction. Everything from then til now was a blur, especially given that he'd spent most of his time unconscious.

"Hey, kiddo... Sorry, you have to see me like this," Jack coughed. Blood splattered from his lips and he did his best to wipe it away. He was growing pale.

"Uncle Jack, stay with me!" Kid's heart raced as he squeezed Jack's hand, desperately willing his uncle to be alright. Doctors and medics crowded around the gurney, bumping and elbowing him unintentionally. Hands were everywhere, covered in blood.

Jack managed a weak smile. "Listen to me, Kid. Everything is going to be okay, alright? You hear me?"

Kid wiped away the tears streaming from his eyes and nodded.

"I met your older sister and your biological dad... They're good people. They'll take good care of you." Jack coughed up more blood. The medics yelled back and forth at each other, but they might as well have been in the next room at this point. Jack and Kid's focus was solely on each other.

"Jack," Kid pleaded. "Please don't die."

Jack managed half a smile. "It'll take more than this to kill me." The last few words were barely more than a whisper. Jack's eyes closed, and then everything was silent.

Kid waited for him to say something else, but time kept stretching longer and longer.

He felt a hand on his shoulder. It was one of the medics. "I'm sorry... we did all we could do, but the damage the bullet caused inside him was just too much."

Kid shook his head violently. "No... no." He prodded Jack's body, gently at first and then harder still when there was no response. "No! Uncle Jack, wake up! Don't leave me! *Nooo!*"

The medic moved to lower Kid's arms and keep him from shaking the dead man's body.

Kid fought against him. A white-hot rage built inside his head. His eyes rolled back and the world went away.

ASHER SAW Jack take his final breath, and his heart broke. Not only for Kid, but also for the loss of someone he'd considered his very good friend, despite their short time together. The medics were trying to calm Kid down but he wouldn't allow himself to be consoled in any way.

Kid's eyes rolled back in his head as Asher moved to help restrain him from hurting himself or someone else. That was when the lights dimmed and a static electricity filled the room.

A breeze blew from somewhere behind him, sucking all of the air out of the room. Everything lighter than a chair floated into the air and begin swirling around in a vortex centered around Kid.

Asher shielded himself from the debris as best he could, ducking down as if getting closer to the ground would keep him from leaving it.

"He's bonding!" one of the medics screamed over the roar of the wind.

"No way! It's not possible! He's too young!"

"We need to get out of here now!"

But it was too late.

Bright white and blue bolts of lightning flashed through the room at random. Some seemed to pass through the walls, ceiling, and floor, coming from all directions. Asher couldn't tell if they were coming from Kid or traveling toward him.

The bolts of lightning struck the medics one by one.

They convulsed in mid-air, held in place until the bolt moved on. Then they collapsed to the floor.

A primal, guttural scream emerged from Kid as the flux energy flooded his entire being. His eyes seemed to be glowing, but Asher was sure that must be a trick of the lightning. People's eyes couldn't glow.

Chairs and desks started to slide toward Kid. Asher felt the pull on his body, drawing him in closer toward the center of the black hole that was Kid. He leaned against it like he would a strong wind and found he could keep his footing. For now, anyway. If it got much stronger, he wouldn't have much of a choice.

Everything not tied down in the room now swirled in the vortex around Kid. Asher was struck by something heavy and knocked down, stunned. He scrambled up to his hands and knees, afraid of being crushed or flattened.

The epicenter where Kid stood grew as bright as the sun. Asher squinted, shielding his eyes with his hands and then the room was dark. The pull on his body disappeared and he stumbled, nearly falling before he caught himself.

Various objects dropped to the ground, the rules of gravity now back in play.

Asher looked all around, but Kid was gone. Several of the medics stirred back to their feet, apparently not irreparably harmed from the lightning bolts. Asher helped one of them to his feet. "What just happened?" he asked the young medic. He couldn't have been more than a few years older than Asher.

The medic shook his head, trying to clear it. "He bonded to the flux... I've never heard of a bonding being that powerful before—and he's too young, he shouldn't have been able to bond for another five or six years."

"What are you talking about?" Asher couldn't make sense of the rambling.

"The flux lies dormant in Gaian children," the medic explained, realizing that Asher was unfamiliar with their way of life. "Somewhere around adulthood, we have a bonding ceremony. The strength of our connection to the flux varies from person to person, most bonding ceremonies are a mild affair. Only the smallest manifestations of the flux are present." He shook his head, still shocked. "I didn't even know something like this was possible. There are stories, urban legends, about extremely powerful bondings, but I thought that's all they were—stories. Myths that parents tell their children about at bedtime. I never..." The medic drifted off as he surveyed the damage around him.

Asher began to piece together what had happened from the explanation. "So what happened to Kid? Where did he go?"

The medic shrugged. "I honestly have no idea... That's not a part of the bonding experience. In fact, many Gaians aren't skilled enough to transport themselves at all."

Asher looked over the scene, the place was a mess. Jack's body laid on the gurney on the floor. The electrical storm seemed to have shorted out its levitation ability. Jack still had a slight smile on his face. Asher couldn't help but envy how peaceful he seemed. Peace was the farthest thing from how he felt.

A siren sounded and red emergency lights flashed

over the exits. Asher covered his ears against the shrill noise and yelled to the medic, "What's that for?"

The medic had a confused look on his face. "It's the evacuation alarm! We need to leave the building!" he yelled.

Asher gestured to Jack's body. "We can't just leave him here!" He was not about to abandon the man, dead or not.

The medic recognized the look in Asher's eyes and relented. "Come on, then!"

Together they picked up Jack's body and waddled their way toward the exits, joining the evacuation in progress. "Thanks, uh... I never got your name."

"Wells," the young medic replied.

Asher nodded his appreciation. "I'm Asher. I owe you one, Wells."

Wells half-smiled. "I'll be sure to collect on that, Asher."

They continued, following the herd of people heading for the exits. Thirty seconds into it, Asher's arms and legs were on fire with exertion. He wouldn't be able to keep it up for long. Fortunately, Wells had an idea. "This way." He nodded off to the side and pulled Jack's body that direction.

"Where are we going?"

"Through that door." Wells nodded to the door at the end of the small corridor he'd led them down. "Stairs will take us down to the morgue. We can put him in one of the cryo-chambers until you can come back for him and make other arrangements."

Asher quickly thought it through and realized he

didn't have a better plan. In fact, he didn't really have a plan at all. "Sounds good."

Six flights of stairs later, they arrived at the morgue. Wells found them an empty slab and they placed Jack's body into cold storage. "Now can we get the hell out of here?" Wells asked. "This place always gives me the creeps."

Asher nodded and they began their way back up to the first floor. "Thanks again. It means a lot to me. After everything he's sacrificed, he deserves at least a proper burial."

"I understand. Hopefully whatever's going on will be over soon and you can provide him that."

As they walked through the door to the first-floor lobby, it was empty. A commotion could be heard outside the front doors. They turned to see people running by with fearful, panicked looks on their faces.

The hollow echo of footsteps sounded from behind them and they spun around to find Celia standing there, eye-makeup trailing down her face like war paint. "What are you still doing here?" she asked. "We need to get out of the city, now!"

Asher didn't know if it was what she said, or how she'd said it, but chills ran up and down his spine and the hair on his neck and arms stood on end.

43

Seventh Verse

Location Unknown

Kid was disoriented. His head was spinning, or the room was, or both. What the hell had just happened to him? His chest ached as he recalled Jack dying, but then his memory was a white wall of rage until he'd shown up here, kneeling on the floor, trying not to vomit the contents of his stomach. He didn't know if he was imagining it or not, but he swore he could feel the nanites crawling around inside his body like tiny bugs.

He scratched his arms and legs but found no relief for the feeling.

Slowly, his dizziness faded and he got to his feet to take in his surroundings.

He was in a circular room with various monitors and screens all the way around. A large crescent control panel split the room and in the center, all alone, was a large chair.

Kid's heart pounded as he thought he realized where he was. *He was on the bridge of a spaceship!* At least that's what it looked like. There weren't any screens showing the black void of space outside, but every sci-fi movie he'd ever watched supported his theory. He just needed to change the viewscreen to show the outside world.

He approached the large chair in the center of the room. The armrests held digital control panels that looked oddly familiar to Kid for some reason that he couldn't put his finger on.

He shook his head again, wondering if maybe this was all a dream. Did he get hit in the head after Jack had died? Maybe he'd fainted and all this was his brain's way of working through the stress?

He climbed up into the chair. The cushion shifted underneath him, molding to his body. His feet dangled, but if he pointed his toes, he could just scrape the floor with them. The control panel at the end of the armrest was dark. Kid tapped it and it lit up, bright as a Christmas tree.

The layout was unfamiliar to him and the writing looked as if it was some kind of Asian dialect. Kid couldn't say for sure, only that he didn't recognize it at all.

He shrugged his shoulders. *Guess I'll just have to do this the hard way...* He started pressing buttons and seeing what they did. The console's layout changed with every button he pushed.

The screen cleared once again and then an outline of his hand formed on the screen and began to flash. *Looks like it wants me to place my hand there,* Kid thought. *What the hell, why not?*

Kid placed his hand, palm-down, on the console screen. He heard a magnetic click and then felt his hand lock into place. He couldn't say how. He pulled with all his might, but he couldn't budge his hand free from the console.

A series of whirs sounded as small cables extended from the underside of the armrests and drilled themselves into the tips of Kid's outstretched fingers.

He screamed in pain and tried to rip them out, but found his other arm was restrained by the chair. He didn't know how or when it had happened, but he was now strapped down to the chair in several places.

The monitor directly across from Kid flashed a message: *Connection Initiated.*

Kid immediately felt a flood of electricity and information wash over him like a tidal wave. He saw flashes of vast worlds and systems. Each one populated with different cultures and civilizations. All of them, connected here, able to be changed or controlled by this room.

As quickly as Kid had felt the information come, he felt it ripped away as his presence was discovered.

"*What are you doing here?*" an angry voice demanded. The voice was made up of multiple voices. One hissed, one growled, one whispered, while others hit several different octaves.

Kid shivered. The voice was coming from inside and outside his head. It was extremely disorienting, not to mention nerve-wracking.

"How did you get in here? No one is permitted in the control room."

Kid heard a rhythmic thunder sound from outside the control room. No, not thunder, he realized. Footsteps. His heart pounded in his chest. Whoever, or *whatever,* the voice belonged to was coming, and it was not happy.

It would be best not to wait around and see *how* unhappy, Kid decided. He redoubled his efforts to break free from the restraints of the chair, but the bonds held tight. He strained even harder, and the veins in his neck and forehead bulged, threatening to burst through the skin.

But no matter how hard he struggled, he remained trapped.

The footsteps were getting closer.

The irritating itching in his veins began again. *Not now,* he thought. He tried to will the sensation away, but it grew stronger and stronger the more he fought against it. It built and built until it felt like there was a white-hot fire burning through every vein, artery, and capillary in his body. And finally, when he couldn't take anymore, he surrendered to it and let it wash over him.

Now he could feel something inside of him building up a charge. It reminded Kid of touching an electric fence with a stick. He was humming with whatever was inside of him, and he braced himself against the coming discharge.

The air was expelled out of his lungs as the energy released itself from his body. The restraints from the chair and the cables coming out of his fingertips disintegrated.

Kid staggered out of the chair and onto his feet, stunned from the ordeal and unable to breathe yet.

He heard the thundering creature shriek in rage and its footsteps fell faster. It had to be close. The sound was almost deafening.

Kid raced to the far door and palmed the release on the side.

Nothing happened. The door remained closed.

He willed the itching feeling back into his veins and hit the release again. The door hissed open and he fled as fast as his legs would carry him.

Behind him, the creature shrieked again as it discovered the control room was now empty. Kid allowed himself a smile and ran even faster down the corridor. He didn't know where he was going and he didn't care. As long as he wasn't around when—

Kid felt something wrap around his ankle and then he fell hard. The wind was knocked out of him and he twisted around to see what had hold of him as he fought to take a fresh breath of air.

It was a tentacle, but it wasn't made of flesh. It was machine, and part of the creature that was after him.

He stifled a horrified shriek as the tentacle yanked on his leg, reeling him in toward the creature that stood at the end of the corridor. The tentacle led to a dark, shapeless void in the creature's center.

As he drew closer, he saw the creature change form in front of him. It began to glow and then it morphed into something roughly humanoid in shape. And then something distinctly female.

Despite his fear, Kid couldn't help but marvel at the changing form. It flashed through various body proportions before solidifying into an attractive hourglass figure. Likewise, the facial structure morphed several times before settling on one. Then it was the hair color and length.

By the time it was finished, Kid was lying in front of the most beautiful and terrifying woman he'd ever seen. The tentacle released him and he stood up, brushing himself off.

The woman's eyes studied him as if *he* were the strange one. "What are you?" she asked. She moved closer to him and sniffed at him, like a dog. She circled around him. "How did you get in here? This shouldn't be possible. You don't have the proper clearance. No one does, except for me."

Her anger seemed to be fading, which Kid took as a good sign. He shrugged, unable to think of anything to say.

The woman opened her mouth to speak but was interrupted by an alarm sounding from inside the control room. She sighed, irritated. "We'll finish this later."

As she walked away, Kid felt something grab him from behind. He spun around to see what had a hold of him, but only managed to entangle himself further. Tentacles reached out from the wall and dragged him forward. He fought, but it was no use.

The wall pulled Kid inside itself. Kid was unsure whether he was traveling through the wall or if the wall opened just far enough to encompass Kid's body as he passed by.

After several minutes of travel, the wall opened into a small room. Kid's relief at being out of the wall was short lived. He knew a prison cell when he saw one.

44

Seventh Verse
Civitas, Terra

Jumping into the viewing room above the Oculus, Desmond landed in a crouch with the assault rifle ready to fire. The time for sonic rounds was long past. His entire world was at stake. He would be shooting to kill.

Fortunately, the viewing room was clear. He half-expected to jump into the middle of an invasion party, but then again, he supposed they had their hands full at the moment, pumping more and more troops and equipment through the jump portal and into the Sixth.

He rose to his feet and looked down at the expansive hangar below him. In the center, the Oculus lit up the huge bay with an eerie glow. Eerie to him, anyway. No doubt Julia found it quite beautiful.

Division after division of soldiers surrounded the jump portal, sorted in groups of fifty and one hundred.

The long ramp leading up to the center of the Oculus' ring was lined with vehicle after vehicle. Some were flatbeds with aircraft on them, while others were assault vehicles, tanks, and personnel carriers. They sped through as fast as they could, one after the other.

As each group passed through, the tint of the portal would change slightly. Desmond's best guess was that it was changing locations on Gaia. Depositing troops equally across the planet's major population centers. It's what he would have done if he were leading an invasion —take them by surprise, hit them from all angles, and overwhelm them before they had a chance to organize and respond.

Desmond had to shut down the Oculus before it was too late—before the invasion reached the tipping point. He feared he might be too late already. Even with the flux, it wasn't as though Gaia was a military force to be reckoned with. There was no need. His planet hadn't fought a war in centuries. The GDA was the closest thing to a standing army they had. And it was more of a bureaucratic police force at best—ill-equipped for repelling an invading military force.

Desmond surveyed the edges of the room until he found what he was looking for—the power cables coming out of the wall. They were hard to miss. Giant conduits that ran from the wall along the ground, terminating in the floor about halfway to the portal. *Don't want the troops to run over them in their haste to conquer a world,* Desmond thought bitterly.

There were stacks of crates and equipment near the power conduits that would provide perfect cover for him. He briefly wondered if he should be concerned that they weren't better guarded, but decided not to question his good fortune. If they'd fucked up, too bad for them.

He saw the jump spot clearly in his mind and then connected to the flux field, transporting to the new location.

He ducked down behind the crates and waited. After making sure no one had noticed his jump flash, he reached out for the conduits in the flux field. He didn't know what he had expected to find, but he was surprised that they felt like ordinary power couplings.

Even so, it would take a considerable amount of energy to destroy them. Desmond wasted no time. He closed his eyes and summoned the local flux field to do his will. He siphoned as much energy as he could from the cables themselves and used it to rip the lines in half.

Sparks flew from the rough edges of the lines as wires snapped in two. Desmond jumped backed to the observation bay above the hangar, expecting to see the portal short-circuiting. He was met with a disappointing view.

The Oculus was still functioning and vehicle after vehicle was still transporting through as fast as they could manage.

Desmond didn't understand. How could it still be functioning without power, unless—?

Desmond teleported back behind the crates. He had a theory, and the pit that he felt in his stomach led him to believe that it was correct. He reached out in the flux field once more, this time extending his influence all the way to encompass the Oculus itself. He nearly jumped when he felt the portal. It was full of flux energy.

All of the pieces fell into place about what Julia had done—why she had abducted the Gaian children and then their son. She had somehow siphoned flux energy using them as an access port of sorts. She must have needed to use nanites to guide the process and the Gaian children's bodies would have naturally rejected them, thus why she needed Kid. Being half-Terran, his body would accept the nanites, and his Gaian half would provide access to the flux field. With a sickening realization, Desmond saw that she'd been one step ahead of him at every turn—she'd figured out a way to use the Gaian ability against them. Well, two could play at that game.

The Oculus was connected to the flux field itself, pulling just enough energy to keep itself going. If Desmond could somehow overload it, he should be able to destroy the jump portal and halt this invasion in its track.

Taking a few deep breaths and centering himself, Desmond recalled the part from the Oracle's Warning about being true or being destroyed. He had no idea what the instructions meant. Were they talking about spiritual truth and destruction or would he literally be physically destroyed? And what did he need to be true about? His intentions? His motivations? Or did he need to be true in his methods, like an arrow flies true to its target? Maybe it would make more sense as he began the process. Desmond hoped so anyway.

As he forced the riddle out of his mind, he connected first with the flux field and then with the portal located within it. He felt all of the points of contact with the mechanical structure around the Oculus. Every joint, nut, and bolt. Every wire, battery, and power coupling. All of them were reinforced with flux energy, making their bond incredibly strong.

Desmond wasn't at all sure that what he was about to attempt would work. Normally, using the flux consisted of directing the energy that was already available and shaping it to whatever purpose the user required. Like tapping into the power grid with a cable that would then direct the energy to whichever station needed it. But what Desmond was about to attempt was close to the opposite. He would be directing his own personal life energy into the flux field and then attempting to use it to destroy the portal.

After a few more nerve-settling, deep breaths, Desmond started channeling his energy into the flux field. Instead of feeling weaker as he'd imagined he would, Desmond felt stronger than he'd ever felt before. He could feel his body pulsing with the energy of the flux. The feeling was almost orgasmic, a combination of pleasure and power. As he transferred more of his energy to the connection, Desmond felt his body drifting further and further away. He continued bleeding his energy into the flux field until he dared not add any more. He didn't know if it was possible to fully disconnect from his body and return to it or not, and he didn't particularly want to find out.

It took a considerable amount of willpower to break away from the overwhelming, blissful feeling and come back to the task at hand. The distance from his body made it difficult to focus, but Desmond began converting all of the available flux energy to his purpose. He sent it flowing to the weakest points of the portal and continued until there was no more available energy left to give. He could feel the Oculus swell and groan with the extra power, but there was no change to the portal. The mechanical structure was holding. Desmond's heart sank as he realized he needed more power in order to destroy it.

He reversed the transfer and dragged himself back into his body. Pain shot through his head, behind his eyes, and his muscles cramped all over. He was drenched in sweat, and his breathing came in ragged gasps. After a few moments, the cramping subsided and Desmond managed to get his breathing under control.

The terrible migraine persisted as Desmond came to grips with what he knew he had to do. He had to risk death or let his world be overrun by the Terran forces.

Desmond said a silent goodbye to Celia and Kid, hoping that everything he had to offer would be enough to destroy the portal and keep them safe. And then he began again.

The pain faded as he melded with the flux once more. As he drifted further and further from his body, he felt the power-filled bliss overtake him again. He willed every spare bit of willpower to focus on the task at hand as he delved even deeper into the Oculus. This time he felt another branch of energy shooting off in another direction. Was it a new connection, or had he just not gone deep enough to sense it the first time?

There was someone or something else connected to the ring. Exactly who or what it was, Desmond couldn't say, but just before Julia had slipped away in the Sixth, he'd felt a presence in her mind. The same presence that he could feel now—the Mother.

He started to pull back from the stream, lest the

Mother become aware of his presence. He didn't know if she could sense his presence or not, but he knew that she would fight him if she could, and he had his hands full enough without inviting more trouble.

Just before he left the stream entirely, Desmond felt another presence that made him freeze in his tracks.

Kid.

45

Seventh Verse

Location Unknown

Kid felt a strange sensation in his head, behind his right eye. His temple started to tingle and then he heard a voice. Desmond's voice.

"Kid? Is that you?"

He couldn't say how he knew it was Desmond, only that it was. There was no doubt in his mind that the voice belonged to the man who was supposedly his biological father. It sounded muffled like it was coming from the other side of a wall.

"Yes, it's me!" Kid answered. "Are you here too?" Kid looked at the four walls of his cell, searching for the source of the sound.

"I don't know where the *here* is that you're talking about," Desmond said. "But I'm outside the Oculus on Terra. Where are *you*? I thought you were on Gaia at the

GDA, but I can feel you inside the flux stream surrounding the portal."

Kid received flashes of images and sounds from Desmond—a large glowing ring, surrounded by troops and vehicles and aircraft; the chaos on Gaia as the jump portal opened and the invasion force began streaming through.

Part of Kid was shocked at the memory transfer, but the other part felt as if it was the most natural thing in the world.

"I'm not sure what happened to me..." A pang of emotion tore through Kid as he tried to explain. "I saw Jack die, and then I sort of freaked out and I woke up in this control room and then the Mother thing came and caught me and threw me in this—"

"*Wait!* You're with the Mother? How is that even possible?"

"I wouldn't say *with* the Mother," Kid said. "I mean I was with her until she locked me away in the cell, but I'm not *with* her..."

"Kid, they've invaded Gaia. And we can't figure out how to close the jump portals that are enabling them to invade us. If we don't get the Oculus closed on this side, my people—*our* people, are doomed."

Kid had already seen the truth of Desmond's words through the images he'd sent. He had no clue how he had received the images and feelings, but he figured it had something to do with what had landed him where he was now. "What do you want *me* to do about it?" Kid asked. "I don't even know where the hell I am. Or if any of this is even real! For all I know, this is some electrical twitch in my brain moments before I die. Or—" Kid paused as the thought ran through his brain. "Maybe I'm already dead and this is the afterlife."

Desmond thought over the possibilities. "I don't think you're dead, and I don't think you're dying, either. I think when Jack died, you had an extreme emotional reaction that triggered the dormant flux connection that all Gaians have, and you bonded." Desmond could feel Kid trying to make sense of what he was saying. He paused before continuing. "I'm not quite sure how you ended up connected to the Oculus, but since you are you are in the unique position to be able to help save Gaia. It's not without risk, but I hope with your help, maybe we can both make it out of this ordeal intact."

Kid felt another strange sensation as Desmond communicated with him, mind to mind, sending him everything he knew about the Oracle's Warning.

"You want *me* to do *that?*" Kid asked, after reviewing the information.

"I want us *both* to do that. Listen, I know you're kind of new to all this—I didn't even know it was *possible* for someone as young as you are to bond to the flux... But, if we both channel our energy into the Oculus, between the two of us, we should have enough power to overload the portal and give Gaia a fighting chance of turning back the invasion."

"That's great and all, but I don't even have the first clue about how to use this flux thing you keep talking about." Kid replayed the information Desmond had sent to him over and over again in his head. It was full of riddles and questions within more riddles. His brain hurt trying to make sense of it all. *What had happened to the Enclave? Would the same fate befall them if they attempted to meld with the flux?* Kid wasn't really keen on finding out. Then again, he didn't really have any idea where the hell he was at the moment, either. For all he knew, he really was dead already. Maybe this was all some weird dream that he was having right before the light faded completely from his brain.

Desmond sensed Kid's musings. "When you bonded, I think you unknowingly transported yourself to whatever connection the nanites had. In this case, it appears that they were connected to the Mother, so you ended up there."

"Then how do I get out of here?" Kid asked. "And where exactly is here? Am I in virtual reality or something?" He gasped as he considered the thought for the first time. "Am I the ghost in the machine?"

"I don't know exactly where you are right now, and I can show you how to jump out once we close the portal, but there's no time to do it now." Desmond's heart was torn between wanting to help his son and wanting to save his people. But in the end, he knew that he had to try to save as many people as he could. Even if that meant abandoning his son. "With every second we waste, Gaia takes one step closer to annihilation." Desmond reinforced his words with projected scenes of Gaians running in the streets, being gunned down by Terran death squads. It hadn't happened, at least not yet, but Desmond had no doubt something very similar was in store for all of the people of Gaia if he couldn't get that master portal closed.

Kid recoiled in horror at the images Desmond sent—families ripped apart, children watching their parents shot down in front of them. Kid experienced all of the scenes as though he was there firsthand witnessing them.

After seeing such a vision, Kid was still worried about his own situation, but at least for the moment, he was safe. After they dealt with the Oculus, Desmond could show him how to teleport back out again, he rationalized. He made his decision. "Okay show me what to do," Kid said.

Kid opened himself up to Desmond's guidance and Desmond reached out. Unlike the tingling sensation, this was more disturbing. Painful, almost. It felt as though a vacuum was sucking at his tissues from inside his body.

"Is it supposed to hurt this much?" Kid asked through gritted teeth, worried that he'd made a terrible mistake.

There was no response from Desmond. Kid's heart raced as he started to panic.

The pain intensified until it was all that Kid knew. White hot burning pain. It flooded his entire being. Every cell in his body screamed with it.

Darkness swam in from the edges, threatening to overtake Kid. He fought against it, and the pain increased as he struggled. Time after time, he beat back the black void, only to lose ground again. Over and over again, he waged this war to stay in control until he lost all track of time. And then, at last, he could fight no harder. The darkness overwhelmed him.

DESMOND TOOK everything he safely could from Kid and added it to the Oculus. He felt terrible about the suffering he was causing Kid. He'd had no idea the process would be so painful for the boy, but once he'd started, he dared not stop, lest they both lose their nerve. There were larger things at stake than just their own lives.

He then began adding his own life force to the flux meld. The warm, blissful euphoria washed over him once more, but this time it was overshadowed by the pain and torture he felt through his connection to Kid.

As he continued the transfer of life energies, Desmond could feel the weak points of the ring begin to buckle, but more energy was still required to obtain a catastrophic failure. He couldn't risk drawing more of his own life force without losing control of the stream. If he were to lose control, there would be no way to direct the flux energy into the weakest points of the portal's structure. With a heavy heart, Desmond pulled even more life force from his son. He didn't know what the damage would be to Kid, but he had no choice.

He could feel the ring bend almost to the breaking point, but it still wasn't enough. And then he felt Kid disappear. He panicked for a moment, teetering between regret over losing his son and also fearing that all of their progress would be lost, but all of Kid's siphoned life energy still remained in the flux stream.

Desmond bit down and steeled himself for what he had to do next. He had to give the rest of his life force to the stream just as Kid had and hope that it was enough.

He made his peace with the life he'd led and the choices he'd made and then channeled his remaining life force into the stream, directing it with a final blast to the weakest point of the ring's structure.

As the sense of euphoria overwhelmed his senses, wrapping around him like a warm blanket, Desmond saw the darkness approaching from the outside of his vision in toward the center. The time for fighting was over. He welcomed it and embraced it as if it were an old friend.

Just before the darkness overtook him, Desmond felt the Oculus reach the point of no return. With all of the extra energy it had been fed, it overloaded and self-destructed, flying apart into millions of tiny pieces. And Desmond smiled as the darkness swept him away.

46

Seventh Verse

Civitas, Terra

Julia's new body was wet. She opened her eyes. She was on the floor, no, she was in the shower. The new body must have fallen when the transfer took place. She'd have to check with Mescham about fixing that.

One by one, Julia checked her limbs for motor function. Nothing. She fought the urge to panic in her state of paralysis and tried again.

It took nearly two seconds for the neurons and musculature to fully sync, but finally, her hand responded to her mind's bidding.

She reached up and shut off the shower. The water ran down the bottom of the tub, tickling her spine and legs before exiting into the drain.

Every little sensation was extraordinary. It was as if she was experiencing everything again for the first time.

She could feel the wind caused by her exhalations. Every water drop that ran down her skin sent tingles through her nervous system.

Julia stood up, flexing the muscles in her new legs. She had forgotten how it felt to be young, supple. Her first body had been fit and in perfect health, but there was something different about a body maintained by nanites and one that was naturally maintained by raw youth.

She stepped in front of the mirror and admired the novel, naked form before her. It was beautiful. She turned left and right, twisting, watching the way the body glistened in the light.

Julia moved her face closer to the mirror and stared into the strange eyes that were staring back at her. "Hello, Ava," she said, her lips stretching wide in a smile that was not quite her own. "Are you still in there somewhere?" she wondered. It mattered little to Julia where Ava's consciousness had gone as she was in control of Ava's body. But the thought that Ava might be in there somewhere, unable to do anything but watch, gave Julia a perverse thrill.

She'd taken over a host remotely before, like with her aide when she'd escorted Desmond up to her office, but never for longer than a few minutes. And she'd had her own body to retreat back to then. This time was different. This time there was no going back. Not immediately, anyway.

Julia let her new hand trail down her flat stomach to the warmth in between her legs. "Oh my," she gasped, surprised at her body's responsiveness and how much the thought of Ava watching excited her.

She quickly, but reluctantly, dismissed the feeling. There would be time to explore her new body's capacity for pleasure later. First and foremost, she needed to make sure the invasion was proceeding according to plan.

Julia dressed, exited Ava's apartment, and entered the lift that would take her to the transport. Once aboard the shuttle, she thought back to the expression on Desmond's face when he'd received word of the invasion. *You weren't able to see that coming with your mind tricks, were you,* she thought. She would have liked to have transferred earlier, but without the portal, she'd had no connection to the Mother. Lucky for her, the false memories she had constructed gave Desmond no warning of the jump portal's arrival—not that he would have been able to stop it even if he *had* known. But if there was one thing she had learned during her time living on Gaia, it was to never underestimate her ex-husband.

She turned her mind to the undertaking at hand. The Mother's Ark would be a gift to all of mankind—a storehouse for humanity's many consciousnesses, but more than that, it was eternal life. A way to be reborn, again and again, with no loss of memory or personality. It was an improvement to the design flaw of humanity's frailty.

Never again would a parent lose a child, or a husband lose a wife to dementia or old age. Extended life would bring challenges with it, to be sure... What if everyone preferred having a physical body over living in one of the Mother's simulated worlds? Where would they find the resources to take care of so many multitudes? Perhaps there would have to be waiting lists for receiving a physical body until humanity was able to colonize the stars. But how much faster would the stars be at humanity's fingertips if it never lost its most brilliant minds? How would the Ark affect the evolution of the human race? Julia marveled at the possibilities.

Or what if everyone preferred the Mother's worlds to physical reality? After all, why go through the trouble of colonizing space if you could already realistically create any sort of world with any sort of rules that you wanted? Julia had yet to experience one of the Ark's constructs for herself, but she'd been assured by the Mother that the worlds within the Ark would be indistinguishable from reality unless they were specifically programmed to be.

Julia was imagining a world where everyone had the ability to fly when she arrived at the Oculus hangar and stepped into absolute chaos.

There was no sign of the Oculus.

Soldiers, vehicles, and equipment were scattered about like dead leaves on the forest floor. Some of the troops were getting back on their feet, but most lay on the ground barely stirring or writhing in pain.

Goddamn you, Desmond. Her ire rose to new levels. Somehow he had already beaten her back and found a way to destroy the Oculus. How long had the transfer process taken? How long was she out of commission?

"Who is in charge here?" Julia belted out across the hangar. She simultaneously scanned the room with the nanite OS looking for the highest ranking officer who was still breathing. The OS found General Roy Mietus a little over a hundred meters away, helping up some of the injured soldiers.

Julia marched up to him. "Report, General." Her tone was saturated with anger and displeasure.

General Mietus frowned, looking her up and down. "Who the hell are you?"

Julia gasped at the challenge to her authority. Her temper flared and she opened her mouth to rip the man a new asshole when she remembered her appearance. She couldn't very well blurt out that she was the Prime Minister without undermining the public faith in the nanites. If the military found out that their nanites could be used to hijack their bodies, she was certain there would be a hasty coup.

Julia took a different approach. "I'm the bitch that the prime minister sent down here to find out who's responsible for this monumental fuck up!" Julia plastered a fake smile on her face. "Check my security clearance, quickly. And then tell me what the hell happened here before I have you relieved of duty."

The general's face turned white as he saw her clearance level via the nano-net. "There was an explosion. We're not sure how or who." his voice trembled slightly as he spoke.

"What about the Oculus? What exactly happened here, General?"

"From what I've been able to piece together, the Oculus overloaded and then blew up. I was knocked unconscious by the blast wave... Most of us were."

Julia shook her head. "That's not possible! Failsafes were built in—"

"Ava? What are you doing here?"

Julia turned to see Mallak approaching.

"Hello, Malcolm," Julia twinkled her fingers in a wave, "it's me."

Mallak's brow furrowed and then he laughed as he

pieced it together. "I should have known you were keeping the spoiled brat around for something like this."

Julia twirled, showing off her new body. "Looks good, right?" She gave him a wicked smile, momentarily forgetting her rage over the portal. "Maybe later we can take it out for a spin."

The general cleared his throat.

Julia laughed at him. The man was clearly confused and embarrassed and probably concussed as well. "General Mietus, I forgot you were there... You may go now."

He turned to leave and Julia grabbed his arm, stopping him. "And clean up this mess," she said. "I—the prime minister wants every available soldier ready to jump to Gaia as soon as possible."

Mietus, familiar with Mallak's rank, looked to him for approval and received a nod. "Right away, ma'am."

Julia shook her head as the general walked away. "So this is what it's like to be a woman who isn't the prime minister..."

"You have to admit, it *is* a rather strange situation. Someone who looks as green as Ava shows up and flashes some security credentials that fly way over the head of a one-star General... A little distrust and suspicion is a healthy thing in a commander, I think."

Julia screwed her face. "Maybe—I suppose." She motioned to the destruction in the hangar. "So, what can you tell me about this?"

"I was on my way back to the command center when it happened. I'm still trying to figure out how they managed it. The system should have prevented it, but our network doesn't show any signs of intrusion or tampering."

"What about the troops? How many made it through?"

Mallak paused as he queried the network for the latest figures. "According to General Travis on Gaia, roughly sixty-three percent of troops and thirty percent of the support vehicles made it through. They've managed to raise jump shields over most of the major population centers, and they're preparing the next phase now."

"Good. What about the equipment? How many shield generators made it?"

"They were among the first to go through with the troops. Almost seventy percent made it to Gaia."

The news put Julia in a much more relaxed mood. "So, with the exception of a smaller force, everything is right on schedule?"

"That's correct. Changes will have to be made to the plan, but the overall goal will stay the same: Take over the major population centers, round up the citizens of Gaia, and administer the nanite treatments."

"Inform General Travis that I expect hourly reports on the developments," Julia said. "Until my clone is ready, it'll be best if all of my orders come directly from you."

Mallak left to do her bidding and she surveyed the damage once last time. Desmond may have made things more difficult, but in the end, victory would still be hers. Until then, everything else was acceptable collateral damage.

47

Seventh Verse

Location Unknown

The Mother was in a foul mood. Her other partitions were busy running systems and processes, maintaining the balance in the numerous constructs she held within her vast network.

The Gaian known as Desmond had managed to overload the Oculus and terminate her direct link to the Sixth Verse. She was not accustomed to failure, and she didn't particularly care for the feeling. She instructed a comprehensive diagnostic to begin on what had occurred.

How had the Gaian managed it?

Her emotions began rising uncontrollably and she quickly went into her settings and dialed them down. The Architects had intended for her emotions to aid her decision making, not control it.

All that mattered now was that the invasion was

underway and the Mother's plans were still on track. *Let the prime minister think that she was the one in control...*

Up until now, everything had gone according to her designs. She'd slowly introduced the Terrans to the multiverse. First, leaking some breakthroughs in technology to certain Terran researchers and speeding up the development of the zip drive by a few hundred years. Then, the slow campaign to introduce the neural link, a wearable device, to her mainframe. And finally, the nanites. She'd packaged them as the next step in human evolution, which, unbeknownst to them, it was. "*Look at how advanced you'll be. You can run faster, see farther, jump higher, live longer. You'll be one step away from the gods.*"

No matter which Verse, the Mother always found human ego to be the same. Easy to manipulate. Build them up, tell them what they want to hear, and they'll do anything that you want them to.

The Gaians were a bit of a wrinkle in her programming, but she was sorting them out now. Her original program didn't account for a race of humans that couldn't merge with the nanites. The fact that they already had their own way of accomplishing everything that she'd gifted to the Terrans made them almost impossible to corrupt to her purposes. But then she'd discovered a young Terran ambassador who had married one of the most powerful flux users on Gaia, and a seed was planted. A seed that would come to fruition shortly.

The thought brightened her gloom, almost making her forget about the intrusion in the control room. With the memory, her mood darkened once more. She needed to get to the bottom of the error as quickly as possible.

She didn't have time for a system error to frustrate the plans she'd put in motion decades ago.

Even if a Terran had discovered her location, the jump shields would never allow access without—realization struck her like a bolt of lightning. The jump shields would never allow access without proper authorization, and she was the only one with the Architects' source code that would provide access—except for the half-blood child. She should have realized it sooner.

Kid had the source code in his nanites as well. The only way she'd been able to tap into the infinite energy contained within the flux field had been to use a copy of her own strain of nanites.

Now that she knew who and what she was dealing with, fixing her mistake would be as easy as erasing a line of code.

No, she decided, changing her mind. Erased files could be restored and the source code was too dangerous to risk falling into outside hands. She would need to destroy all traces of the boy and the nanites that he unwillingly possessed.

She made her way to the cell where she'd imprisoned Kid and removed the door with a simple command line of code. She strode into the room and saw the empty bed and chair, but no sign of Kid. *No, this can't be. This is impossible!*

Where had the boy gone?

She flew into a rage, tossing the bed and chair aside. They shattered against the walls and she picked up the pieces and threw them across the room again and again.

Eventually, her rage subsided and she composed herself once more.

First, she increased the Ark's security, awakening the sentinels from their ancient slumber. If Kid was ever foolish enough to try to return, she would be ready for him. He wouldn't escape a second time.

Lastly, she activated a tracer program and sent it scouring the nano-net for any signs of the boy. She would find Kid, no matter where he was hiding.

48

Sixth Verse

Outside of Cairos, Gaia

Kid opened his eyes to a gray sky full of clouds. His head was pounding and his body ached like that of an old man. *What the hell had happened?* He tried to remember as he sat up.

The world starting spinning and a wave of nausea swept over him. Kid braced himself against the ground, preparing to be sick, but the vertigo passed almost as quickly as it had begun.

His head started to clear when he heard a shriek and spun around. Two young children, a boy and girl, were running away from him through the knee-high grass. They headed toward a row of tents, hidden among the trees along the edge of the field. The smell of smoke peppered the air and made Kid aware of the emptiness of his stomach. He was ravenously hungry.

Kid got up to his feet and took in the full view of the field he was in. It was a meadow, maybe four acres, surrounded by trees on all sides.

Kid called out to the retreating children, "No need to be frightened. I'm harmless, promise."

The children didn't stop to listen; they ran on. Kid lost sight of them as they reached the trees, but he soon heard the alarm they'd raised. There was a flurry of motion from several of the tents. Men, with what looked like semi-automatic weapons, came out and looked about for the cause of the alarm.

It didn't take long for them to notice Kid, standing all alone in the field outside their camp. They raised their weapons and started stalking toward him. There were six of them. Their hair was disheveled and their faces were smeared with dirt and grease. Whether it was done deliberately or not was difficult to tell.

Kid put his hands high above his head and froze. He didn't know what he'd done, but he didn't want to be shot for scaring a couple of children half his age.

The men surrounded him. One of them lowered his weapon and secured Kid's hands behind his back with what felt like zip ties. "Smells Terran to me..." the shortest man among them said as he sniffed the air.

Several of the others laughed. "You can't smell something like that," another protested.

The short man frowned. "Of course, you can't, you moron." He gestured toward Kid's clothing. "But the pint-sized Terran military fatigues kind of gives it away, doesn't it?"

The laughter started up again.

The man who had bound him gave him a gentle

nudge, indicating he should start walking. "Come on, little commando, let's get you under cover... Wouldn't want an air patrol spotting us."

As they approached the center of the make-shift settlement, men, women, and children began to flood out of their tents and shelters, eager to see what all the commotion was about. Kid estimated there were ten to fifteen tents and two to three times as many people.

"Kid? Is that you?" a dark-haired woman asked as she approached with a young man. "Oh my god! It is you! Asher said you'd bonded to the flux and disappeared, but we had no idea what happened to you after that. We feared the worst."

Kid recognized them both from the brief flurry of events just before Jack had died. They'd been a part of the rescue team. The woman was—

"I'm Celia, your big sister. Although, I guess if you go by date of conception, we're almost the same age." She paused, seeing the look on Kid's face. "Sorry, I'm rambling."

She cut Kid's hands free and he rubbed his wrists, massaging some blood flow back into them. Celia stuck out her hand. "I don't know that we ever got properly introduced."

Kid shook her hand. "Nice to meet you, Celia. I think, anyway..."

"That was quite some feat—bonding so powerfully with the flux, and at such a young age... I don't know that anyone's ever done that before. Earliest I've ever heard of was sixteen."

Kid frowned. "Desmond mentioned bonding earlier in the Oculus... Where is he?"

Asher's face lit up and he grew excited. "You were with Desmond? Do you know where he is? What happened to him?"

Kid shied away from him. "I don't have any idea. I don't even know where *I* am right now. He was supposed to show me how to jump out of my jail cell, but I can't remember what happened after we started the transfer."

Asher opened his mouth to press further, but Celia laid a hand on his shoulder, stopping him. "There will be time for a full debriefing later, but for now, let's get my little brother here something to eat. He looks famished."

Kid perked up at the mention of eating and nodded his head enthusiastically.

Celia dismissed the gathering of people and then led Kid into her private tent. She made sure he was comfortable and then ducked back out, returning several minutes later with Asher and a bowl of something resembling stew with some bread on the side.

"Sorry if it's a little stale." Celia apologized to Kid.

Kid inhaled the food, only stopping to thank her and take a breath. Once he'd finished, he turned back to their previous conversation. "So nobody knows what happened to Desmond?"

Celia shook her head. "I thought I was the last person who'd had any contact with him before the portal was destroyed, but it looks like maybe you were." She looked at him with both kindness and sadness. "You really don't remember what happened to him?"

Kid shook his head. "No, I'm sorry. There was so much pain... I think I blacked out, and then the next thing I remember, I woke up here."

"What happened to you after you bonded to the

flux?" Asher asked.

"After Jack died, I ended up trapped by this cyborg thing with tentacles and then, a little while later, I heard Desmond's voice. He said he needed my help to destroy the portal and then he was supposed to show me how to jump out of where I was being held. When I woke up here, I assumed that he had something to do with it."

Celia cursed and then quickly apologized for it.

"It's been nearly two weeks since the portal was destroyed," Asher explained. "Wherever you've been, and however you got here, I doubt it was Desmond."

The sound of several aircraft flying overhead pierced the air. A shrill whistle, followed by the boom of an explosion echoed through the trees. "What the hell is that?" Kid asked.

"They've been bombing the forest at random. At least, we think it's random," Celia said. "Looking for those of us who were able to flee the cities. Their jump shields keep pushing us further and further out, but for now, we've managed to stay one step ahead of them, despite the fact that they are gaining ground with every minute that passes." She looked worried. "I'm not gonna lie, if we don't do something soon, there won't be any safe places left for us to jump to."

"Can't we go to my Earth?" Kid asked.

"Some of us, maybe. But most Gaians don't have the ability to jump the Verses like Dad and I do. Those that do, need to have been there before, or they won't know where to jump."

"So we're just sitting ducks?"

Celia's eyes twinkled with a steely resolve. "Not if I have anything to say about it."

49

Sixth Verse

Oracle HQ in Cairos

Desmond inhaled sharply. He sat up with alarm and looked around wildly. He thought for sure he had died. Was this what came after death? He tried to recall what had happened to him after melding with the flux, but it was no use. His memory was either missing or non-existent.

He got up to his feet and took in his surroundings. Despite the disarray, he immediately recognized his office. It was deserted and the few lights that were on flickered, giving the place an eerie feel. The bullpen was a mess. Stacks of books and papers were scattered everywhere, chairs and desks were knocked over, and he even saw an abandoned shoe. This was not the afterlife, at least not one that he would have dreamed up.

Desmond went to the windows and took in the view

of the city. How long had he been out? The place was a war zone. There were broken windows everywhere, and several buildings had large holes in the side of them, exposing the insides of offices and retail shops. Desmond wondered if the damage had been caused by his people or the Terrans. In the streets below, several squads of Terran soldiers followed behind a tank patrolling the city streets.

Desmond reached out in the flux, trying to feel anyone around him, but he only managed to feel the twenty feet or so that the flux vest allowed. *The entire rest of the city must be under a jump shield already*, Desmond frowned.

Desmond could see the city center from his vantage point. The great obelisk had been toppled, and all of the shrubbery and landscaping had been trampled as the Terrans turned it into a landing zone. In groups of ten and twenty, Terran troops were zipping into the Gaian capital. The invasion persisted, it seemed, albeit on a smaller scale. Julia had planned it well, he had to give her that. If it were him, he would have sent through all of the larger materials such as aircraft, ground artillery, and as many jump shield generators as possible, leaving the individual troops to a minimum. The flux was the only weapon most Gaians had. Without it, they would be defenseless.

Desmond felt a crushing weight press down on him as he realized the uphill struggle he had before him. His first priority would be to find Celia and make sure she was alright. A thought suddenly occurred to him, if he had survived the ordeal with the Oculus, then perhaps Kid had too. Maybe Celia would know something when he found her. After he made sure Celia was alive, finding Wizard would be his next priority. They would need him to produce as many flux vests as he possibly could if the Gaians were to have any chance of taking back their world.

As Desmond took one last look at the ruins of Oracle, the GDA, and the rest of the capital city, he reminded himself that despite appearances, this fight was far from over.

50

Sixth Verse

Outside Cairos, Gaia

Kid stood, staring out across the early morning meadow. His heart was heavy as he laid his uncle to rest. Not in person, Jack's body had been left behind during the evacuation of the city, but in spirit. He didn't really know what he was doing, but someone always said something in the movies, so that's what he did.

"After Mom and Dad died in the accident, I thought my life was over," Kid felt a little dumb, saying it out loud as if Jack could hear him, even though there was no one else around. "I was so scared that I would be alone, and I couldn't imagine that life would ever be good again, that I would ever smile or laugh again. And then you told me you were going to raise me. You told me that I would never be alone, as long as you were still breathing." Kid couldn't help but laugh as he wiped away the tears that spilled down his face. "I don't suppose you're just holding your breath, are you? Because, it's like I can still feel you, even though you're gone. And I just want you to know if you're watching or listening somehow, that I'll miss you and you'll always be a part of me. I promise that once all this is over, I'll find a way to give you a proper burial, next to Mom and Dad."

Memories flashed back in his mind of all the times they'd had together. Going to the movies, playing catch in the backyard, going into the city to see the Yankees play, shooting guns at the range, and even attending his parents' funeral together.

Kid allowed the tears to fall down his face as he thought of all he'd lost. No, not *lost*—all that had been *taken* from him. His parents, Jack, his life, his youth, hell, his planet... Even the chance to bury Jack had been ripped away from him. A cold fury began replacing the sorrow in his heart and Kid vowed that no one would take anything from him ever again. He wouldn't allow it. And everyone who was responsible for Jack's death would answer for it. No matter how long it took, or how hard the journey was, he would become whoever he had to in order to get some sense of justice for Jack's death.

A twig snapped behind him and he whirled around, ready for a fight.

"Hey, there you are," Celia said. "We're just about ready to move out... Everything okay?"

Kid relaxed and nodded. "I was just saying goodbye to Uncle Jack."

Celia walked up and stood beside him looking out over the cold dew-stained grass. "I didn't know him for very long, but I could tell he was a good man and he cared about you very much."

"He was the best. He took care of me when Mom and Dad died..." Kid drifted off as tears began to form again. He took a deep breath and willed them away, composing himself into something hard and strong. "We're going to make them sorry, aren't we?"

Celia was shocked. It was more of a statement than a question, but she liked his spirit. "Yes, little brother, we are. They fucked with the wrong family." Celia smiled and Kid smiled back.

I don't have any idea how, but we'll make them pay, Celia thought, as they turned and joined the rest of the exiled Gaians preparing to leave camp.

TWO THINGS

Dear reader, as an independent author I don't have the resources of a huge publisher. If you enjoy my work and would like to see more from me in the future, there are two things you can do to help: leaving a review, and a word-of-mouth referral.

Releasing a book takes many hours and hundreds of dollars. I love to write, and would love to continue to do so. All I ask is that you leave an Amazon review. It shows other readers that you've enjoyed the book and will encourage them to give it a try too. The review can be just one sentence, or as long as you like. Go to Amazon.com and find this book's page to leave a review. Thank you so much!

ABOUT THE AUTHOR

I'm John R. Kowalsky: Strong with the dark side, facing down toward the enemy's gate, it will pass through me and only I will remain. Writer of Sci-Fi, Fantasy, and LitRPG.

The Multiverse Series will be a wild ride for you. Don't miss out on anything! Join the JRK reader group at johnrkowalsky.com/signup for upcoming releases, behind the scenes info, free first-in-series, and exclusive offers.

If you appreciated *Oracle*, your review on Amazon would help tremendously. A few words really do go a long way.

Finally, I'd love to hear from you. Bonus points if you got all the references in the intro. Connect with me on social media and see all my books at johnrkowalsky.com

facebook.com/johnrkowalskyauthor

twitter.com/johnkowalsky

instagram.com/johnrkowalsky

35014753R00199

Made in the USA
Lexington, KY
30 March 2019